ALINA MARTYN

Embracing My Future

Contents

II   Other works by Alina Martyn

I

Trigger Warning

In this book, there are mentions of sexual abuse, thoughts and talk of suicide, suicide, non-consensual sex, emotional abuse, neglect, death and dying, stupid old outdated men and their misogynistic thinking, human trafficking, murder, and graphic sex scenes.
Enter at your own risk.
Go on, you know you want to.
(But really, do what you need to. Your mental health matters.)

The Save

Cillian

"Go, Cillian," Kieron snarls, and I run from the room, intent on finding rope or something sturdy that can hold Hector from the rafters. A quick glance at Trent tells me just how much he is seething, barely keeping it together.

I can't say I would fare any better if my girl had been beaten and almost killed. I try to rush—I don't want to make this any more difficult for Trent or Auggie than I know it already will be.

Trent, who called me earlier tonight and told me all about how his charge, Kieron's sister-in-law, Auggie, was taken from their safehouse, was... well, he was a wreck. But not for the reason I thought he would be. I thought I'd get to the safehouse and he'd be shitting bricks because he lost a power member of the game, but he was raging and scared because *his girl* had been kidnapped.

It changed everything.

When we finally got to where Hector, the newly appointed

leader of Los Muertos; a powerful street gang, was holding Auggie, Trent was savage. Nothing was keeping him from her. I ran in with him to keep him from dying before he actually got to save her.

The poor girl is naked and bloodied, she's obviously been thrown around, and with the threats we heard while hiding, waiting for the perfect moment to announce our presence.... Well, I don't know how Trent hasn't killed the fucker already. I know I want to.

I realize after I'm already out of the room that Kieron probably has zip ties on his person, as they're his preferred way to restrain someone. The fucker never comes to a takedown without them. Him having them in his back pocket has saved my ass more than once so I'm not going to complain.

I really need to start doing that though.

I remember seeing extra office supplies in the room Trent and I broke into, but it was on the first fucking floor. And there's not a chance in hell that I am going to climb all those stairs again. Not a chance. Plus, we took out everyone but Hector so, the elevator should be good.

Pushing the button, I take a deep, unsteady breath and wait for the steel doors to open. Luckily, it's not even thirty seconds of waiting for the elevator before it dings.

Objectively, it's a nice building. Stainless-steel elevator with floor-to-ceiling mirrors and carpeted hallways with warm lighting make it feel like a very fancy hotel. It's close to headquarters, so I can't help but idly wonder how much rent is. Obviously, I don't want that... trauma in my life. I'm not actually thinking about moving here, but I can't help but wonder.

It'd be nice to get out of the standard apartment at headquarters.

Hitting the first floor, I walk swiftly toward where we entered and find the abandoned room. There are chairs stacked and lined against all the walls, broken lamps, unused desks, shelf-less bookshelves stacked here and there. There are plastic storage tubs pushed in between everything, so I start there.

Jackpot.

The first tub I look into is just wires and cords, so I grab two handfuls, stuff them in my pockets and get out. It should be enough to make a strong temporary hanger and bind. I'm sure that if Trent doesn't kill Hector here, we'll be moving him to the basement where Trent will have a torture table, chains, and a ruthless mafia jail cell to hold him until he's ready for Hector to die.

Making sure to close the door as softly as I can to not alert anyone potentially walking by, I walk to the elevator. Right as I turn the corner that would bring me to the steel doors, I jump back, flattening myself against the wall as much as possible while still being able to see exactly what's going on. Two dark-haired men are holding up a limp, naked woman by the biceps and dragging her to the elevator. Clocking the weapons at their sides instantly, I wait.

This poor girl. She's shaking and shivering, curling in on herself, maybe trying to shield her naked body from prying eyes. Her long black hair is falling in knots down her back, touching the dimples above her ass. Bruises cover every inch of her body. She goes to stand up as much as she can, and the guy on the right smacks her with the gun in his hand, snapping, "Be still!" in a hushed tone. The rage I'm feeling is severe, deadly, and incredibly welcome at this moment.

The other guy brings out a radio and starts speaking Spanish quickly. High school Spanish was a long-ass time ago, so the only words I really get are: "here, girl, Hector, alone".

But it's enough for me. This is the girl they thought was Talia.

I take a deep breath, centering myself for the fire fight. I quietly check the magazine of my gun, ensuring I have enough bullets to take them out. Just as I'm about to open fire, the girl's head rolls to the side and her eyes meet mine.

And it feels like I've been shot.

A jolt runs through my system as those electric, almost unnaturally blue eyes meet mine.

She's beautiful. Gorgeous. Breathtaking.

But under all that, there is a look of defiance for her captors while also pleading for help at the same time.

This girl is a fighter.

My feet move without my conscious thought, and I raise my gun swiftly, aiming the barrel at the skull of the man holding her. With one pull of the trigger, barely any effort, his blood and brains spray everywhere, covering the woman with blood. She immediately moves as fast as she can behind me. The other guy tries to grab her before she slips from his grasp, but his attention is too focused on me.

His arm comes up to take a shot, but my fist pops out and hits him quickly in the nose, knocking off his aim and making more blood splatter. While he's holding his nose and struggling to keep his eyes open, I elbow his chest—hard—and rip the gun from his hand, all in a matter of seconds.

"What the fuck? I think you broke my nose!" he screams at me.

I take pride in the fact that I actually do think I broke it. It's already bruising and is definitely sitting crooked.

"Don't worry, it won't hurt much longer," I tell him, taking aim again.

His eyes narrow, his thick eyebrows furrowing in confusion before I smirk and pull the trigger again. This time I put a nice, neat little hole right between his eyes.

As his body joins his friend's on the floor, I turn to look at the girl. I was expecting her to scream, or cry. But all she did was stare. The defiant look in her eyes turned to one of justice and I know that whatever they've done to her was truly horrific. She didn't bat an eye at their deaths, and didn't seem to feel anything but relief from it.

"Are you okay?" I ask, slowly putting my gun away and holding my hands up to show her I don't mean any harm.

Silence.

"What's your name?"

Silence.

Fuck, I don't know what hell they've put her through, but if what Hector said is true, she's been in their hands for a month. There's a lot of ways to break and bend a person in that amount of time.

She looks around quickly, alertness slowly creeping in. Her pupils are sluggish and she's breathing faster from the exhaustion of holding herself up.

What is she on? Or what did they give her?

"Hey, it's okay. I promise. Here." I pull my jacket off, then slide off my dark henley, holding it out for her to take. "It's okay, cover up. I need to go help my friends, can you come with me?"

I realize I'm speaking to her like she's a wounded animal, but I don't want to spook her. While she seems like a fighter, she's been through trauma and doesn't know me yet. I need to prove that I'm one of the good guys.

Thankfully, she accepts the shirt, but struggles to lift her arms.

"Can I help you?" I wait for her to give me consent before I do anything. I leave my hands up in front of me, frozen in space until she nods.

Consent given, she lifts her arms as high as she can and I help slide the soft material over her head. She's tall, taller than average, but still shorter than me, so the shirt gives her a little bit of coverage. As long as she doesn't bend, she'll stay covered.

"I promise, you're safe now," I tell her earnestly. Those blue eyes look at me, and her head cocks to the side slightly as if she's trying to figure me out. Figure out my motivation for helping her. But she still doesn't say anything.

Very slowly, I reach out to take her hand. I expect her to jolt or jump away from me, but instead, she grabs hold and lets me lead her to the elevator. She's shaking and I put my arm around her to help support her as she walks, but other than that, she's standing strong. Once we're inside, she grabs the handle on the wall to move herself to the farthest corner and I don't blame her. Just because I killed the people that had her, doesn't mean that I'm her savior. I'm no one's savior. I have a short fucking temper and I'm quick to have words and let my feelings run the show. I refuse to let it hinder me during missions, so usually when I'm not working, emotions fly high.

I push the button for the penthouse and we slowly ascend.

It's slightly awkward; she's naked except for my shirt, and she's shivering. It fucking kills me not to be able to do anything more for her. I want to reach for her and hold her close. Just to make her feel safe for a moment.

Taking an experimental step closer to her, I hone my attention, zoning into her body language. When her arms tighten around her middle, I step back. She's not comfortable and I get it.

"What's your name?" I say softly.

Her voice is barely above a whisper, and I have to strain to hear it. But with the one word she utters, I know my life will change forever.

"Mila."

The Rescue

Mila

They didn't drug me this time.

Why?

My two jailers are speaking Spanish quickly, but the amount of time I've been forced to spend in their presence has taught me more than they're aware of. The tall one speaks about me like I'm not even here. Like I'm not even a person. He's bragging about having had me earlier, about screwing a drugged-up woman like it's a fucking prize. The other one says something about if I know it was him.

I want to scoff. I remember him, *I remember all of them.* Each son of a bitch that creeped into the cell to violate me in the darkness. He'll be the first one I kill when I can. He can't be older than me, just hitting his mid-twenties, and he fucked me like he was a virgin, so... he talks a big game, but can't exactly back it up.

I hate that I'm shivering, I hate that I have to play this part of a whimpering mess, but I can't let them know who they have. I can't let them know who I really am.

No one can know.

"Oh, I know. The fact that he's kept her drugged is smart as shit though," the other one, the kinder one, says.

Both of them have a tight grip on my arms, holding me up. I've lost so much muscle, so much endurance and stamina, while I've been held captive. I've been with Los Muertos a long time. Too long.

It shows me that The Bratva has given up on me.

Or they just don't care.

The second is far more likely.

Movement catches my attention out of the corner of my eye, but I let my head drop forward, hanging down so that I can see what's coming better.

It's a man. He's very obviously not a part of Los Muertos. He's tall, got a buzz cut with dark hair covering his head, a jaw that could cut glass and tattoos up his neck. He's wearing a black leather jacket, and holding a gun with a silencer on the muzzle.

The elevator dings, and I know I have to give this new guy time to help me. I don't know if he's here to help or hurt, but my choices are limited and I'd rather take a chance than stay where I'm at. I whimper and let my feet drag. The tall one lifts his hand and backhands me across the face with the butt of his gun.

Ow. That one hurt.

Everything in me wants to smile up at him sinisterly, letting the blood drip from my mouth like the animal that I am and have had to contain.

"Be still!" he snarls, pulling me harder and snapping to the other guy, shit-talking me all over again.

I turn to the man hiding, desperate for him to help before I have to step onto the elevator. The adrenaline coursing through my incredibly tired body gives me the push I need. When our eyes meet, I can feel my heart beat harder. He's the most handsome man I've ever seen, a bright savior.

His dark-brown eyes have a lighter caramel-colored ring around the iris that sucks me right in. I see the unbridled rage in those gorgeous, inherently kind eyes.

He steps toward me quickly, pulling his gun up and aiming straight for the tall fucker holding me. Before I can even blink, brains and blood explode in my face, and the world is rid of one more evil.

The other guy holding me releases my arm for just a minute and I don't waste the moment. I run as fast as I'm able to with the drugs wearing off in my system. I hobble toward my savior, hiding behind his back. The two face off, and my savior isn't letting the remaining jailer have any space to get close to me.

The new guy pops the other and there's a very audible crack as his nose breaks. Then my savior speaks.

"Don't worry, it won't hurt much longer," he growls. The timber of his voice is low and gravelly, very American with a hint of something else. English accent? Irish? There's definitely something more there.

With one more silenced shot, it's done.

I'm free.

They can't get me. Not with this guy in front of me.

"Are you okay?" he asks.

I'm too stunned to answer.

Trying a different tactic, he questions, "What's your name?"

Yeah, right. Like I'm going to tell him my name right now.

I look around, watching for signs of any more danger. I'm half expecting this giant man to pull a syringe out and drug me himself.

But he doesn't.

In fact, he starts to take his jacket off and I instinctively step back. I don't even think about it, I'm just so used to only being used for one thing. It's been a month of being tortured, raped, hurt, *abused* by those men. But they didn't break me completely.

No, I made sure of that. I played the part as if their torment was working, only to keep my true self hidden away. Preserving it. Compartmentalizing who I am with who I pretended to be.

It doesn't mean that the fear wasn't real, as much as I hate to admit it.

"Hey, it's okay. I promise. Here," the man says, taking his jacket all the way off and ripping the shirt off his back, holding it out for me. "It's okay, cover up. I need to go help my friends. Can you come with me?"

I take it, but with the drugs still in my system, everything is so hard. I used all my energy to get away from my captors and now it feels impossible to do anything else.

Everything is so heavy. My head, my arms, my legs. Everything. I'm barely keeping myself from falling to the ground.

"Can I help you?" he asks, waiting patiently for me to answer. Not seeing any other option and really wanting to not be naked, I nod. Unfortunately I do need help.

He helps me lift my arms and slides the soft material over my head. I relish in the warmth of the fabric. It is still heated from his body and I can't help but sniff the collar. *Mint, amber, cinnamon*. And something else I can't place. Something that must just be him.

His shirt is long on me, but not long enough. I should be fine as long as I don't try to shift too much.

My savior smiles kindly at me, and I step closer to him.

"I promise, you're safe now," he says softly, like he's trying to portray just how much he means that. Slowly he reaches out and takes my hand in his. Threading our fingers together, I can't help but feel that it's right. Holding his hand feels more like home than anywhere and with anyone ever before.

What the fuck does that mean?

We step onto the elevator and I need space. I need time. I need to get away. The only problem is that I don't know what I'm up against, I don't know if there are more members of Los Muertos here or if they're going to still be after me. There are too many unknown variables. I pull my hand from his and hold on to the handle, resting my body weight against the corner.

The guy is staring at me with pity, and I try not to get offended. He's a nice guy, but one who has no problem shooting people or killing in cold blood obviously, so I'm nice enough to not tell him to fuck off. I open my mouth to take a deep breath and that's when I realize that my teeth are chattering. There's a chill so deep in my bones that I don't know if I will ever warm up. I've gotten so used to it, the darkness and coldness being the only constants in my life.

"What's your name?" the handsome man asks, and I'll give him this one thing. Even if it's the only information I can give him.

"Mila." I whisper.

The Savior

Mila

I pull the blanket that someone wrapped around my shoulders tighter to me as I try to slow my breathing. At the very least, I'm not naked anymore.

The guy who saved me, Cillian, I heard someone call him, is hovering over me. Strangely though, as much as I've been watched and leered at by all the fuckers before, this man's gaze didn't make me want to gouge his eyes out. I welcome it, in fact. I can't explain it, I just feel safe with him.

Maybe it's Stockholm Syndrome setting in already, but he's just… he's like a big teddy bear wrapped in a strong, tattooed, giant of a man. Watching Cillian kill my captors point-blank with no hesitation or compassion… I haven't seen that from another person in years. I'd be lying if I said it didn't turn me on a little.

I really am fucked up in the head.

He came along and took care of my problem for me, and I'll be grateful for that eternally. A life for a life, that's the debt I owe him now. That's what my family believes in, and what I've always believed in as well.

"Are you okay?" Cillian asks me, leaving the other guy that looked quite a bit like him. A brother maybe?

I nod, looking up at him through my eyelashes, giving him a slight pout and shiver to really sell the image. Before I look away, I take in as much of him as I can.

This mammoth of a man is at least 6 foot 5 inches and wide, so built with muscles I'm sure he could pick up a refrigerator with ease. He's handsome in a conventional way; sharp jaw, sharp cheekbones, cropped brown hair. But what really gives me pause, and what makes me drop my act for a split second, is his eyes. His eyes are peering at me like he'd fight the rest of the world for me if I said the word.

He's gorgeous and kind, even while being merciless.

I nod again, letting him know that I heard him. I'm scared to speak, because once I do, I don't know how much I'll give away. And I can't let anyone know who I am. Who I *really* am.

"Give me some space, guys," Cillian says to the other men in the room, and I can see that it falls on deaf ears for all but one of the other three. He's shorter than Cillian, bearded and brawn like a lumberjack. He's been staring at me in between taking care of the girl passed out on the floor. The redheaded man leaning over her is beside himself with worry, snapping at the lumberjack to help him. But still, his eyes continue to find me.

Cillian sits by me, still shirtless under his leather jacket, and clicks the safety on his handgun.He slides it into the back of his waistband, an attempt to keep me comfortable, I guess. It's a pretty gun, the HK45, and I know I could take it from him in two moves.

"Are you okay?" he asks.

I don't say anything.

"Stupid of me to hope you'd say something again."

I don't even shrug.

"I can only guess you've been through hell. But until we know more about who you are, why they took you, Kieron"—he gestures to the tall guy with long, dark hair arguing with the redhead as he tries to take the unconscious girl from him—"my boss, thinks it's best if you stay with one of us."

Terror runs through me, and it's not part of the act when my eyes widen.

"I volunteered," Cillian says quickly. "If you're okay with it. If not, then we can put you up in a safehouse apartment. Either way though, you'll be close by."

I'd rather be back on my own, living in my own fortified apartment, and bathed in anonymity, regardless of the fact that my fucking family runs The Bratva. But obviously, they could care less.

"You," I say softly. I'd rather be with him. Until I can figure out an escape, I'd rather have the devil I know isn't going to hurt me than chance it on my own in an unknown place with who-the-hell-knows watching over me.

His smiles tightly at my words and I try not to let my own heart beat faster at how obviously controlled his happiness is.

"Okay, then." He smiles brighter this time, a bright white row of teeth peeking through despite his attempt to be neutral. "Kieron and Trent are going to get Auggie to the hospital with Bryan." He waves at the guys, and I can finally put names to the faces around me. "And you and I are going to head to my place," he says, standing up and offering me his hand.

When I don't immediately grab it, I can see the panic that visibly takes over his body. Cillian's eyes widen, his mouth drops, and he pulls his hands back.

"I didn't mean… I wasn't trying to…. You'll have your own bedroom, your own space. You don't even need to see me if you don't want to," he babbles.

I keep my expression neutral, but stand up, still very shaky, and tug the blanket tighter around me.

I don't speak, I don't need to. My actions speak for me.

Cillian nods, lets out a deep breath, and puts his hands in his pockets. "Let's go," he says, and tilts his head back behind me, toward the elevator.

My eyes turn toward the group behind him, Trent and Kieron still arguing while the lumberjack—Bryan—shakes his head and huffs before bending down to pick up the girl and stomping past the both of them. She hangs limply in his arms. Her hair is highlighted with different colors so it looks like a rainbow shimmering in the light with each step he takes.

I wonder what happened to her and hope she's okay. We arrived too late for me to see what went down. I only know that these guys took out every fucking dumbass gang member. I count five dead on the ground, including Jonas, Hector's right-hand man. Hector himself may be dead, but I don't think so based on how tightly Cillian wrapped him up in the cords he had stashed in his pocket.

If I had it my way, I'd slit Hector's throat right then and there. The table in the middle of the room is made of glass, one swift kick and I'd have a sizable shard, big enough to cut him open and watch the blood pour from his body. It'd be a far-too-kind end for the evilness Hector showed me, but at least he'd be gone for good.

I take a step toward the elevator, waiting for Cillian to walk forward first so I can follow him. But he doesn't.

"Killer! I need your help!" Kieron yells from where Hector lays. The redhead, Trent, ran after Bryan who still had the girl in his arms. Hector looks bad. Really bad. Kieron's already tied his ankles and wrists together in a hogtie, and Cillian shoots me a sheepish look, before he runs off to help drag the gang member around.

The elevator dings, signaling its arrival after dropping the two men and one woman at the ground floor.

"Mila," Cillian says softly, speaking more gently with me than any man I've ever known to do, while dragging a battered body. "Go ahead and get on, Kieron and I will be right behind you."

He doesn't need to tell me twice.

* * *

"Home sweet home." Cillian twists his key into the lock and opens the door with a flourish. The building his apartment is in is magnificent. It also happens to be the well-known headquarters for the Irish Mob in Boston.

Fuck.

It's immaculately decorated, the building. It makes you feel as if you're staying at a luxury hotel and not an apartment/office building that undoubtedly has a 'playroom' in the basement for their victims and enemies.

I know we have one.

As I step through the door, one thing strikes me. It's painfully obvious that Cillian lives here alone. Everything is designed and decorated for one. A long sofa with one blanket, one side table, no photos or mementos where I can easily see them, one bowl on the counter. Just everything for one. If someone has a girlfriend, or boyfriend, they will usually have things around them that remind them of their significant other. At least another set of dishes. At the *very* least.

There's nothing here. No pictures, no ticket stubs, nothing personal.

Nothing that would give me more information about this man. Nothing that would tell me more about him. Nothing to give me something to defend myself with if needed.

"Sorry it's kind of messy." Cillian starts to walk around wiping tiny crumbs off the surface of the coffee table, refolding the blanket on the couch, picking up the lone coffee cup on the side table by the arm of the couch. My mouth drops slightly in surprise while looking around at the immaculate space. It looks like the showroom of a model home with absolutely not one fiber out of place. 'Kind of messy', my ass. He must be a neat freak like I am.

"Let me show you to your room, " he says, quickly depositing the cup in the sink before walking into the hallway. I had to hold myself back from running my fingers down the walls, anxious to feel the smooth, cool texture. But if he thought a coffee cup and slightly misfolded blanket was messy, running my hand across his walls could be pushing a boundary of his.

"Here is the guest room. It's nothing much, but the bed is clean and warm. There's a bathroom attached and a dresser over there." Cillian points to the door across the room and I assume it's the bathroom he promised. "My room is across the hall down there," he says as he leans back from the doorframe and flicks his head to the side to gesture where it is. "If you need anything, let me know. Towels are under the sink and there's the basic toiletry stuff in the drawer, but tomorrow we can get Cara—our assistant, well really she's Kellan's assistant—to go get you what you need. And a change of clothes. Oh shit, I forgot..." The big man snaps his fingers and leaves the door frame. The moment he's gone, it's like the sun and all its warmth evaporates.

It's off-putting and worrisome.

"Here," Cillian says brightly as he returns and the light comes back into the room. He shoves a stack of warm, dry, soft clothes in my arms with a smile. "They're going to be big on you, but at least they're warm and clean."

I grab a t-shirt from the top of the pile and as it unfolds, I know it's easily going to go past my ass. It's a long, gray, very-well-loved t-shirt and I want to moan in comfort from just looking at it.

He's kind. So kind, in fact, that I'm starting to question it.

Is he always like this? Is he only acting this way because he wants something from me? A piece of my darkened soul that so many try, and have before, to take and use? Does he want me to do something *for* him? *Be something* for him?

"Are you hungry? I have some stuff to make sandwiches. Or would you like a snack, some tea? Do you need anything?" He looks out the door as if he wants to run out and prepare everything he has to offer for me, and my heart threatens to thaw more.

When I first saw him, I knew he was a gentle giant. Then I watched him murder the lackeys and I realized that he's demented.

Just like me.

I shake my head slightly, trying not to drool over the sight of the bed that beckons my name. I haven't slept on more than a hard floor covered with a few threadbare blankets in over a month. I adapted, but it sucked. But then again, the shower is so, so tempting. An actual shower, with actual soap. Yeah, I have to do that first.

"Okay. I'll leave you to it." Cillian puts his hands in his pockets, turning to leave the room. My eyes lock on the bathroom door as I wait for the second that I can stand under the spray, but then I hear Cillian sigh.

"I want you to know you'll be safe here. With me. I don't know what happened, but I can guess, and it makes me murderous. If Trent didn't have dibs on that fucker, I'd have killed him the moment I stepped back into that room with you behind me." He sighs again, but this time it definitely seems like he's trying to control his breathing. "I don't want to scare you more, so I won't tell you what I have planned for him. But know that no harm, no forcefulness, no danger will come for you here. Not with me. I promise."

The weight of his words makes my chest tighten.

Cillian takes another deep breath, and puts on a fake, shaky smile before leaving. The door stays open; giving me the choice to close myself in, or wander.

A choice I haven't had in so long.

Stepping forward, I reach for the doorknob and slowly close the door, letting the latch click as it closes.

I have to get some space. Some distance from this man. If I'm not careful, we'll ruin each other.

The Adjustment

Cillian

Three weeks later...

Living with Mila was much easier than I thought.

She's quiet, tidy in the common areas, and respectful. She doesn't ask any questions, or demand to know where I've gone. Fuck, she doesn't even bat an eyelash when I walk through the door covered in blood. In fact, she nods and her eyes gleam in excitement.

What the fuck is that about? I think, and not for the first time. *What goddamn horrors has she seen that make her comfortable and even kind of giddy at the sight of someone covered in blood?*

Kieron found out very quickly that Mila is in fact, Mila Smirnova; niece to the Head of the Bratva. Since then, he's made some kind of comment every time I see him, about getting information from her. And I know he's right. We can't just send her back without getting some kind of info on the Bratva. Something that we can use in case they come back at us for harboring Mila. But, this chick has to have had some kind of training because nothing—and I mean nothing—of use is coming out of her. She's not even giving me anything with body language. When I ask questions about her family or her time with Los Muertos, it's like talking to a wall. No blush, no eyes widening, no pupil response, no shifting in her seat, no changes in breathing. *Nothing.*

I open the door as quietly as possible, seeing as this mission didn't ever fucking end and it's so early in the morning. My back hurts, my knuckles hurt, I'm sticky as shit from the blood drying on my body. Normally, I wouldn't be the one doing this shit, but Trent's taking care of Auggie, and trying to find her a new place to live and Kieron and Talia just found out they're having a baby, so he's taking more time off. That leaves Bryan and I to keep shit running smoothly so that Kellan, our Skipper, stays off our back. The four of us; Kieron, Trent, Bryan and myself, work best when given freedom to get shit done. None of us handle micromanagement well. In fact, that's when shit starts going sideways. So, Kieron makes sure we get what Kellan wants done, and Kellan stays away.

Win-win.

Right now though, it's fucking hard being two men down and still working at the same level of efficiency as four.

All the lights in the apartment are off, but that's nothing new. Mila barely leaves her room, and even when she does, she doesn't leave a trace that she has.

I hobble into the kitchen and pull down a glass to fill with water. That dickhead got a few hits on me, and I'm not exactly happy about it. I'm going to have a black eye. Groaning in pain as I roll my shoulders back and down the water in one gulp, I turn on one of the under-the-counter lights, hoping not to disturb the sleeping beauty.

Even though she's in a completely separate room.

With her door closed.

Asleep.

Fuck, I have it bad for her already.

"Cillian?" Her soft voice floats through the air and I fight every instinct in my body to jump.

"Mila, why are you up? It's late." I look down at my watch. "Fuck, it's really late."

"I heard the door open and close. It was nearly silent. Made me worried," she says quietly.

Her whole body is glowing from the soft lighting and I fight a moan. This girl, fuck *no*, this *woman*, is exquisite. Her long black hair falls over her shoulders, knotted from sleep and framing her face so beautifully. But, fuck, Mila's wearing my shirt again. It's way too big for her, slipping slightly off her shoulder and giving me a teasing glimpse. Two weeks in and I've never asked for it back, and she's never offered or slipped it into my laundry.

I don't mind. Not one bit.

"Light sleeper." I put the glass behind me, rest my hips against the counter and wince before flinching in pain. The cheating fuck got me with the brass knuckles. I'm sure I've got a deep bruise, if not a crack in my hip bone. Doesn't matter, I've had worse.

"Are you hurt this time?" she asks.

"It's nothing. I need to wash this off," I say, gesturing to my red-spotted skin and clothes.

"Wait." Mila steps forward, one arm crossed over her chest and the other out in front of her to stop me from leaving. "Where are you hurt? You normally just have busted knuckles."

"It's just my side. And probably the rest of me." I weakly chuckle. I don't want to make a big deal of it, but I also crave her hands on me.

Her big blue eyes stay locked on me as she steps closer, getting right up in my space. It's like electricity zaps through the air between us. I don't breathe, I don't move. Especially when I want to tense up as she reaches out, and puts a cool hand on my chest.

"Please, Cillian. Let me help you." Her voice is strong and sure.

"Really, I'm—" I start to say 'I'm fine', but the look on her face is so sincere, I close my mouth and accept the care. Because that's what this is. Someone caring for me for the first time in a long time. "Thank you."

She smiles—actually smiles, and her whole being seems to light up in the darkness. It's beautiful, *she's* beautiful.

"Come sit on a stool, I'll get the first aid kit. You should take some pain meds." She flits around, more confident and commanding than I've ever seen her. I nod numbly and reach for the bottle in the cabinet above the sink.

This isn't the first time I've been beaten up badly. And it's definitely not the first time I've won.

Mila comes back into the kitchen area, holding the old, weathered kit that has a permanent place in my bathroom. She's pulled her hair back into a thick, black braid that drapes seductively over her shoulder. I can see the short sleep shorts that she's wearing peeking out from beneath my t-shirt as she hurries back into the room, her pale strong legs going on for miles.

A vision.

"Did you take something?" she asks.

I nod, parking myself on a stool like she told me to.

"Good boy."

She smiles and I jolt. A long-since dormant, hidden side of myself that I never show anyone begs to be let out.

I know she's teasing me, but those words…. those words do something to me. Make me want to fall to my knees and worship her.

"Take off your shirt."

The way she's saying it, it's clear she's not asking. If I'm not super fucking careful, I'm going to get a hard-on and scare her away. This is the most she's talked to me yet, and trust me, I'm keeping track. I do what she says, pulling the neckline up of my shirt and reaching behind to pull it off my back.

Is it just the dim lighting or did her eyes widen? They're fucking locked on my body and I love that I've pleased her. That my body is something she enjoys looking at.

"For fuck's sake, Cillian. Did they have a bat?" At once, her hands are on my body. They sweep softly over my chest, my sides, my shoulders, my arms. Every last bit of skin is covered in tattoos, pieces of art that bring me joy or have meaning. There are a few fucked-up ones that I got just for fun, or on a drunk dare. Kieron's big on drunk truth-or-dare and his dares usually always have some permanence to them.

"No," I whisper.

"Brass knuckles, then. Your tattoos are all purple and blue, instead of black and white."

She prods a spot on my pec. I wince, when really, I want to growl in pain.

"I'm sorry. I need to check for internal bleeding," she says softly, her face grimacing sympathetically when she hears my discomfort. "Oh fuck, that's a bad one." She gets to my side where I can feel a massive bruise already.

"I have bruise cream in the kit. Other than that, I just need ice and to get some fucking sleep." I start to stand up, but she pushes me back down.

"Let me take care of you. Please."

I feel the need in her tone. I don't know why she feels so strongly about this, but I'm not going to take it away from her. Selfishly, I want someone to want to take care of me.

"Okay. Okay, fine." I put my hand over hers that's laying on my chest, trying to keep me in place. "That would be nice."

Another wide smile blooms across her face. "Good. Then stop being so stubborn, and let me see what's wrong." After that, the only sounds that fill the air are the opening of bandages and an occasional hiss from me when she hits a sensitive spot.

I don't dare break the little bubble we're in. It's all soft, slow touches, her gazing up at me from under her eyelashes every time I move, small smirks or looks of anger when she finds another bruise or cut. Mila works quickly and effectively. I'm sure the whole exchange takes no more than fifteen minutes, but it feels like it spans days. Or maybe that's wishful thinking. I could spend days under her hands.

"All done. You need to put some ice on that one on your hip, and don't shower just yet, but hopefully in the morning, you'll be feeling better." She wipes her hands on a towel to get rid of the medicine before going to the freezer and picking out two bags of frozen peas.

"Thank you." I take them from her and stand up, the dredges of the relaxing spell she had me under still wanting to pull me into her. "It's been… just, thank you." I smile sadly. I don't need to tell her all my bullshit. She doesn't want to hear it anyway.

"Anytime." Mila steps back, the space that's always been there quickly returning and I can feel her walls being built back up, maybe even higher this time.

"Goodnight, Mila," I whisper before she slips out of the room and back to her isolation.

"Goodnight, Cillian."

The Breaking Point

Cillian

One month later...

"I don't know what to do, man. She'll talk to me, but not *talk* to me. It's all surface level." I'm getting sick as fuck that Kellan, Kieron, and everyone else thinks that just because Mila decided to stay with me, it means she actually tells me anything. I've barely gotten her to come out of her room since the night she patched me up. Forget telling me about her family.

"Surface level? Like her likes and dislikes?" Kieron presses.

I shove the phone in the crook between my shoulder and ear, needing both hands to start cooking dinner. I'm sure Bryan will come by soon, just like he has started doing in the evenings to see Mila. She doesn't talk to him either, but we figure the more people she's around, the more comfortable she'll become.

It annoys the shit out of me though. He's so kind and patient with her… and she smiles at him. Not a full smile, but I swear, my heart lurches every fucking time because I don't want her to smile *at him.* I want her to smile at me.

I grab a pot and start filling it with water for the pasta. "Not even that anymore, man. I tell her when Bryan's coming over and ask what she wants to eat, if she needs anything, if she wants to call her family, and I get nods or ignored. She needs more time, and you need to back off just a little."

The moment the words leave my mouth, I want to retract them. Aside from being my cousin, Kieron is the Second-In-Command for the Irish Mob in Boston. He's in charge of a lot of shit and deserves the respect that comes with his position. Never mind that he is my cousin who I look at as more of a brother. We've been close all our lives, with me being only a couple years younger than him, and both of us basically living at Headquarters with our fathers. Sometimes I forget my place, and mouth off when I shouldn't.

Even though we're like brothers, he can, and will, pull rank and make me do grunt work or some shit for my disobedience. That happened to me a lot before Kieron took over. I don't like authority figures. Imagine that. But Kieron has always been able to lead without demeaning others. He's always been fair.

He's silent on the other end of the phone, and I sigh. I turn the water off and lean my free hand on the cabinet above the sink. My head hangs as I try to figure out what to say to fix this. Fix all of this.

"Sorry, man. I'm… I don't know what to do to help you guys without forcing her to open up somehow." Even suggesting that makes my stomach hurt.

Mila hasn't told me much about her time with Los Muertos.

Just that they'd taken her from outside her workplace. She's kept the details to a minimum, and I can understand why. From what little she did say, after they took her, she didn't see the light of day until I saved her.

After she'd told me that, I made sure to change out the blackout curtains in her room to sheer ones. That way she'd have privacy, but always have fresh air, sunlight, and a view. Even at night, she'd be able to see the stars and moon.

"I get it, Killer." Kieron sighs heavily through the phone. "But, seriously Cillian, if she's from the Smirnov family… we're inviting a war by keeping her."

"She doesn't want to go," I whisper into the speaker. "I've told her time and time again to give me an address I can drop her off at, a name of a person she wants to see to bring her home, but she refuses. The last time I offered, she cussed me out in Russian and told me never to ask again." Running my hands through my short hair, I sigh. I'm in between a rock and a hard place. I want, desperately for some unknown reason, to keep her comfortable and safe. I want to be the one she runs to for safety and care. I need to be that person for her.

Don't ask me why, I don't fucking know.

It's like something shifted the moment her ice-blue eyes locked onto mine. Something in my DNA was rewritten to put her above everything else. It's a tricky line to walk, especially since she seems to want nothing to do with me.

"She should understand the risk we're taking by keeping her. You need to sit down and explicitly tell her what will happen if we don't tell the Russian Bratva that we're harboring a daughter of theirs. Not just any daughter. One that was *taken* and held hostage. What happens if word gets around? It looks like *we* did it. Like the *Clan* did it. How do you think that's going to go?" Kieron says, and with each word I can hear the stress he's under.

"I get it. I'll take care of it. Give me a week." I barter for more time to figure this shit out. To figure out how to get Mila to talk, without making an enemy of the girl I'm trying to save.

"You have four days, Killer. That's the most Skipper would give me before he takes it into his own hands. And based on how he was speaking, he's not going to handle it in a way that you'd want him to."

Fuck.

I'm so screwed.

* * *

After hanging up the phone with Kieron, I need at least three beers.

Maybe a few shots of whiskey too.

As I lean against the marble countertop in my small kitchen, my forehead hits the cabinets above, and I groan, letting out all my frustrations and stress with the sound.

How am I going to do this? How am I going to not fuck up all the progress I've made with Mila?

"What did he say?"

At the sound of her voice, I flip around quickly to see the girl in question. She's fucking gorgeous, just standing there in one of my sweatshirts that's so big on her it could be a dress. I can see she has shorts on underneath, but they're the shortest fucking things ever. Barely covering her ass. Not that I mind.

She's taken to wearing my clothes and I fucking love it. Her black hair is pulled up into a messy bun, and she has not a stitch of makeup on. She's natural. Beautiful.

"What?" I already forgot what she asked. My brain was too busy short-circuiting from the sight of her.

"You sounded upset. I wanted to make sure you were okay," she says softly, wringing her hands together. They're covered with my sweatshirt sleeves, and it's so endearing. "I assume that was your boss. What did he say?"

"Nothing really." I shake my head and move to the island in the middle of the kitchen. I'm not going to force the issue yet. "Are you hungry?"

Mila shakes her head no, but her stomach growls. An adorable blush covers her cheeks, and she looks down self-consciously.

"I'll take that as a yes." Gesturing for her to sit at the stool under the island, I say, "I'm a terrible cook, so does spaghetti sound okay?" I open the fridge to pull out all the ingredients I need.

"You don't have to."

I ignore her and try to hide my smile when I see that she sat down.

"What kind of host would I be if I didn't feed you when you're hungry? Plus, Bryan will be here soon for dinner and you know that man can eat." I dump the spaghetti noodles in the boiling water and pull out a smaller pot for the sauce.

"I'm sorry," she says softly, so softly that I barely hear it.

"Why are you sorry?"

"Because. You have to deal with me. You have to feed me, clothe me. You're giving me shelter and safety. You're so patient with me, Cillian. You have no reason to be so nice and understanding, but you are. I don't deserve it. I'm not used to this. I know that me being here with you is putting you in a bad place and I… I'm sorry. I don't deserve your kindness."

My whole body tenses as I hear her start to cry. I don't know what to do, what to think, so I turn my brain off and let my heart do the talking. It's the most Mila has opened up to me in days. I turn around to face her cautiously.

"I don't mean to be such a mess. I just don't know how to face it," she whispers.

I turn around, doing my best to put a neutral expression on my face. "Face what?"

"My family."

"And why is your family some big bad thing?" I press. I'm already pushing too much, I can tell. She's revealed more in the last few minutes than she has in weeks, and I don't know how much more she's going to give me. I don't want to appear too thirsty for her information, but I need more. Besides the order from Kieron, I'm desperate to know more about her. This mysterious girl who has taken over my every thought.

"They… Well, let's just say that I'm safer here than with them." She looks down at the marble countertop, running her fingers over a pattern. "They're powerful and ruthless. But they're my family. Even if I wish they weren't." She sighs. "What happened with Los Muertos? Are they gone?"

"There aren't any survivors, we made sure of that," I say, and take a deep breath. I know exactly how she feels though. The Clan in Boston is fierce and to be feared. I've always known that I'd be inducted into this life, regardless of what I wanted. The only thing that's made it somewhat bearable is that I work for Kieron, with Bryan and Trent. The four of us form our own little unit and Kellan has stopped trying to pull us apart for missions. He knows that no matter what, we'd bring in the others.

"I understand that actually." I nod, turning back to preparing the food. "My family is also powerful and ruthless, as you put it. They've been known to do a lot of bad shit, but in this instance, they—we, are trying to help."

"You realize that if I contact the people you want me to, they're going to think that you were the one to kidnap me. Your family might be big and powerful, but if it's just you and whatever little gang inside the Irish Mob the four of you have going, you'll die. They'll kill you before you can even say a word."

"I think me and this 'little gang' have more sway than you think," I say softly, my back still turned to her.

"What do you mean?" Mila asks, just as quietly.

It feels like a pinnacle moment. A moment that's going to change things between us. The only question is; will it change for the better?

I put the spoon down and pick up a rag, wiping my hands slowly before I turn to face her. I'm sure she's well-versed in the world of organized crime, but we still don't know exactly what she knows. She probably doesn't even realize that she's been saved by the Second-In-Command and his unit, but I guess telling her the whole truth couldn't make things *worse*. She's already not talking to me, barely eating, hiding in the spare room.

"The small, wannabe gang that took you was Los Muertos. They were the uncoordinated, small-fish-in-a-big-pond type group, with a leader with goals that were way too stupid and lofty for them to attain. They weren't even on our radar. That's how inconsequential they were. My family, the four of us, well baby, we're the top of the Mafia chain here. Kieron is the Skipper's son and I'm his cousin."

I let that information sink in, turning my back to her again and dumping the sauce into the pot to heat up while her mouth opens and closes as she tries to think of what to say.

"You're just the cousin, too?" she says after a few moments of silence.

It wasn't uncomfortable silence, I realize, just companionable and understanding. I know I should've watched my back after I told her… not turned and left myself vulnerable. But, I have a feeling that Mila is just like me. Like we're two people misunderstood and overlooked by our families, forced into doing things that we don't necessarily want to.

"Not the heir, but the spare?"

I nod.

"I have to leave," she says suddenly, pushing away from the table and turning to run to her room.

She's quick, but I'm faster. My hand darts out to grab her wrist, stopping her from running.

"You can't leave, Mila."

"Watch me." Her eyes narrow, challenging me.

I take in all the small changes about her as she seems to prepare for a fight.

She straightens her spine. Her naturally pink lips press together as she pushes her jaw out slightly—showing me just how annoyed she is—and she rips her arm from my grasp.

She may be part of the Bratva by birth, but I've been living, breathing, and being an integral part of the Clan for my entire life. I've been taught how to fight since I could walk, so if she wants to think that she could get by me, I have to give her a pat on the back for effort. But she's not leaving.

"I can't let you do that." My words aren't meant to come out as menacing as they do, but when her foot slides back and she shifts into a fighting stance as quick as a blink, I know I'm in trouble.

"I won't let you get hurt by the Bratva, Cillian. Not after all you've done for me. The only way to avoid that is to walk away." Her leg darts out and a small, but fucking mighty kick knocks me in the back of my knee.

I go down *hard*. My knees hit the tile and my hands dart out to break my fall.

What the fuck was that?

I'm sure the look on my face is as ridiculous as I feel. "We can work together, Mila."

"You don't know them like I do," she says. Her piercing, beautiful blue eyes are full of terror and fear as she looks down at me before turning away again. I don't want to fight her, I don't want to hurt her, but I can't let her leave.

I jump up and sweep my leg so she tumbles to the ground with a breathy *oompf*, but she rolls so she's facing me in the beat of time that it takes me to get to her. Her leg kicks out at me and I wince when it makes contact with my shoulder, knocking me back.

How is she so fucking strong? She's tall, sure, but petite.

"Will you fucking stop?" I snap through my teeth.

She doesn't answer me and instead swipes her leg at me to try to kick both of my arms out. I'm ready for it this time. I grab her leg and pull her body to me until her ass hits my knees. Mila's thrashing and I can tell that she's putting up a hell of a fight, but she's no match for me. I have at least five inches on her and at the very least fifty pounds.

"Are you going to keep fighting me, or do I need to pin you

down?"

She growls, *fucking growls at me*, and I can feel my cock start to harden. She's feisty and strong and squirming all up on me.

Focus, Cillian, this isn't the time.

I shake my head to clear it and shift so that I pin her thighs under my knees, putting just enough pressure to keep her still, but not enough to hurt her. Grabbing her wrists, I pin them to the ground. Her chest is rising quickly, with exertion and anger, and I feel every breath she takes.

What the fuck am I thinking? This will do nothing but turn me on more. Her tight body under mine, her muscles clenching and shifting to fight me, her breathing heavily in my ear.

Fuck.

"Can we talk about this?" I say suddenly, doing everything I can to not make her uncomfortable or poke her with my hard-on.

"There's nothing to talk about, Cillian! I'm trying to protect you!" she yells at me, but her words are anxious and desperate. "I'm trying to protect you!" she repeats, more desperately than before.

"Why?"

"I—"

I jump up and wrap my arm around her waist before she darts out of my way.

"Just fucking talk to me, Mila," I snap.

I feel her chest rise with a sob, and she opens her mouth slowly, like she really doesn't want to tell me.

"I..." she starts, but then, right at the worst fucking time, Bryan walks in. Like a bear coming out of hibernation, he stomps his way through the apartment and I secretly wonder how the hell he stays so silent on missions because each footstep seems to rattle my apartment.

He comes to a stop when he sees us on the floor and his eyes quickly avert. "I, uh, I didn't… I can leave," he says.

I give him a second look because something seems odd with him. Bryan's never one to chat a whole lot, but I'm usually able to tell what he's feeling. Right now is no different. He's trying hard to cover his feelings, but I know this guy too well. His cheeks are red, he's clenching his jaw, his hands are curling tightly into fists by his side. He's upset and pissed off.

"Bryan," I start to say because something is bothering him and I can clearly see it.

But Mila uses it as an excuse to twist my arm and force me to let go of her. She wiggles her thighs and after getting one free, rams it up into my side, forcing all the air from my lungs, before jumping up and running to her room.

"Fuck. *Fuck,*" I wheeze, rolling over to follow her.

"What the hell is going on?" Bryan grumbles, but I don't answer him.

I can't let her leave. I can't let her go.

"Mila!"

The Breakdown

Mila

He might be in the Irish Clan, but there's no way he knows what the Bratva is like. There's no room for love, for caring, for softness. If I don't get away from him, then the Bratva will destroy them all. I can't let that happen. I can't let Cillian be harmed because of me.

Not when he's the only person I've ever met who seems to care without needing something from me, without using me to get something else.

Not after he's the first person I've felt some kind of care for.

"Mila!" Cillian booms as I run to my room.

My toes grip into the hardwood to propel me further. I bolt to the end of the hallway, and grab the door frame to pull myself into my room just as I see a big imposing figure quickly making up any time I'd gathered by my few second head start.

I have to get out of here. *I have to get out of here.*

I slam the door shut, twisting the lock, giving myself mere

moments to try to figure out how to escape. *Think, Mila. You've been in tighter spots than this before.*

Boom! A kick to my door rattles the whole thing, but it stays intact.

"Mila, please. Please, let's talk about this. I know you're scared, but running away isn't the answer!" Cillian yells.

"You dont know them like I do, Cillian. You don't know what will happen if they think it's you and your family who took me. Even if they left me to rot, it will still start a war. A war I can save you and your family from," I try to explain. My uncle, the leader of the Bratva for the Northeastern US, didn't get to that position without bloodshed and torture. To this day, he doesn't spare anyone his cruel treatment. Not even his brothers or sons who work directly under him. Especially not his lowly niece. "They won't let it go if they feel they've been disrespected."

All of us—all blood relation to Uncle Sergei, no matter what rank or position, are forced to go through a training program. I never wanted to be a part of that awful, evil dynasty. But I wasn't given a choice. I quickly figured out that the only way to survive was to hit harder, run faster, be stealthier.

I became the *Prizrak,* or Ghost. Assassin for the Bratva that no one knows about. So the fact that Los Muertos got the jump on me, keeping me drugged and powerless, tells me that they weren't stupid. They just didn't know what they'd caught.

"I'm not running. I won't let anyone hurt you. I promised. And I keep my promises." Cillian knocks harder on the door.

"He does, Mila. It's a very annoying, very loyal trait of his." A gruff voice joins Cillian's by the door.

There's a vent up by the ceiling that I could fit through, but

I don't know what security systems they have in place. Lasers, gasses, maybe metal grates further in? I've seen them all and would be able to figure it out, but I'm not at 100% health yet.

Boom! Another shoulder to the door. "I don't want to take your privacy away from you, I don't want to be that person, but I did swear that I'd keep you safe no matter what. Even if that means breaking down this fucking door." Cillian sounds desperate.

I know the feeling.

Running to the window, I see I'm way too far up to consider jumping.

Fuck. Fuck!

"Come on, Mila. We aren't the bad guys here." Bryan's calm but growly voice floats through the space. Like I don't know that. They might be part of the Mafia, but these men aren't evil.

I've shown my hand. Ruined the meek-demeanored character I was playing for my own safety.

"One, two…" Cillian counts loudly, letting me know right before his shoulder is due to slam into the wooden door again. I pull it open before he gets to three.

Cillian has both hands clasped together and his shoulder braced to hit into the door once again. A quick glance shows me that one more hit would have cracked it enough for them to get in.

"Mila?" he asks, breathless. His eyes are focused, but I can see the determination in them.

Bryan stands to the side, in the middle of pulling off his own black leather jacket like he was going to help Cillian break down my door.

"Okay, boys. Let's talk."

* * *

There's obviously no way in hell that Cillian isn't going to watch my every move from now on, so I'm not surprised that I somehow manage to be placed in between Bryan and Cillian as we walk single-file down the hallway.

They may be good guys, but they're still adept in the world of danger, stealth, deception, and protection.

We walk to the living room and Bryan breaks off, hustling to the kitchen.

"Goddamnit, Cillian. Can't even make spaghetti without burning water," he grumbles under his breath.

I notice how Cillian's once nice and clean kitchen is now covered in red splotches everywhere, but at least it smells good.

I plop onto the overstuffed gray couch and await my interrogation. There's no reason to share everything with them just yet.

"What the fuck was that, Mila?" Cillian throws his arms out like he's exasperated with me.

Finally, an emotion from him that isn't so kind and understanding.

"What are you talking about specifically?"

"I mean, the calm, shy, scared girl who's been living in my house suddenly kicks my ass out of fucking nowhere? What the hell was that?" He sounds pissed, but I can see the confusion and a bit of pride in his eyes.

"I grew up in the Bratva. We all learn to fight." I shrug my shoulders, leaning back into the cushions.

"Don't do that, don't act like that wasn't more than basic

self-defense."

"What do you want from me, Cillian?"

His nostrils flare slightly with each quickened breath he takes. Like always, I take in as many details as I can. He's clenching his fist like he wants to point a finger at me accusingly. He's kept the other hand pulled back a bit, probably to keep it closer to his gun if he decides I'm a threat. The window is to my right, but I'm still much too high up to escape that way. I hear Bryan take soft, measured steps from the kitchen area, and the zing of something—probably a knife—across the counter. If this goes wrong, I'll have to disarm Cillian first, then focus on the knife. Bryan probably has a gun as well, so watching my back is crucial.

Not that I want it to come to that, but I have to be prepared.

"Cillian." I put both of my hands up and stand. Both men adjust themselves around me, making sure that I can't escape them. "I'm Mila. Mila Smirnova. The same person I was fifteen minutes ago."

"Who are you, really?" he sneers.

I've always known a softer Cillian. I knew he could be brutal, especially after how he saved me. But his brutality was never directed at me.

He's a completely different person.

And I respect it. I'm a threat right now, and he won't let anything or anyone harm his family.

Taking a deep breath, I bite the inside of my cheek. I don't know what to do. But what I do know, what I've felt since the very beginning, is that I can trust him. "Okay, I'll tell you but can you both stand down? Bryan, put the knife down. Cillian, inch away from your gun. I'm not a threat."

"That's not for you to decide," Bryan says.

Cillian's eyes narrow even more.

"If I wanted either of you dead, you'd have already been dead," I say with a shrug. And that is as honest as I've ever been. If I wanted them dead, the moment they brought me into headquarters, I would've snapped their necks before they turned around to check on me.

The two burly men in front of me look at each other. A silent understanding passes between them, and then Cillian looks at me. "The moment I think you're lying to me again, you're dead."

"Understood."

There is an anger coming from him, that's warring with frustration and intrigue within. I'm sure his mafia training is screaming at him to kill me and be done with it. So, I can't blame him for his sudden change in personality. I've thrown a massive surprise at him.

"Please, sit down and let me explain. Ask your questions and I'll do my best to answer." I gesture with my head to the couch, moving back toward it with my hands still up, proving to them I'm not armed or going to harm them.

Slowly, so achingly slowly, I see Cillian unclench his fist, bringing his other hand forward to rest on his hip. He moves to the far edge of the couch. A loud metallic clattering hits the floor and Bryan stomps over to stand behind Cillian.

I fucking wish I had someone to back me up unconditionally like these guys have with each other.

"Talk," Cillian snaps.

The Truth

Cillian

I brought a fucking wolf in sheep's clothing into headquarters.
Into my fucking home.
Mila Smirnova is meant to be Bratva royalty. Meant to be a Princess sitting up on a throne with her cousins and uncle. Away from any of the foot soldiers who do the dirty work; a girl whose only concern should be staying out of danger, hitting on her next boytoy, and shopping. But, instead, here she sits, dangerous and deadly with just her bare hands. We aren't going to talk about how that thought alone gets me hard. I shake my head to rid myself of the vision, or fantasy, I usually have but never let myself fully indulge in.
A strong, lithe woman, dressed in all black, telling me to be a good boy and get on my knees. *Fuck.* Now the woman that I usually see in my fantasies, someone without a distinctive face, morphs into her. Mila could be the one that makes that come true. She's strong enough, that's for sure.
She'd make me feel safe enough to try.

She fidgets with the ends of her black hair, gnawing on her lip. I can't tell if this anxiety she's exuding is genuine or part of her game.

"Talk," I bark at her again, crossing my arms over my chest and staring her down.

"Look, there's a reason why I didn't want to tell you. I didn't want you to tell my family. I'm trying to protect you."

Again with this protecting *us* shit. I roll my eyes, and look back at her just in time to see her gaze harden.

"It's the truth."

"How would I know?" I snap back. I can feel the anger build in my chest again, threatening to explode. Deep breaths aren't cutting it now.

"Okay, okay." Bryan steps in, putting his hand on my shoulder to ground me. "Just get to the point. Why were you taken, and who are you, really?"

It's annoying as shit that he felt he had to step in, but he's the voice of reason. I'm too close. This reaction, and my reluctance to simply blow her head off right now, tells me that my feelings are fucking involved. Even though I tried to keep them neutral. I didn't try hard enough, I guess.

"I am Mila Smirnova," Mila says earnestly, genuinely, telling us what we already knew. "But I *am* more than just the niece of the Bratva leader."

"Obviously." Grinding my molars, I do my best not to roll my eyes again. It's hard for me to see all that she's done as sincere, as if she does actually care about how it goes down between the Clan and the Bratva.

"I think what Cillian means," Bryan cuts in, *again*, and his eyes narrow at me—telling me to calm the fuck down—"is that its fairly obvious from everything that just went down that you aren't simply the Bratva Princess. Unless they put you through combat training for a specific reason."

His words sit heavy between us. The air is thick with tension and waiting.

"They did have us all go through combat training. Each of the heirs. Marek, Ivan, and myself," she says. Mila's staring out in front of her, her eyes trained on the floor, unseeing, dark and dim. She's twisting her long fingers together nervously. "Marek and Ivan…. It was expected of them to be trained, to go through initiation. They were Uncle's sons. The true Heirs. But my father insisted that I be trained too. He felt it prudent that I, as his oldest child, receive the same skill set as my cousins. Unfortunately, Uncle agreed."

The way that she said 'initiation'…. It made my skin crawl. I'm no stranger to the brutality and cruelty, the impossible choices that we were forced to make in our own training for the Clan. To join the Clan, to show how dedicated we were, to survive; we all had to do things that still keep us up at night.

The guilt lessens, but never really goes away.

Our hearts and souls just darken more and more over time.

"Those sorts of lessons are not intended for a woman of our world," Bryan mutters.

I immediately tense up.

"And what is that supposed to mean?" Mila's eyes snap to Bryan, hooded and narrow. She looks as if she's about to pounce, like she would snap his neck before I'd be able to blink. Gone is the demure, soft-spoken kitten. In her place is a sharp, fierce warrior.

Don't get me wrong, I like both sides of her. But, this fierceness is bringing out something in me that I can't control.

"That you, the niece of Sergei Smirnov, should have been

treated like a princess in a tower. Unattainable. Used only for political influence and union. It's the way female heirs are handled. They're kept safe. Protected," Bryan says, shrugging his shoulders.

I want to say something because I can see the fire building behind Mila's eyes, but he's not wrong. It may be barbaric and outdated, but it is usually how girls born into the mafia are treated. Unless the leader of the crime family wanted to use them for something different, or the woman wanted to fight for a different life. The women that did that didn't usually didn't stay in favor.

Or alive.

"I'm not saying it's *right*, I'm saying that's how it's done," Bryan clarifies gruffly, crossing his arms over his chest.

Mila shoots up from her seat, silently and deadly, with fire in her eyes. She points an elegant finger in Bryan's face, making sure he listens.

Not that she has to, we're both enraptured with her. Bryan looks more intrigued. Guarded, but still interested. Whereas, I'm slipping into obsession.

I'm not forgetting her lying, but damn, she's beautiful.

"Don't you dare try to tell me about the outdated and patriarchal customs of men in power. I'm well-fucking-aware. My entire life has been nothing but keeping men happy, bowing to men, letting them touch and use me as they want. Just because I'm a woman. Sending me to be trained, to be initiated, was a risky move by my father, but he knew what could happen. He knew he couldn't protect me if Sergei decreed I be sent off or married to a bad man. Teaching me to fight, that was my father's one and only kindness. I may have been used for a different purpose, but I was never thought of as a political match again." Mila's chest is heaving fast with her deep breaths.

"How were you useful to the Bratva then?" I ask. My words, while they may sound callus, show how accustomed we are with the way this mafia life works. If you aren't useful or in favor, you're disposed of.

Mila's eyes slide to me slowly, hurt swimming in the blues of her irises.

"They turned me into a ghost," she whispered.

We're all silent as she lets go of a deep breath and sits back down.

"The Ghost. The *Prizrak*." She speaks so softly I'm not really sure I heard her.

"No," Bryan says, chuckling humorlessly. "There's no way. The Ghost is a nightmare we're told about in the Clan. A way to keep us in line."

I remember the stories Kellan would tell us when we were younger about how if we didn't follow through with what he wanted, he'd 'send The Ghost after us'. That we would be dead and forgotten before sundown. It's a way to get recruits to fall in line. Ghost stories.

"You're my age. I've been hearing about The Ghost since I was a preteen." It doesn't make any sense.

Mila sighs. "The *Prizrak* is a mantel. Given to the best of the best. Every generation, there is a new one. The previous *Prizrak* works under Sergei's rule until the newest one is ready, and then the honor is passed down. They stay active in the Bratva, always lurking, always available if needed, but the newest generation is roped in at eighteen years old. The *Prizrak* has been around for decades. Lifetimes. I am the current *Prizrak* for the Bratva, although I'm sure since my kidnapping, I've been disgraced and they replaced me. Thank god." She whispers the last words as if she's relieved.

"Why should we believe that you're not a plant? That this isn't some elaborate plot of the Bratva?" I ask. There's a part of me, okay, a big part, that hopes she's being sincere. I know full and well that she is Mila Smirnova, part of the Bratva, but this… It just seems a little too coincidental that she, the feared *Ghost*, pretty much arrived on our doorstep. I want to believe her, I really do. But I'm not careless or stupid.

"Because I've been disgraced. Going back to the Bratva and telling Sergei that I was kidnapped and defiled by a gang that's so far beneath them, I'll be thrown out. More than likely killed."

"Then why were you trying to run before?" I have to know. I have to know why she'd voluntarily go back to them when I've been begging to protect her.

"Because, Cillian, if they find out that I'm here, even if the Clan saved me, they'd send the current Ghost after you. Then after me. I can't let that happen to you, not after everything you've done for me. I can't have them manipulate me with another person I care for." Her blue eyes lock on mine, and I see the truth. I'm sure that she has more secrets, I know I do, but she's on my side.

* * *

Mila went back to her room after she told us her story. The exhaustion was written all over her face and when I saw her body slump forward, I told her to go to bed. Not before reminding her that I have sensors and cameras installed and I'm now activating them.

She nodded sadly, and left. I don't want to become her jailor, but I can't trust her right now. Not after everything I just heard. Not now that I know how good she is at espionage.

"What are you going to do?" Bryan asks, cutting off my train of thought.

"What do you mean?" I stand up, pushing off the couch to get a drink. A strong one. The spaghetti is a lost fucking cause. It burnt to a black, crusty mess on the stove a long time ago. The white-and-gray backsplash is coated in marinara sauce and I just know it's going to take me forever to clean that shit up. The noodles are one big clump in the water. Nothing is edible.

I'm not going to worry about that right now. That's a problem for a different day.

I open the cabinet and pull out a bag of chips, just something fast to munch on while I'm thinking about all the shit that's gone down.

"You know what I fucking mean, Cillian. Kieron's been at you to get information about her so we don't start a war. She just trusted us with information that will definitely start a war if we don't play this right."

With a sigh, I run my hand down my face. I'm too tired for this shit. This is not how I thought today was going to go.

"I don't know, Bryan. I don't know yet. I need to think."

"You need to tell Kieron or Kellan," Bryan pushes. I know he's right, I know I should tell Kieron, but something is telling me not to. At least, not yet.

Rubbing the nape of my neck to release some of the tension

that's built up, I shake my head. I've always trusted my gut with big things, and this time is no different. I shouldn't—can't—break her trust right now. Not without getting to know her more. The *real* her.

"Tell me that you understand that, Cillian." Bryan sounds exasperated. I pull the tumbler of amber liquid down from its spot in the cabinet, and grab the glass I drank from earlier. I stay decidedly silent. I'm not going to lie to him, but I need him to stay quiet until I figure it out. My back stays to Bryan, and the whiskey sloshes into my empty cup.

"Dammit, Cillian," he sneers.

"Just give me some time, Bry," I snap, turning to face him and taking a long drink. The whiskey hits my throat, warming me. I'm hopeful the buzz will hit soon and keep me calm.

"Time for what? For her to slit your throat in your sleep? For Sergei to storm headquarters, thinking we've stolen his Ghost? His niece? Think of the Clan."

Another sip of whiskey down the hatch. "I understand that, Bry. But something feels off here. I need to figure it out first."

I can see the disappointment in his eyes as I stand my ground. Grumbling, Bryan turns and starts to stalk toward the door.

"Bryan…"

"I'll give you a day, Killer. Twenty-four hours. Figure it out in twenty-four hours and tell me what I need to do. But don't tell me that after those hours are up, I can't take matters into my own hands."

"And what does that mean?"

His eyes lock on mine and I can see the wall he's building in his mind through the brown irises. "It means, I'll make sure the Clan is taken care of. I like Mila, I do, but I can't sit back knowing we have 'The Ghost' under our roof without letting the appropriate people know."

"Understood." I nod once. I can't blame him, in fact, I should be happy that he's giving me any time at all.

He shakes his head and slams my front door, leaving me alone with an impossible choice and hard feelings I need to sort out and fast.

"Fuck. *Fuck!*"

The Real Conversation

Mila

Another time limit for Cillian.

Because of me.

Because of what I'm putting him through.

Bryan and Cillian aren't in the wrong here, I know that. I tricked them without any ill-intent; I just wanted to be safe. I just wanted to get away from the Bratva. From the *Prizrak.* From all the terror, danger, stress, and anger. Constant anger. Constant fear. Constant disappointment.

I just want to be safe. Safe and loved. Loved for just me. Just Mila. And for the whole time I've been here with Cillian, under his roof and under his care, that's all I've felt. I don't know if he ever felt anything more for me, I haven't dared to hope that he would return any feelings, but at least I've felt his care.

I get where Bryan and Kieron are coming from though. Finding out my history, I knew that they'd throw some guards up. You don't survive in our world without suspicions and high walls.

I don't hide myself in the short hallway, but I stay quiet as I watch Bryan leave. He slams the door so hard, the paintings shake on the walls. I hear Cillian roar in frustration, and try my best to shut off my feelings. Be as icy and impartial as possible. But I can't. My normal compartmentalization tactics aren't working.

Why?

Normally, I have no problem being able to switch off my emotions. A useful trick I was taught in the torture chamber as I was made into a new creature for Sergei. Being able to differentiate the fear and agony, the need and the humiliation; all while hiding who I actually was so they couldn't touch and destroy my soul, was and still is, an incredibly useful tool. It's been the only way I can survive, the only way I *continue* to survive through everything they made me do. When things get too hard, *click*, emotions go off.

But with Cillian, I don't want to. I can't.

I watch him knock back the drink in his hand and immediately go to refill it.

"I wouldn't blame you, you know?" I say softly and watch his back muscles tense. If he knew I was there listening, he hadn't let on.

"For what?" His voice is flat, frustrated and tired.

"If you told them what I told you."

He's silent as I watch him pick up the tumbler and pour another drink. Normally, I'd be wary of any man drinking like this because in my experience, it only leads to hurt and pain for me. But Cillian has proven to me over the time we've spent together that isn't him.

He's struggling.

"What I need to know, Mila, is why you decided to tell me the truth. Is it to take down the Clan?" He turns around quickly, his eyes accusing me with every movement.

"Of course not."

"Is it to embarass me?"

"What?"

"You've told me all this, proving that you've been able to infiltrate the Clan and trick me all this time?" He growls, his drink forgotten on the counter as he stalks closer to my position at the end of the hallway.

"No!"

"Then why? Why do this and why tell us? What kind of mind games are you playing?"

His words ignite my own frustration and I push off the wall to stand toe-to-toe with him.

"Is it so fucking hard to believe that I thought I was safe here? That you'd provide me some kind of safe harbor from the Bratva? You promised me when you saved me, you promised that nothing would harm me." I throw his promise in his face, knowing that he meant what he said, but that he isn't proving it now.

Cillian steps into my space, leaving barely any room between us. I can feel the heat from his body, the tension radiating from him. He's practically vibrating. Whether from anger or something else, I don't know. "You wanted safety? The Ghost? The feared *Prizrak* wanted saving? You expect me to believe that?"

How dare he? How *fucking* dare he?

"I expect you to believe the truth, Cillian. I expect you to understand the pressure and expectations I was under. I expect you to empathize with me because you may be in control of your family in some ways, but I've always been under the thumb of mine." My finger pushes against his hard chest, poking him so hard I'm sure he'll have a bruise. I don't care.

The anger dissipates in his eyes as I see the truth dawning on him.

"I expect you to understand how badly I want out," I whisper.

Cillian brings both of his hands up to hold mine. "Enough to be kidnapped?"

My head hangs with shame.

"I didn't intentionally set out to be taken. Los Muertos, one of their goons, drugged me from behind in broad daylight. Cocky fuckers. They just didn't know the prize they had once I'd been captured. They kept pumping me full of tranquilizer every time I regained consciousness so I was never able to regain my strength enough to leave. Until the night you found me. I wasn't wanting to be taken and raped, but I'm so fucking happy that it was you that saved me."

Cillian's jaw tightens. His nostrils flare. His eyes narrow. "If those fuckers weren't already dead, I'd track them all down and kill them myself for even thinking of touching you against your wishes." He snarls at me, like the mere thought of me in pain or danger was enough to push him over the edge.

"You mean that?" I whisper, looking up at him through my eyelashes.

"Every word."

It's like the room is pushing us together. There's no choice, no option for us not to close the little bit of space between us. My body calls to his; our energies feel like they're intertwining. Like there's never been a choice, even when I tried to pull away for my own good. For *his* own good.

But I never stood a chance against this.

"Cillian," I whisper. My breath comes quicker, and the fire in my body burns hotter with his proximity. With each breath, my chest rubs against his and I can feel my nipples start to harden.

"Are you going to fuck us over?" he whispers back, his eyes trained on my lips. I feel so guilty, not because I'm planning on screwing them over, but because he feels that he needs to ask.

"No." I meet his gaze, pushing as much sincerity into my voice as I can. "I won't, wouldn't, do that to you *or* yours."

Cillian takes a quick breath. "Do you promise, Mila? Because, doll, once we start this, whatever *this* will become, you'll be mine." He dips his head closer. His words are husky and quiet.

They elicit a very strong reaction. My nipples are completely hard and straining against the thin fabric of my borrowed shirt. I feel the heat start to build between my legs, the anticipation building between us as this is about to go further.

"Do you understand? *Mine.*"

Boom, my panties are drenched.

"I'll be yours, but really, you'll be mine," I say softly, licking my lips and eliminating any space between us. I wrap my fingers into his short hair and pull his mouth to mine. I take the kiss from him in a loving, desperate, dominant way. Just how I like it.

Cillian doesn't fight me for dominance. Instead, he slides his hands around my waist and pulls me in tighter. One of his big, warm hands slides up in between my shoulder blades and presses my chest into his.

"You're not wearing a bra." He pulls back barely, just enough so that his lips aren't on mine.

"No," I say with a smirk, "I'm not. What are you going to do about it?"

Without missing a beat, a change goes through Cillian. Like a mask sliding over his face. His mouth shapes into a snarky, cocky grin. The grip he has on me becomes more dominant, more pushy, and he starts to crowd me in a way he hadn't before. For anyone else, I'm sure it would have seemed like he was taking control of the situation. Becoming "the man" in charge.

But it feels false to me. Like he's putting on a show.

"Show me," he demands.

But it feels off to my ears.

If he actually, truly, really, wants to be in charge, that's fine, but I'm good at reading people. I can tell it's not genuine. He wants someone to take care of him. To let *him* follow directions and just be in the moment.

"Do you think you deserve to see?" I let my words hang, letting the tone of my voice, the way I phrase the question, linger between us.

Cillian steps back slightly, like my question is a test and he's trying to figure it out.

In a way, it is. I want to see if he really feels like he needs to take over, or if he would be okay with *me* taking over. More than that, I *need* him to be okay with me taking over. I need to have some control back after Los Muertos took it from me.

Sex, *good sex*, I've found needs push and pull. Someone to take the lead and another to be told what to do. There needs to be electricity, connection, understanding between them. Two people with the insane need to be together, to explore together, that *want* each other.

"Do you think you've earned it?" I push Cillian a little further. Biting down on my bottom lip, I wait for him to answer. To choose.

His eyes darken, and the cocky look on his face melts away. The tight grip that he's had on my body slackens a bit. His touch is still there, still holding me, but it's not dominant. It's not demanding.

He's waiting for me to tell him what to do.

"Well?" I say. "Do you? Tell me why you've earned it." My voice is low and husky as I look at him and watch every detail of the way his body changes. I've been trained to notice minute changes in body language, to be able to understand people's weaknesses and their strengths.

Cillian's eyes blaze. He bites his lower lip like he's both nervous and excited.

"Come on, big guy, tell me," I whisper, sliding my fingers down his arms until I reach his hands. I take one and thread our fingers together before maneuvering our clasped hands to rest over my heart. He's able to feel every thump of my heartbeat, and he's able to be honest and real with me.

"Because." Cillian speaks as softly as I did. "I want to take care of you. I want to serve you and keep you safe. Please."

"You're right. You have kept me safe. You have taken care of me. But serve me? How do you expect to serve me? That's a very specific word, *serve*."

"I want to be what you want, Mila. I want to hold you, I want to pleasure you, I want to fuck you, I want to take care of every need, wish, and want you have," he says, his eyelids hooded.

There's an unspoken 'but' hanging between us. Like he

wanted to say something more, but stopped himself.

"But…" I lead, hoping he'll keep talking.

"I think I've exposed enough of myself right now. I answered your question, now I want to see."

I step back a bit, and hold my hands out to my sides. "Go ahead, Cillian. You've earned it. But don't think we won't continue this conversation at a later time."

Cillian smirks. "Yes, Ma'am."

Oh, I like that. I like that *a lot*.

The First Act

Cillian

I saw how her eyes darkened when I said, 'Yes, Ma'am.'

I can feel how her breathing increases, and that's when I know for sure that she likes taking control in the bedroom. I've never really had a woman act like this. They're always first to hit the mattress, lay back, and let me do whatever. They don't talk, unless it's to sound like a phony-ass pornstar, and when they do talk, it's to tell me to fuck them harder.

It's never soft and tender. It's never to praise me.

Her arms are out, waiting for me to undress her. But I want her to give me permission. I want to show her I can be good for her.

"Can I take your shirt off, Mila? Please?" I ask, and even I can hear the breathlessness in my voice, the raw need.

"Good boy, asking permission," she praises me. The sultry tenor of her voice makes my eyes roll back into my head as I groan.

If I wasn't so fucking turned on by her tone or by her words, by being called a *good boy*, if this wasn't such a secret fantasy of mine, I might have been offended by her forwardness. Instead, it makes me feel comfortable, like I can shed my worries from the day, from the weight I carry from the Clan, and just let her take it all for me.

I drag my fingers down her sides, and pray she doesn't see how my hands have started to shake. The worn fabric of the t-shirt is soft under my fingers and I can feel her strong curves under it. When I reach the hem, I drag my attention up to her eyes. Not before my gaze catches on her hardened nipples straining against the fabric. My mouth feels dry, and all I want is to have her nipple in my mouth and *suck*.

"Please?" I whisper, licking my lips.

She stays silent.

She keeps me in panic, in suspense, like she's emotionally edging me.

The tease.

And I fucking love it. I want more.

Just as I'm about to ask, no, *beg*, Mila to let me undress her, she nods.

Mila just simply nods. But the look in her eyes is magnetizing. It's amazing how just her gaze tells me she wants this as much as I do.

Without skipping a beat or giving her—or myself—a chance to change our minds, I rip the shirt over her head.

And *fuck me*. She's gorgeous clothed in baggy sweats, she's gorgeous in everything I've seen her in, but, fuck, this is my favorite look on her. Eyes full of passion and desperation, hard nipples, a taut stomach and tight waist. She's wearing plain cotton panties that cup her ass in the most tantalizing way I've ever seen. I never thought plain cotton panties could be so sexy.

"Do you like?" she asks as if she can't see how hard my cock is straining against my jeans.

"So fucking much."

"I think you should show me how much you like what you see." Her gaze dips down to my groin and she bites her bottom lip. "Get naked."

I have to force myself to remember what she's gone through. Even if I want to fuck her against the counter, and the wall, and anywhere she will let me, really, I need to remember the trauma she's recovering from and not push her. Bringing that reminder to the forefront of my mind, I take a small breath and vow to not suggest anything, not push her to anything, to let her guide us.

I'm here for whatever she needs.

Whatever. She. Needs.

I pull my shirt over my head without any hesitation, but when I get to my jeans, I pull the button open and kick them off. I feel a strange sense of vulnerability as I stand almost naked before the woman that has completely taken over my mind, my home, my everything. *Everything* is filled with Mila now.

And after this, after whatever happens, I know I'll need more. I'll want more.

"You're so handsome," she coos, taking a step forward to run her fingers over my chest. "So strong. So sexy. I love the tattoos, and the muscles, and the you-ness of the vision in front of me. But what really gets me is how much you're willing to let me take care of you like this. Like such a *good boy.*"

A shiver takes over my body as I stand there, letting her

inspect me as she wants to. I stand there, completely at her mercy.

Mila starts to slowly walk around me, taking survey, but her fingertips never leave my body. My dick is hard as fuck, pressing against the black briefs that aren't doing much to hide my erection. Her hand cups my ass and she squeezes, just for a second, before releasing me.

"Now, let me be clear, Cillian," Mila says as she returns to my view.

And god, do I like it. It's obvious she's feeling the same insane need and desperation that I am. That even though she has more of a hold over herself, she's breaking apart on the inside.

Just like me.

"I want you. I've wanted you since the very beginning. And I understand that you're upset with me right now but I promise you, I want you. I want this. And I won't do or let anything be done to jeopardize it. Do you understand?"

I nod, not to brush what she's hidden from me aside, but because I'm sure as shit that I'm not in the right headspace to have this conversation. I'm not stupid, I know she's scared of her family, of *something* back in the Bratva.

And I need to figure it out before I make any decisions.

"We will talk more about it. But before I give either of us permission to give in, I wanted you to know." She smiles softly, sheepishly, like she's uncomfortable being vulnerable. But as fast as that look came, it vanished. In its place is the dominant, confident woman from before. Her fingers slip underneath the waistband of my briefs, toying with me.

I groan, my eyes falling closed for one second before I rip them open to see her reaction. To see if she likes it. To see what being with me does to her. My breathing is shallow but needy as I let her tease me torturously. I stay still. As her fingers slip deeper into the front of my briefs, it takes everything in me to not move. My abs clench and the tiny, unconscious shift of my hips makes me still.

Like a deer frozen in headlights, I stare at Mila to see her reaction.

"Do you want more?"

I nod so fast I feel my neck pop.

"Do you want me to touch your cock?"

My heart beats faster, and my mouth dries up. Hearing this vision of a woman say that shit to me… spank-bank material for sure.

"Do you want me to make you feel good? Come all over my hand? Watch me lick it off?"

"Yes," I say, my voice hoarse and deep. "So fucking much."

With a smile that makes me shiver, her long fingers take my dick in her hand and slowly start to pump me. Her warm palm slides up and down my shaft with *just* the right amount of pressure. I moan softly, trying to keep my composure.

One of my hands is clenched at my side, while the other inches forward to touch her exposed hip. I marvel at how big my hand looks cradling her hip. My fingers, as I spread them out to touch more of her, span from maybe an inch from her belly button and I can feel the dimples of her back on my fingertips.

"Touch me," she whispers, her warm breath fanning across my lips while her hand moves faster.

I don't need to be told twice. I surge even closer, desperate to grab her, touch her, feel her as much as possible. The hand on her hip squeezes tighter, and the other one slides up her back, touching all the smooth skin available to me. I crush her upper back to me and her lips move to mine.

We meet in a blur of passion and need.

And let me tell you, this woman's lips are the softest I've ever kissed. I never want to stop. I think it might hurt me to stop.

I push deeper, begging for entrance to her mouth to taste her completely. My tongue licks the seam of her lips and she opens with a sigh.

Her hand keeps moving over my cock. Each stroke brings tingles to my spine. The confident and commanding way she's working me over, I'm going to come and I'm not going to have any fucking control over it.

We push and pull with our kisses as they get more intense, more desperate, more sloppy. I fucking love it.

I feel my orgasm coming in way too fast, and pull back.

"Wait, wait," I whisper, but she doesn't let me move.

In fact, she starts jerking me off faster. "You're going to come on me, do you understand?" she pushes. "I want to feel your cum sliding down my stomach and dripping over my wet pussy. Can you do that for me, Cillian? Please."

"Oh god,"I moan. Her words set me off. One of my hands goes to the back of her head and I thread my fingers through the loosely braided dark hair, crushing her mouth back to mine.

Her other hand cups my bare ass and squeezes, while the one on my cock twists over the mushroom-shaped head, gathering my pre-cum and sliding it all over before doing that twist again. There's no chance that I can hold back. That I can make this as good for her before I come.

There's no fighting this.

My lips rip apart from hers, and with a deep groan my muscles throughout my body tighten and release as my cum spreads all over the front of her pussy and lower belly. Mila keeps pumping me, but thank fuck, she slows down and isn't squeezing so hard. It's not overstimulating, but just enough that it extends my orgasm.

"God, Cillian." She sighs.

My eyes open lazily, I'm firmly in that post-nut haze, and I watch her. Her blue eyes are full of want and lust, of satisfaction and gratification, even though I hadn't done enough to get her off.

"That was… that was amazingly sexy. And look at the mess you made." She smirks, and her hand leaves my softening cock, but trails through the cum slowly sliding down her. My gaze locks onto the fingers of the hand that's slowly tracing through the sticky mess I've made of her.

Biting my bottom lip to stop from moaning, I feel my spent cock twitch as she brings her fingertips to her mouth. Mila inspects it, the cum she's gathered there, and her eyes meet mine with the same curiosity. What is she going to do?

Slowly, she licks off every bit. She licks until her fingers are clean and moans. *She fucking moans at the taste of my cum on her tongue.*

"That's so sexy. Fuck. *Fuck.* If I hadn't just come, I'd come straight into your mouth to see this all over again," I say, my voice low, husky, and still breathless.

"Next time, big guy." She rubs my chest with her damp fingertips, and smiles. Her smile… god, it takes my breath away. I've seen her smirk, I've seen her grin, and when I've seen her smile in the past, it's always been guarded. But this… this smile is bright and electric. It's full of hope and another emotion I don't want to try and label. Not when we have all this unknown, lies, danger, between us.

"Your turn," I say, turning my attention back to her and her pleasure. But as soon as I do, she steps out of my reach.

Her quickness shows me that Mila will only be in my arms when she wants to be. Holding onto a ghost is impossible, unless they want to be held.

"Oh no, Cillian. This was all about you. About you letting me take charge. About letting yourself be vulnerable and doing as you're told, not being what you think you need to be." She steps into my space and kisses my lips softly. Like she knows she has me stunned, exactly as she does. "Damn, it's late." Her eyes dart over my shoulder to the electronic, illuminated clock on the stove.

"We need to talk about all this," I say earnestly.

Mila bends down and picks up the shirt I took off her not long ago, slipping it over her head. I follow her lead and pull my briefs and jeans up, leaving them unbuttoned but resting around my hips.

"I know we do. I know. But can we just have this moment? Please?" She pulls her long, dark, braid through the head-hole in my shirt.

I love seeing her in my clothes. Fuck, I love it. Almost as much as I love seeing her out of them.

Taking a deep breath, I try to push my anxiety aside. We've... well, we've revealed a lot in a short amount of time. On one hand, she might run. She tried to run before, she tried to get away the minute she decided that her family would come for mine if they discover we are harboring her. But on the other hand, she promised.

She *promised.*

That means something in our world. You're only as good as your word, and when someone—especially someone that is as high up in the food chain as we both are—promises something, it's as good as a contract. At least, that's how it's *supposed* to be. I could sit here and ask her to assure me over and over that she's not going to run, that she's going to actually give me a real conversation in the morning. But that would suggest that I don't understand the value of her promise.

I nod hesitantly, never taking my eyes off of her. Mila is a super-spy assassin. I realize now that even though I think she's showing her emotions, she might not be.

But if I want to learn more, if I want to give this… attraction, a real shot, I need to give her this little bit of trust. Maybe not trust exactly, but a test of sorts. If she's still here in the morning…

Well, if she's still here in the morning, let's just say it'll be a nice testament to how she actually feels.

The Test

Mila

There are eight recessed lights in the ceiling. Twenty slats in the air-conditioning grate. Twenty-seven books on the bookshelf in the corner. I didn't sleep all night.

I had to physically keep myself rooted to my bed. Every single part of me was screaming to leave. That the longer I stay here, the worse it will be for everyone. Especially Cillian.

I laid there staring at the ceiling, at the grate for the air conditioning that I could've probably escaped from. My mind raced constantly with the different ways that I could've left, and of the different ways that my father, or worse—my uncle—could retaliate wrongly on the Clan.

But I know, I *know*, that if I had done anything other than stayed in my room ruminating over everything, it would've destroyed all the progress I'd made with Cillian last night. I want to prove to him that I'm on his side. That whatever he's thinking, whatever he's wanting, I'm on board. I just don't want to get him hurt in the process.

73

I know my word means something to him, and I'm going to prove to him that I mean it. That I'm not just 'The Ghost'. I'm also a woman who wants a man. Badly.

I look at the clock on my side table, wondering if five am is too early. I've heard Cillian leave this early before. Maybe I can catch him before he goes.

I crack the door open, and peak my head out just in time to see Cillian's sleepless face do the same out from a crack in his door down the hall. I bet I look as tired as he does, if not more so.

"You're still here." He speaks the words as he breathes. Like he's relieved, skeptical, and surprised, all at the same time.

"I promised you I would be. When I promise something, I mean it." Pushing the door open, I stand in the darkened hallway with my upper back leaning against the wall. After our little dalliance last night, I went right to bed and did my best to ignore the mess in my panties. I didn't take care of myself and the image of Cillian watching me clean his cum off my pussy played in an endless loop. *Fuck.* His normally genuine and joking demeanor had been so dark, hungry, and obsessed. I knew if I even so much as brushed my clit, I would've come just from the look on his face.

"Did you get any sleep?" he asks, stepping out of his room, still in the jeans he was wearing last night and a rumpled white shirt.

"A little."

He gives me a pointed look.

"Okay, okay. Not at all."

"Why? Is the bed not comfortable? I can get you a new one."

Before I can say anything, he whips his phone out and starts to type something.

"The bed is great. I couldn't sleep because I was worried about you. About the talk we have to have today."

Cillian locks his phone and slides it into his back pocket, then shoves a hand in each of his front pockets."We do need to figure this out. I'm kind of on a deadline from a few people." He gestures with his head toward the living room. "But first, I need coffee. Copious amounts of coffee."

"Oh my god, please." I moan at the thought of the hot, caffeinated liquid touching my lips.

Walking quickly into the kitchen, Cillian immediately gets to work on his fancy coffee maker. "Have a seat." He points to the kitchen island stool before turning back to the cabinets, pulling down two mugs and the various things he needs to make the coffee taste so good.

The dark wooden stool squeaks as I drag it back and sit on the cool leather cushion. I kept my sleep shorts on, and Cillian's baggy shirt from the night before. Regardless of whatever happens, I know I'm keeping his shirt. At the very least, every time I slide it on, I'll remember his expression every time he saw me in it.

"So..." I drum the light marble top with my fingernails. "Where do you want to start?"

"The beginning is usually a good place."

"This story will take forever," I mutter self-consciously. No one needs to know all the boring details. My life... my life hasn't been pretty. It's never been safe or calm. Ever.

Cillian looks back at me seriously, his eyes making contact with mine as he abandons the coffee for a moment to make sure I listen to him.

"I have nowhere else to be. Nowhere else I'd rather be. So, please, start at the beginning and don't leave anything out."

———-

After Cillian made us coffee, we moved to the couch to be more comfortable.

"Well, you know I'm Mila Smirnova from the Russian Bratva. We work with people in many areas of trade. Many areas that I wouldn't enter into willingly. You know that in our world, men reign supreme. So being a woman in a man's world… I knew early in life I had two options: become the silent head of my house, letting the men think they had all the ideas and power while laying on my back but having all the power they naturally held, or, I could become a weapon. Thankfully, my father made that choice for me and as you know, I became 'The Ghost.'" I take a sip from the warm cup, trying to organize my wayward thoughts before I continue.

"I told you last night about why I did it, why I trained so hard, and became such a treasure for the Bratva. Not that I had much choice. Once it became time for Sergei to choose the next Ghost… well, I had far outpaced my cousins. My father, so proud of his lowly, useless daughter, recommended me to become the new *Prizrak*. The initiation process…. Well, I'll never forgive myself for that."

Cillian tentatively placed a warm hand on my knee, but didn't push me for more. Still, I kept talking.

"I don't know how the Clan handles initiation. From what it sounded like last night, Bryan made it sound like your guys' initiation was just as bad as mine. They use whatever means necessary to determine the thing that you hope to never have to do, the thing they know will darken your soul, the thing they know will break you. And then they make you do it."

My heart clenches and I take a deep breath. "I don't know how they figured it out, I don't know how they determined that it would kill me inside. I've never spoken it to anyone. I've never written it down, I barely even thought of it because of how uneasy and sick to my stomach it makes me." I pause, worried that if I tell him exactly what I had to do, he'll never look at me the same way again.

"What did they make you do?" he asks.

"They brought me into a dark room with a bag over my head so I didn't know where we were. I walked for what seemed like hours. I was taken down into a dark cellar and I can still feel the damp, broken stones under my bare feet as I walked down deep into a cave, holding on to some unknown person to try not to fall. It smelled like… death, decay, rot, mold." I take a deep breath to center myself, to keep myself here with Cillian and not back there. "I hear sniffling and crying from the corner. They trapped young girls down there. When they ripped the bag off my head… It was obvious from the look of them that they'd been there for months. Maybe years at that point, and my heart immediately sank. But I couldn't let anyone see it. Because I had to be the strong *Prizrak*. If I wanted to take them down from the inside out, I couldn't let them know that I wasn't on their side, so I kept a blank face. I pretended with everything I had, everything I learned, everything within myself, that it didn't bother me, even though I was dying on the inside. On one side of me was Sergei, and on the other side, was my father. Holding a gun to my baby sister's head. Like she wasn't his own flesh and blood. I knew at that moment that I would do anything they asked of me as long as she was safe. My initiation task or the task where I had to prove my worth to them, to become 'The Ghost'… It… I had to assassinate all the girls they had trapped."

I'm going to be sick. The guilt tears me up. I haven't let myself think about this for years. I'll never forgive myself.

And that's exactly why they made me do it.

"But, of course, it wasn't enough. I still had to prove that I wasn't soft. That because I was a woman, I wouldn't let my emotions about my family get in my way again. Because they knew, *they knew*, that the only reason I'd completed… what they'd asked, was because they threatened my sister. They made me prove to her and to everyone else that I was ruthless. That I needed to become hard, strong, and cold like steel." I gulp. "So I had to kill my cousins. All while my sister watched me. And I couldn't do it cleanly, with a bullet to the head for each person. No, that would be much too easy. Too clean for my fucked-up father and uncle. They made me skin them each alive. People I'd grown up with and people I loved."

I take a deep breath, trying to center myself, and sneak a peek at Cillian's face. I don't think I want to know exactly how he feels, but I have to know how disgusted he is.

His expression is blank. There's not an ounce of emotion that I can name. If I didn't know better, I'd think I'd just told him an incredibly boring story and he was begging for it to be done.

Cillian clears his throat slightly and says, "I take it you did?"

"I had to. The other cousins… I know they were trying to get out of this life. That Irina, Sasha, and Aleksander were doing everything they could to get out from under Sergei's control. And that was a threat to Sergei, a rejection that he couldn't take. If I didn't take care of them, our family would be taken care of instead."

"Wait, wait, go back. Who are Irina, Sasha and Aleksander?"

I take a deep breath, shaking my head softly because my

family tree… Well, it's complicated.

"So, I think it's easiest if we start at the top. Sergei, as you know, is my uncle. He's my father's brother. My uncle and father also have a sister; Svetlana. She was married off to a terrible, awful, disgusting man but their union provided his gang with protection and our mafia with land and allies. Svetlana was forced to carry his children to seal the union; thus Irina was born. And Sasha. And Aleksander. They had similar choices to what my sister and I had, but because we had the Smirnova name from birth, we were favored more. Aleksander… he hated how Svetlana was treated, how his sisters were treated, so he went off and learned a valuable trade."

"Accounting," Cillian said.

My mouth dropped open. How the fuck did he know that?

"Accounting." I nod.

"I don't fucking believe it," he mutters.

I'm just about to ask him, but then he motions with his hand for me to continue.

"The three originals; Sergei, my father, and Svetlana, were close at one time, but once Sergei gave Svetlana to a man who she knew was going to harm her, they never talked again. In turn, my father clutched closer to Sergei, especially after the only heirs he had were female. Svetlana's fate was a big neon sign to all of us girls what we were in for if we went against Sergei's rule. And I knew my father wouldn't stand against him. He'd gladly hand me over. So the fact that he pushed for me to be trained with Ivan and Marek—Sergei's sons—was a kindness that I didn't know I'd ever have. He ruined it when he held a gun to Maria's head, though."

"So tell me, how does it turn out that you had to brutally kill your three cousins and your aunt and uncle, but Aleksander is still alive, doing the books remotely for Los Muertos?"

Cillian cocks his head and my world stops.

The Other Shoe Drops

Cillian

"What?" Mila breathes the word out like I've punched her in the stomach.

"Aleksander, he's the reason why you were taken. He's why they took Auggie, thinking she was working with the Russians. Kieron told me that before he killed each and every one of the gang members from Los Muertos, that Hector—their leader—said that they suspected the Russians had infiltrated their gang and killed their previous leader, Auggie's ex. Because of their paranoid suspicion, they took Auggie, and her 'sister'—you."

"Are you sure they said Aleksander? There's a million Russian Aleksanders."

"There are, but Hector specifically boasted about how he had one of the great Smirnovs doing his finances."

"How? How is that possible? I killed him." Her mouth drops and her eyes fill with tears that I know she won't let fall.

Taking the coffee cup out of her hand, I set it next to mine on the table, and pull her by her bare thighs so she's closer to me. "Did you see their faces when you killed them?"

"I… it was… the cellar was dark. I was told that I had to prove my scalping skills by doing it with minimal light. All I could hear was the screaming, the crying. Sergei and my father had lights on them, but the other five were in the dark," she confesses.

"So you don't know for sure that it was Aleksander. It could've been anyone. You might not have killed him, Mila. And that means, we'll have a mafia war on our hands."

* * *

"I… I don't know what you mean. There's no way they wouldn't have done that to me… They made me kill all those girls first, why would they… why wouldn't…" Mila doesn't complete a single thought. She's shell-shocked.

"We can't tell for sure what they would and would not do. Are you really telling me that you think that the head of the Russian Bratva wouldn't use your compassion for others and your love for your family? You said it yourself, they wanted to take everything from you to make you a loyal soldier. To make you a better *Ghost*. There's one thing I know about our world: it is not family-oriented."

And how fucking lucky am I to have such a solid relationship with my cousin and uncle? Shit, my life could have turned out completely differently if I'd been born into a different Clan. "They're willing to do whatever it takes. They were willing to break you down in any way. Shape you into the person, the soldier, the *weapon* that they wanted you to be."

I watch her as she sits there processing my words. They were probably harsher than they needed to be.

As she lets a single tear fall down her cheek, she says, "I know I've done multiple other soul-sucking things for Sergei as 'The Ghost'. But maybe I didn't kill my family. My sister won't even look at me anymore because she had to watch the entire thing. Everything I did to protect her, to keep her alive, to keep her and I in compliance with our Uncle, and she won't even look at me. Won't even talk to me. And she's right not to. I'm… I'm an awful person with no chance of redemption."

"If anyone understands what it means to do what you have to do in order to keep your family safe and alive, it's me. It's Kieron, it's Bryan, hell, it's even Trent. I know you didn't get to talk to him or his girl much because everything was going down when you met, but Trent literally went against every rule we have in place to get Augustine back. To protect her, he ran straight into the building, guns blazing, to make sure she was okay. And that's before they were serious. The point is, we don't abandon our family in this Clan." I wrap my arms around her upper back and pull her into me. I know she won't ever let me see her cry openly so I try to offer her this little bit of privacy and comfort. It breaks my heart when I can feel her body shake from the sobs.

"It's always been me against the world. I've had no back-up, no one that cares if I come back from a mission. No one that wants me for me. They only want the weapon, the mighty deadly 'Ghost'. And now I don't even have that anymore." She sobs into my shirt. "And all that is left is me. Some useless girl that's good for nothing except giving men heirs or killing people on command."

My entire chest tightens with the anger that I feel toward

her family for making her ever feel that way. Don't get me wrong, the females in the Clan aren't treated equally or given the same opportunities, but they're allowed to make their own choices, especially when it comes to love, even though it may mean that they need to make sacrifices in order to be protected.

The fathers always protect the daughters. The brothers always protect the sisters. The Uncles always protect the nieces. In the Clan, family is family. Even family brought in, like Talia for Kieron or Auggie for Trent. If one of us decides that is our person, they're protected with the weight of our name and our Clan. I never thought that the Bratva wouldn't be like that.

"I'll kill them all," I say tensely. My jaw ticks with the anger and frustration that I feel because I just want to keep her safe and happy. I never want to see Mila cry again. If I have anything to fucking do with it, I'll make sure she only ever cries happy tears.

"Everything I'm doing, and everything that I'm trying to do, is to protect you. I'm trying to protect you with everything I have, even if it means that I'm in danger again," she says softly.

Oh, that won't do. That certainly will *not* do.

"Listen to me," I say firmly, pulling her away from my chest so I can see her beautiful blue eyes even if they're filled with tears and her cheeks wet. "I need to know right now. I need to know right now what your plans are and what side you're on, because I'm willing to give you the protection and the strength of my name in my Clan to keep you safe and hidden. But if that's not something you want or you're just using me for some game I need to know now. Are you planning to go back to them? Are you planning on using my family to make your family stronger? Are you planning on screwing me over irreversibly?"

As much as she's trying to choke back her tears, it's proving to be too much.

"Cillian… No," she whispers. "I don't ever want to go back there. I have nothing, no one, waiting for me back there. Only darkness and death. The Bratva is what I was born into, but I've wanted out every single day of my life. Everything bad that's happened to me, it's all because of my family. Family." She scoffs the last word, disgust dripping from her tone. "Family isn't meant to hurt you, it isn't meant to be a chain around your ankle, dragging you down into the deep, dark, frozen sea." Another tear slides slowly down her cheek. "At least, I don't think it is. I've felt more cared for in the weeks I've been with you guys than I have for the decade and a half I spent under my uncle's roof. I'm not asking you to start a war for me, I won't do that. But I'm asking you to trust me when I say that I will never choose them over you."

Her words are beautiful, just what I want to hear. Does that mean I shouldn't trust what she's saying? She must see my hesitation because her sad, blue eyes harden. They become determined. Like a flip of a switch.

"How can I prove it to you?"

The million-dollar question. How does one prove that even though they've lied to you before, and are a master manipulator, they're telling the truth *now*?

There's only one sure way I know.

"You'll have to tell Kieron. Bryan. Maybe Trent too, if he can pull himself from Auggie. And without a doubt, you'll have to tell Skipper. *My* Uncle. Head of the Irish Clan. If you're willing to do all that… well, it's proof enough for me."

I say, shrugging my shoulders and dipping my head to look her square in the eye. "Don't get me wrong, doll, I believe you. But if you understand me even a fraction of what you say you do, you understand that I need to protect my family, too."

She nods vehemently, relief and hope evident on her face.

"Anything," she gasps. "Anything to show you how much I want *you.*"

* * *

"I need you to come over here," I tell Kieron through the phone.

Mila went back to her room to shower and put on what she said were 'real clothes', much to my dismay. Maybe I can talk her into wearing another one of my shirts, then that would really tell the guys that she's mine.

Even if she says she wants to be, agreeing to be with me is one thing and completely breaking away from her family is another. I've decided I'll give her my protection, even if it's bad for me in the long run. From everything she's told me, all the bullshit, trauma and abuse she's gone through, if I'm able to get her free from her family, and she decides I'm not what she wants long-term, I won't hold it against her.

I'll let her go.

"This better be some serious information from your house guest, Killer," Kieron grumbles through the phone in his pissed off, you-just-interrupted-me-getting-laid tone.

"It'll be worth your time. I'm calling Bryan and Trent too."

"It's okay, baby, I'll rock your world as soon as I get back,"

Kieron says, obviously trying to cover the microphone and failing.

Yuck. My cousin and my good friend fucking is not something I like to think about. Although their kid is pretty damn adorable.

I'd like one of those of my own.

Someday. With the right person.

"Gross, man," I groan.

"Oh, shut the fuck up, you little shit." My older cousin chuckles. "Don't think I haven't seen exactly how you look at your temporary roommate. We can talk about that over a whiskey at another time." I can hear him shuffling around and getting his stuff. "How big of an information bomb are you about to drop on me, Cillian?"

Taking a deep breath, I pinch the bridge of my nose and look down the hallway to Mila's room where I can hear the shower running.

She's naked in there. Water cascading over her bare body. The gorgeous, strong body that I saw without a single stitch of clothing on, not even fourteen hours ago. I consider ending the call, telling Kieron I'll call him back and going into the shower with her. Pushing her up against the shower wall and—

"Cillian!"

Kieron's harsh tone breaks the fantasy that I desperately want to make a reality.

"What?" I snap, reaching down with one hand to adjust my dick so it's not pushing against the rough denim of the jeans I changed into when we decided that I needed to let the guys know what's going on.

"Yeah, yeah, go ahead and give me shit for loving on my

wife, but in the meantime you're stuck in fantasy-land about a girl you've just met."

I can hear the laugh in his voice and know him well enough to know he's rolling his eyes.

"But, seriously," he continues, "this better be good. The time is ticking for me to report to Skipper."

"Just get over here," I say, ending the call.

I dial Bryan's number and repeat the conversation. Only to then dial Trent's number and repeat it yet again.

"Fuck me. Should've just sent a group text. That would've been easier," I mutter to myself.

Don't get me wrong, I love the guys, but in situations like this, I just need them to get the fuck over here so I just have to say it once and they have all the same information.

"Are they coming?" Mila's voice is like a shot of peace through my system. I can feel my shoulders drop and my chest lighten.

"They are. Soon, I would say." I turn around and am blown away by her, yet again.

It's like she read my mind because instead of any of the clothes I got her weeks ago, she's found a clean shirt of mine and paired it with a pair of soft leggings that wrap around her sculpted legs. Her hair's still wet, and pulled into a braid that drapes down over her shoulder.

"You look beautiful."

Mila smiles, or smirks rather, and pulls at the hem of the dark gray, faded shirt that she has on.

Mine.

"Is it okay that I borrowed it?" This bombshell of a woman, a woman who told me what to do, how to do, and when to do it, a woman that is a weapon herself for a whole fucking mafia, is asking if it's okay she borrow my shirt. And she almost sounds shy about it.

"It's very okay." I try my best not to sound like I'm begging her to always wear my clothes, but I'm sure I do. Because I basically am.

"Well…" She smiles, bringing the neck of my shirt to her nose and cuddling in deeper, "…good."

Fuck me, she might be sexiest when she's shy. It's a toss-up, because I know for a fact that she's outspoken, dominant and commanding when she wants to be. I shift myself from side to side so that hopefully my dick doesn't spring to attention again.

"Okay, I'm here. Let's get this shit sorted so I can get home to my wife." Kieron's voice booms through my apartment as he storms through the front door. From the sound of boots clomping, I know the other two are right behind him.

"You know, you're not the only one with a girl to get home to." Trent shoves Kieron playfully before plopping down on my couch.

"Don't talk about my kid sister like that," Kieron snaps.

"She's not *actually* your sister. It shouldn't bother you knowing how much she turns me on," Trent teases, just trying to wind up Kieron.

Auggie might not be Kieron's biological sister, but she is Talia's and he protects Auggie like she is his full-blooded sister.

Kieron looks murderous and opens his mouth to snap back, but Bryan beats him to it.

"Oh shut up, both of you," Bryan says, going straight to my coffee machine and starting a pot.

"Hello to you all, too. Like a herd of fucking buffalo clambering into my home. Jesus."

The transition from soft, comfortable Mila that was just blushing about wearing my shirt, is immediate. Mila straightens her spine, her eyes narrow, and she stands tall with her hands behind her back.

"Relax," I whisper, and put my hand on the small of her back for support. "They're just my family. You've met them before."

"Yeah, but now I'm spilling all my secrets. I'm essentially the enemy, even though I don't want to be," she whispers back, not looking at me, keeping her eyes on the door and the three new people in my home.

"By telling them everything, you're gaining their protection as well as mine. You're making a choice here, a big one. And this is the last time you'll be able to change your mind. Are you sure you want to do this?"

Mila breaks her watch to look at me, and I can't even begin to decipher what she's thinking. What she's going to say. But I know if she wants to leave, I'll let her. If she simply wants to go into hiding with a new identity and shit, I'll help her get that. Whatever she needs, I'll be, I'll provide.

"I'm sure."

The anxiety in my chest loosens at the two loaded words.

"Then, come on." I gesture with my head for her to follow me into the living room as the three of the closest men in my life bicker about stupid shit, giving me and Mila a moment to talk.

"Are you ready?" Kieron says, as we enter. He's speaking to the room, but I know his words are pointed at Mila.

She knows it too, so she takes a deep breath and nods, continuing to stand in front of the four of us as she clears her throat, and begins to tell her tale.

The Plan

Cillian

I knew the moment she opened her mouth that Kieron wasn't going to go easy on her.

As 'soft' as he thinks he's gotten from marrying Talia and welcoming their kid, I can tell that the anxiety of keeping his family as safe as possible has deepened. Before, it was all about the Clan, keeping the four of us working, safe, and together. Now, he still has those same values, but he uses the Clan as a protective shield for his girls.

As I would.

Mila's story comes through like a debriefing. The emotion that she showed to me, and even a bit to Bryan, is gone. Vacant. She's presenting information without any bias.

"And they kept me drugged, so even though I'm 'The Ghost' for the Bratva, they never let up the tranquilizer enough for me to escape. The first time that they let up even a bit was the day that Cillian saved me before I could save myself." Mila ends her tale by putting her arms over her chest, even though her eyes stare over Kieron's head. She's cold, aloof, guarded, not making any sort of contact with anyone.

I don't like it.

She's obviously curling into herself like she thinks if she says something wrong, she'll be thrown out.

"Holy fucking hell," Trent says, running a hand through his cropped red hair to cover his face and scratch his beard-covered chin.

"You don't really think that Aleksander, who you think is running from the Bratva by working for Los Muertos, would be so stupid as to use his real name with them? It would be like a neon arrow for the Bratva to follow and see that one of their captives somehow escaped execution." Bryan had moved from a lounging, kicked-back position on the couch to leaning his elbows on his knees the minute Mila mentioned Svetlana.

"I'm not sure. Maybe he did it for another reason," Mila states.

"Fuck. *Fuck*," Kieron mutters, never looking away from Mila before letting out a sharp breath and taking his phone out of his pocket. "Hey baby, yeah, it's going to be late. I'm sorry. I'll help with Rosie when I get home, promise. Just sleep. Yeah, yeah. It's going to be okay. I love you." We all sit silently until he hangs up the phone, shoving it back into his leather jacket.

"It's obvious this whole thing was pinned on you and you're lucky that they took Auggie," Kieron starts to say before Trent scoffs.

"I was saying—" Kieron smacks Trent in the arm and rolls his eyes before continuing."—You're lucky that Auggie was taken and our paths crossed. Not that I wanted Auggie mixed up in this shit, she was my little sister before she was your girl, Trenton, remember that. Jesus."

Trent huffs and crosses his arms over his chest. Those two guys get so protective and possessive of the Jones sisters that in moments like these, I want to roll my eyes and holler at them to get back on track.

This isn't about their girls now, it's about *mine.*

"Focus, please," I snap.

Kieron nods. "Yes, okay." He sits back and I can see the gears turning in his head. "Killer, what do you think?"

One of my eyebrows raises in confusion when he, and the rest of the room, turn to me. He's the one in control here, he's the leader. Not me. But, he's giving me the chance to change her future. He's giving me the chance to give my protection to her publicly. Or, maybe he's trying to see how far I'll go to protect her.

Kieron stares at me, his gaze calculating. One of his eyebrows rises in challenge. He was willing to start a war for his girl before she was even *really* his girl. He was willing to go against his father's wishes when he wanted to bring her into his home. Hell, Kieron even married Talia as soon as he could, just to give her his name and the full weight of protection as his wife. And from his stare, I can see him asking me if I'm willing to go that far for Mila.

He should know that I've already decided to give her that if she wants it.

I square my shoulders, turning to face him straight-on, and return his stare with my own. I can feel the tension from Bryan and Trent, and I can tell without even looking that they're extremely tuned in.

It hits me once and for all that I believe her. I believe

she's telling the truth and that she's not going to use this to somehow harm me or mine.

And I feel like I can take a full breath again.

Her eyes sparkle, a full-blown smile that I know she won't let me see in front of the guys behind her eyes, hidden in her expression.

"I believe her. I think there's something sketchy going on with Aleksander, I think someone is targeting Mila, and she can't go back to the Bratva." I stand up from the couch and move next to her. Her blank expression has melted off and I can see the fear in her eyes. Our gazes lock and I feel the same sense of peace that I had earlier. I know right then, that I'll do whatever she needs, vow whatever is needed, *be* whatever she needs.

"I promised her I would protect her. That I'd do whatever it takes to make sure she's happy and no longer under their rule. Under *anyone's* rule." I emphasize that she is the one with the power here.

"I agree with Cillian." Bryan speaks up, his voice deep and scratchy. "In all the time Mila has spent with us, I haven't seen or heard anything—other than The Ghost bomb she dropped—to make me think that she would be a threat to us. The fact that she's telling us all these things, it means she's serious. I'm good with her staying," he says, looking at the floor, and his last sentence has me on fucking edge.

'I'm good with her staying.' What does that mean? And why the hell isn't he looking at anyone as he says it?

"Well, Trent, do you have anything you want to add?" Kieron changes direction, his eyebrows raised and his arms spread across the top of my couch. The way his dark eyes flicker from Bryan to Mila to me, has me feeling uneasy.

"No, man. I think these two know her well enough to vouch for her and her intentions."

Before I can open my mouth to say that *I* know her best and *my* word should be enough, Kieron claps his hands and rubs them together the way he does when he is about to give us a shit -ton of work to do. "It's settled then. Majority rules. You passed the first of many rounds to stay here, and know that Cillian and Bryan's words can only take you so far. Before I bring all of this to Skipper, I need your word that you'll tell your information to whoever I deem necessary. Answer quickly and answer correctly." He looks pointedly at Mila, and I can see the threat there.

I step forward to tell Kieron off, to remind him once again what I'm willing to do if I think she's being fucking threatened, but Mila's hand grabs at mine, pulling me back.

"I will."

"Good. That will make this much easier. Kellan, our Skipper and my father, tends to ask questions even if they are painful. Cillian, I'll let you know when that meeting is going to happen. But in the meantime, you're her main guard. If the Bratva doesn't know we have her by now, they will soon. They aren't stupid, especially if they have someone working from a technological angle. And if they've given up looking for her to bring home, that means she has a death warrant on her head."

Mila cringes, and I thread our fingers together. With all the information she's told us about her family, it's probably true. Especially with as long as she's been kidnapped and not found.

"Trent, you're going to be looking into the new Ghost. See if we have any information or can get any information from our spies about if there's a replacement." Kieron keeps delegating.

"'The Ghost' is a scary story, Kieron. How am I meant to find information about someone that's not ever said to actually exist?"

Trent has a good point. Before meeting Mila, I thought the same.

"Instead of asking about The Ghost, try asking if there have been assassinations where a lock of skin and hair approximately half an inch tall and wide was taken from the back of their head," Mila whispers, and all eyes dart to her.

It's not that what she said is the most horrific thing we've heard, hell, we've all done so much worse, but the fact that she had to take trophies of her kills.

"That's... oddly specific," Kieron says, turning to her and waiting for an explanation.

"Sergei requires DNA to confirm that his target is eliminated. Half an inch in the back of the head, especially with individuals with thick hair, usually goes unnoticed," she explains.

"And if the target is bald?" Trent's eyes widen slightly.

"The sample is taken from other, more private places," she says simply with a soft shrug.

"Oh, that's nasty as fuck." Trent grimaces. "But good to know. I'll reach out to the others and see what I can find out."

"Bryan," Kieron says, moving on, "you're in charge of finding out everything you can about Svetlana and her kids. But focus more on Aleksander. Especially the person that did the books for Los Muertos. I agree with you, Cillian, it does seem like there's specific targeting going on. There are a lot of moving parts here, and we need to get to the bottom of it all. Now."

There's a beat of silence, where we all look at each other, a knowing look that's loaded with tension and understanding. We're taking on another mafia, potentially putting ourselves and our family in the line of fire. Kieron looks at me, nodding with fire in his eyes.

He's doing this for me. I know it. Just like I did it for him.

"Trent, Bryan and I are going to go get started on the information gathering. You're going to fortify your apartment as much as you can. Not that I think there's been a breach, but we thought security was top-notch when the Italians came for Talia. I'm learning and moving on."

"Sure thing, boss." I nod to Kieron.

"Let's go, guys." He gestures to my other two friends and they all move toward the door, leaving their coffee cups on the kitchen island. Trent offers a half-hearted salute to Mila and me as he walks out the door, pulling his phone from his pocket and dialing up one of his many contacts. Bryan, who *still* hasn't made fucking eye contact with me since he vouched for Mila, sets his cup down and hurries out of my apartment, stuffing both of his hands in his pockets.

Kieron watches Bryan leave and smirks at me, shaking his head. His eyes go to where our hands are still holding each other's tightly.

"Mila, welcome to the family. Unofficially, of course." He winks and walks to the door, shutting it behind him.

And with their exit, a quiet calmness comes back to the room.

"What the fuck was that?" I ask, chuckling a little as I point to the closed door.

"They're your family," Mila says with an easy smile and a shrug. "Thank you."

"There's nothing to thank me for. I haven't set you free yet."

She looks at me with such care and such hope, that I can't help but pull her close.

"You're doing all of this for me. You believe in me. You vouched for me with your family when it would've been ten times easier to let me leave. I still think I shouldn't be selfish and go before you're even in the line of fire." Her eyes drop from mine to my chest, and it hurts. It hurts, but I understand.

I slide a finger under her chin and tilt her head up slightly, just enough for her to look me in the eyes again. "You're it for me, Mila. My girl, the one that I'm willing to put it all on the line for."

She gasps, her soft lips parting. "What?"

"I know we've only been truthful with each other for a short time. I know that. But, when it counted, you were honest. You're strong. You're stubborn. You're willing to fight *alongside* me. You're… you're just… everything I want."

Her eyes glisten. "Even if it's hard?"

"Even if it seems impossible," I vow. "But you have to want it, too. You have to want me and us just as much as I do, baby."

The expression on her face morphs from awe to a challenge, as if I'd just told her I didn't think she wanted me. And she was going to prove me so very wrong.

"Trust me, big guy, I want you more than you know. You say I'm it for you? Well, you're like the sun; shining safety and brightness, after being in terrible, frightful darkness forever. You're everything. Do you hear me?" Mila's fingers dig into my shirt roughly as she pulls me closer.

"Everything," she whispers, finally taking the kiss that I've been fucking dying for all day from my lips.

The "Finally"

Mila

Cillian gasps against my lips as I kiss him roughly.

I need it. I need him. Gentleness will come later.

My fingers grip his shirt to keep him from moving, but honestly, I could be pushing him away from me and he still wouldn't move. Cillian's in complete control over me, over us, over the whole situation that I've started.

As scary as that was before, we've been through enough for me to know that Cillian would never push me farther than I wanted to go sexually. I'm good with letting him take over.

At least for now.

One hand tangles in my hair, while the other slips under the hem of my shirt. Or, really, his shirt.

"I want to fuck you, baby. I want to take that step. But only if you're okay with it," He whispers in my ear, and his breathlessness makes me shiver. The hand that was behind my back slides around to the front of my leggings, slipping in between my thighs. I shiver again, shaking with anticipation.

I want to know what he feels like against me. His fingers slide lightly against the outside of my leggings, and I know he can feel the heat coming from me.

I moan, I can't help it. Feeling the touch of a man, *wanting* his touch on my most intimate places, is such a welcome feeling. "Please," I beg.

"Say it."

"I want you to fuck me," I admit without missing a beat.

Cillian leans back so he can look at me, look at the havoc he's caused, and I feel myself getting wetter at the raw lust clearly written on his face. With my words—even though they are not as dirty as I would like to say or hear—I'll admit, Cillian looks like he's about to go feral. The cocky, playboy façade that I saw on his face last night is back, but in his eyes, I still see Cillian. My Cillian.

"Please, Cillian, please."

"Oh god, doll." He groans, and it's like we're magnetic. Two opposite forces that can't stay away from the other. We clash together in a mix of teeth, lips and moans as he deepens the kiss, pushing me to open my mouth so he can take it further.

I love that when we are this close and he's kissing me, I have to lean my head back as he pushes me backward. Our legs tangle as he walks us toward the back wall, and I trust that he'll keep me safe as we move through the room. He never lets up. If anything, his kisses grow more intense with each step as we move and just as I think he's going to shove me against the wall, he pulls back.

"Yours or mine?" he asks. His lips are red and swollen, his eyes wild with promise.

Instead of answering, I lean forward and nip at his swollen lower lip.

"Yours it is, then." He answers his own question. Cillian bends down and wraps his hands around my thighs, lifting me roughly so my core is pressed against his hips. And fuck, does it give delicious friction on my clit every time he takes a step. The wetness between my thighs grows with each movement and it brings me so close to the orgasm I've been denying myself all night and day, that when he throws me on the bed, I groan. But not from being turned on —although I am—but from being denied—which I'm not used to.

"Patience, baby." He chuckles, obviously understanding the subtle differences in my tone.

"I don't have a lot of patience, especially when it comes to you."

"I'm going to take care of you, like you take care of me." Cillian smirks, pulling the waistband of my leggings torturously slowly down my legs. I reach to pull my shirt off, but he pushes me back down onto the bed with a soft thud. "Keep it on."

"What?"

"Keep. The. Shirt. On." He enunciates each word and growls.

Poof. There goes the last shred of hope I had that my panties weren't ruined.

"I like it a lot when you wear my clothes. Like you're telling everyone you encounter that you're mine." Cillian slips off his own shirt by pulling the back of the collar over his head, taking it off in one gesture. "I want you like this, all the time. Comfortable, safe, happy. I like the braid, I like the sleepy eyes, the leggings or shorts with a baggy shirt on. Especially when it's my t-shirt."

"I like wearing your shirts too. They smell like you," I

confess softly. My eyes are glued to him, wondering what he's going to do next. His hands slide up the outside of my legs before his long, thick fingers reach the thong I'm wearing.

"Take them off me," I order, my need to control the situation starting to come out.

"Is that what you want?" Cillian looks at me through his eyelashes, a new kind of desire on his face. "What else do you want?" he whispers, suddenly self-conscious, like he wasn't just throwing me around the room.

I sit up on my elbows, the movement forcing his chin to rest on my leg. "Do you want me to tell you explicitly what I want you to do?"

This has to be his decision. We can talk about it later in more detail, but if he's not wanting me to top him, then I need to know now. I'm content with letting him take over, but if last night was any indicator, Cillian has some serious submissive hopes.

He doesn't answer me verbally, but I can see the excitement in his eyes as he nods.

"No, no, big guy. That's not how this works. I need you to tell me you want this. Out loud." I'm not taking any chances. I may be the one that has gone through abuse, some sexual fear, but I know enough about who I am. I know what I like. And I won't take that discovery away from Cillian. The experimentation of what he really likes and the vulnerability from us both that we can discover more about our sexual relationship together.

"I want you to tell me what to do," he responds, without hesitation.

The amount of excitement and trust that flows through me is amazing. "Good boy," I whisper. I cup his cheek softly, and lay back down.

His eyes sparkle with the praise and it seals the deal for me. I know what he needs and right now, it's me talking him through everything. It's telling him exactly what I want, and what I think will bring us both pleasure.

"Will you be a good boy for me, and do what I say?" I bite my lip and look at him through hooded eyes of my own.

"Yes, Ma'am," he whispers, leaning into me and embracing me.

"Then, take my panties off and suck me off of them."

Cillian wastes no time. He sits up, bringing his knees under him and rips the seams of my thong.

Literally rips my underwear from my body.

My mouth drops open. It's sexy as fuck, the pure strength and need…. *Fuck me, and fuck me now.*

"Put them in your mouth," I tell him, fire and lust flowing throughout my entire body. I have to see him do it.

Please.

I mentally beg him, but Cillian doesn't make me wait. He adjusts the cloth so that the spot darkened with my wetness is right in front of his lips.

His eyes meet mine and tension fills the air before he licks the entire center slowly. Like he's savoring it. I watch, not breathing, as I see his eyes flutter close when the slick spot hits his tongue.

"Oh god. Fuck. You taste so good." He moans and dives back in, more ravenous than before.

I observe him for a few moments, watching his eyes close as he savors it and makes the dark patch larger with his spit as he sucks my taste from every spot on the cloth. I bend my knees and let them fall open wide so Cillian can see what he's doing to me. A reward for following my directions.

"Come on, big guy. I'm watching you do all that skilled work with those, but I'd really like to feel how good you are at eating pussy. Come lick me." My voice is strong and dominant, but I'm so turned on that there's a level of huskiness that I wasn't expecting.

Cillian pulls the fabric from his mouth and stuffs it in his back pocket. "Yes, Ma'am." He smirks at me, and without any prompting at all, he slides his hands under my thighs and pulls. He pulls me hard, to the end of the bed, and wraps my legs around his head.

I just know this is going to be life-changing.

And it is. Goddamnit, it's amazing.

He licks my lower lips before sucking on the hood of my clit. I cry out, the stimulation is almost too much with how long I've been on edge. Cillian slips onto his belly, and really dives in. His tongue enters me as far as it can go and I feel a finger join his tongue, curling inside me in a come-hither motion.

"Suck my clit, but keep your finger doing just that," I gasp.

Without skipping a beat, he does exactly what I ask. Cillian's other hand pulls the hood of my clit back and he starts to do a mixture of sucking and licking while his finger twirls and twists within me. He hits just deep enough that I lose control of myself faster than I intended. I really wanted to prolong this just a bit more, really be able to experience it, but my body has other plans. And Cillian's just that good.

My back arches as I come, orgasming right into his mouth. Cillian slows his movements, keeping me going until my body stops throbbing. I'm breathing deeply, trying to recover from the much-needed orgasm, as Cillian kisses his way up my body.

He hovers, kissing my neck, nibbling my pulse point. "Did you like that?"

The way he asks catches my attention. He's not asking me for validation, but more out of curiosity. Like he really wants to know if I enjoyed it, if he did it right.

"I did. You did such a good job." I kiss his lips, tasting myself on them.

Such a turn-on.

"Good," he says around my kisses.

I do love the feel of his weight on me, pinning me down and grinding against me.

"Why are your pants still on?"

"You didn't tell me to take them off." He raises an eyebrow in challenge.

I chuckle. "You're right. Take your pants off. Take *everything* off."

Cillian pushes off of me, and wastes no time unzipping his jeans, pushing his briefs down with them. His cock is thick and long, *perfect*, and jutting straight out in front of him. I bite my bottom lip, pushing myself up off my back, and onto my knees. His shirt drapes down, barely covering my messy, wet, pussy. My braid is no longer neat, big chunks are falling out.

I don't think I've ever felt sexier.

"Lay down." I move to the side, and watch as he does what I say.

Cillian's all toned muscle, tattoos covering his skin, the beloved 'V' cutting into his lower abdomen leading to his erect cock.

"Hands to the side. No touching. If you touch, I'll stop," I tell him, but my eyes don't quite meet his. I'm already making plans on how I want this to go. How I want to blow his mind.

Cillian nods, fisting the blanket beside him, but never taking his eyes off me. His gaze feels like a warm caress moving over my skin.

"Good boy," I whisper, straddling his calf, and taking his dick in my mouth.

I hear a gasp, and take him in deeper.

"Oh fuck, Mila. That's so good," he babbles.

I hollow my cheeks to get more suction. I bob my head up and down, over and over, harder and harder. It's impressive how he's holding back. I can feel how Cillian's trying not to move his hips, trying to keep himself completely still. The small tremor under his thighs is enough. Pulling back, and sliding up his body, I let my wetness trail up his leg before I get up and hover right where his cock meets my slit.

"Are you sure you want this?" he whispers. He's mistaking my hesitation for nerves.

"Completely sure." I kiss him deeply, messily. "I was just trying to think of a way to ask if you want to use a condom."

"Do you?"

"Where are your condoms?" I ask instead.

"I want to feel you bare. Please, Mila." He growls, a fierceness taking over him.

"Where. Are. Your. Condoms?" I ask, shifting forward and letting his cock drag along my wet slit with each word.

"Side table, right side, top drawer. Hurry," he says, his words heavy and needy.

Just like I feel.

"Don't move." I slip off his body and make my way to his room to see the completely made bed before me. He didn't sleep last night. Was he worried I'd leave? Was he staying up all night thinking about what happened between us, like I had?

A conversation or thought for another time.

I need to get back to him, as soon as fucking possible. I rip open the top drawer on the nightstand and giggle when I see loose cough drops, receipts, a mini Snickers, five or six condoms, and an eye mask. Just a drawer of randomness. I pull the condoms out, taking them all because I'm not sure we're going to be satisfied after this one time. Before I close the drawer, I take the Snickers, opening it up and eating it. I suck the chocolate off and swallow the candy on my walk back to my room.

"You listened. What a good boy you are. I can't wait to reward you," I coo, bringing his attention to me instead of the ceiling. His cock looks redder and more pronounced, beckoning me to come help him.

I let the roll of condoms fall in between my fingers, showing him that I got what we needed. His fingers twitch against the bedspread, unclenching and clenching again.

"I can see how hard you're fighting to move, to take over. And the fact that you're trying so hard to listen to me... It turns me on, to see you like this." I pull apart the top condom, setting the others down on my dresser for later. A promise.

"Good, because it's fucking killing me." He groans.

"It'll be worth it, baby."

He shifts a bit, but without flipping over or moving his hands, he isn't going to find any relief without my permission.

"Let me take care of you, like you take care of me," I say, repeating his words back to him. I roll the condom over his cock slowly, and yes, I may have tugged a few times unnecessarily because I just can't help it. I may have just come, but I need to feel him. I need him as close as possible.

Leaning over to kiss him, I press downward, and feel his cock spread my pussy to fit him. There's absolutely no space inside me as I stretch around his girth. Our mouths are pressed together, but we both moan as I take him inside me. His tongue slips in my mouth, and our kisses become deeper and more insistent than before, like he's trying to eat me up.

"Chocolate?" he whispers, the moment I let him breathe.

"Your top drawer was very odd. Snickers are a nice touch though." I smirk, sitting up straighter. I swear to fuck he's touching my cervix in this position.

"I like it. Your kisses are addictive by themselves, but fuck, add in chocolate and I'm never going to stop."

Maybe chocolate is the way to this guy's heart.

"That's the hope." I smile down at him, and circle my hips, before rocking back and forth. The smile drops from my lips as I grind my clit on his pelvis. "Touch me, you can touch me. Hold me closer."

"Fucking finally." His hands grab my hips roughly like he wants to move me.

"Do it, move me. Show me how you want me to fuck you." I want to encourage him to talk to me. I might want to be more in control in the bedroom, but I also want him to show me what he likes.

Cillian starts to thrust up into me while still holding me down so I can grind and rock against him.

"Oh fuck yes." I let my head fall back. "I know you like the shirt, but I want to feel your skin on mine." I give him a moment's warning before I pull his shirt over my head and drop it beside us.

"You're so fucking gorgeous." He moves one of his hands from my hip to my breast, running his thumb over my pebbled nipple. Before I know what he's doing, Cillian moves us into a seated position and I cry out in ecstasy, this position making me feel even fuller.

"You like it like this?" he asks, bending to take my nipple in his mouth. It's like I'm on fire and his hands are spreading the flames. His other hand cups my ass to remind me to keep grinding against him.

"Yes!" I moan and keep riding him, faster and faster.

His lips move to my other nipple, giving it the same attention and care. He sucks hard, and nibbles on the erect nipple, sending shivers down my spine.

I can feel that Cillian's trying to thrust, trying to move in some way, but in this position, it's all about me. I cup the back of his head, holding him close as he gropes, sucks, and pushes me closer to coming just by playing with my nipples.

He pulls away from my chest, releasing my nipple with a pop and wraps his hands around my back."Come for me, Mila. Come for me, gorgeous. I need to feel it against my cock. I bet when you clench around me, you'll scream. And when you do, you'll scream *my name*. Do it. I need to hear you."

His words push me closer and I speed up, needing to come again so badly.

"That's it, baby. Take what you need. I'm yours. Just like you're mine. You know that now, don't you? Use me to make yourself feel good." He growls in my ear, then leans down and sucks, hard, on the pulse point on my neck.

The zip of pain is just enough to push me over the edge and I detonate.

"Cillian! Fuck, Cillian!" I scream his name like he wants

and the sparks of pleasure move from where we're joined. It starts to take over my entire being, heat and fire spreading through my body as I surrender to it. I'm clenching around his cock, over and over, harder and harder, as I milk him for every moment of pleasure I can.

"Yes, babydoll. Yes." He moans, his eyes running over every inch of me hungrily. Cillian flips us over, thrusting back inside me as quickly as possible, finding his own pleasure.

He's quiet while he slams into my fluttering walls, but the moment I run my fingers through his hair and pull lightly, a delicious, deep moan leaves his mouth.

"You feel so good, Cillian. You're taking care of me so well. I need to feel you come inside me." I babble in his ear, and feel his back tighten with tension. Sliding one of my hands from his hair down to his ass, I squeeze. The strong, sculpted muscles clenching in time with his thrusts is amazing. He's so strong, so built, so… it shows me how protective he is. And he's all mine.

"Come for me, big guy. I want to feel it. I want to be stuffed full with *you*," I whisper, kissing his ear and sighing. I fucking love feeling his weight on me, feeling his cock thrust hard inside me. I know I will always crave this. Crave him.

"Mila, *fuck.* Fuck!" Cillian roars, snapping his hips one last time before he groans. He turns into my sweaty neck as he comes into the condom.

We both stay quiet, catching our breath and holding onto each other. His hands slide around me, hugging me even tighter to him.

I was wrong before. I'll always crave sex with him—always—but this, this right here… I need it. I can feel the parts of myself that were shoved into the dark, the parts of myself that I've been forced to ignore, the parts of myself that I thought no one would ever like, start to heal. His lightness healing all the traumas that have happened to my soul.

Cillian brings his mouth to mine in a kiss. It's a different kiss than before, almost lazy, but I can tell.

I can tell it's forever.

The Talk

Cillian

That was…

That was… something I'll never fucking forget for the rest of my days.

It just reiterated everything I've been feeling.

I'm not a saint by any stretch of the imagination; I was a playboy in my teens and early twenties, willing to screw anyone and anything. But I can't remember many encounters. They felt good at the moment, but left me feeling hollow. When I'd wake up, I'd feel more alone and like a bigger piece of shit than ever.

But with Mila… with her, it's completely different.

"You're amazing." I kiss her again, licking her lips to taste the lingering chocolate. "I never want to leave your body." I punctuate each word with a kiss across her body, any part I can reach without moving off her at all.

"I want that, too." Mila's hands wrap around my shoulders, sliding over my neck and up to my hair. "I do want to talk a little bit about it, if that's okay."

"What do you mean?" What could she want to discuss? Was it not as good for her as it was for me? Shit, was it *bad*? I thought I was pretty good at this, but if she tells me I'm not, I'll never recover from the humiliation.

"Don't sound so nervous, big guy," she says with a chuckle. Her voice is teasing, and I relax a little.

"What am I supposed to sound like? I just had the best sex of my life with a girl who I want nothing more than to make my own, and she says she wants to talk about it."

"I didn't say that because I didn't like it, I really liked it. Coming twice isn't something that happens a lot for me." Her cheeks redden adorably and I try not to let my chest puff with pride too much.

"I just want to talk about what you specifically liked about what we did…" Now she looks nervous. My soft cock slips from her wet pussy and we both gasp. "Maybe first we should clean up?"

"I'll be right back, don't move," I tell her, poking her nose with my forefinger and kissing her quickly before rolling out of bed. After I get to the bathroom, I tie off and dispose of the condom before washing my hands. I grab a clean cloth and wet it with warm water for Mila. The whole time, I'm trying to figure out what exactly Mila is meaning when she says she wants to talk about it. Was it not good for her? Coming twice is usually a surefire way to determine that the sex is dynamite.

I make my way back to her; she's laying out in the middle of her bed with a smile on her face as she's looking off to the side. Her braid is barely holding on, falling out and framing her face so nicely. And even though I like her in my clothes, I really fucking like seeing her naked breasts rising and falling with each breath, watching the red, abused peaks harden as her body cools.

"You're beautiful," I whisper, speaking the truth.

"Thank you," Mila says shyly, moving to cross her legs.

"Let me clean you up." I sit on the soft mattress and push her creamy thighs apart to see the shiny center, the proof of what I've done to her. I so fucking wish it was my cum seeping out of her pussy, mixed with her own.

Soon. *Soon.* Slowly, I wipe her folds, touching her softly. When I get close to her clit, Mila jumps slightly.

"Shhh, babydoll." I shush her, showing her how calm and slow I'm being. I don't want to rile her up again, not yet at least. Taking my time, I clean her reverently before I deem I'm done and throw the wet towel to the side where it lands in the hamper with a *splat*.

"Thank you," she says with a soft smile.

"Anytime. Now, you've gotta put me out of my misery. What do you want to talk about?" "First off," Mila says, scooching back to rest against the headboard, "I want to tell you that being with you was..." She seems to struggle for words, opening and closing her mouth a few times before settling on something. "... life-changing. Finally taking that step with you, I know. I know now."

She's being cryptic. I don't know what she means, but she's smiling so brightly that I don't ask. I just let her think through it all and talk to me.

"Second, I wanted to talk about how our personalities mesh when it comes to the bedroom. Be honest with me, Cillian. Do you like it when I take charge?"

I sit back, blinking once or twice, thinking about her question.

"Does it make you feel even better when you do what I've told you to do? Do you like being good for me?" she asks quickly.

I snap my mouth shut. My chest is tight. It's so hard to admit this, but… I nod. Because I did. I do. I like when she turns dominant. I like when she lets me just… feel. I don't have to worry about anything other than what she's telling me to do. But I also like being a little rougher with her. I like it all.

And if I'm being honest, I love hearing her call me a good boy. I love the way her voice changes when she tells me that I'm doing good for her. My cock starts to swell a little just remembering when she whispered it in my ear as she rode me.

Fuck.

"Do you like it when I take care of you? And do you like taking care of me?" She puts both hands flat on the bed, pushing her chest out, all while never breaking eye contact with me. It's intoxicating.

"I do." My voice sounds hoarse, but I don't care.

"Have you ever had a partner dominate you?" she asks, cocking her head to the side.

"No. No one I've ever slept with, any relationship I've had, no one's wanted to take care of me in that way. I'm six-foot-six, covered in tattoos and an enforcer for the Mob. No one would think that I lean toward being submissive. That I want to be. That I wish someone would just take over in the bedroom and tell me what to do, let me fully be immersed in the moment. So, I got really good at being dominant. At being what others wanted me to be. At being what others expected me to be."

"That's why you change," she says softly.

"Excuse me?"

"Your whole energy changes when we start to be intimate. Like you put on a mask."

"I have to." I pick at an invisible thread on the rumpled bed. "How would it look if someone like me told a girl outright that I wanted her to tell me what to do? To call me her good boy and praise me? To take care of me so I can take care of her in turn? It would make me the laughing stock of the Clan if anyone found out. It would make my cousin second-guess my abilities as his enforcer. He'd think I'd gone soft. So to answer your question, no. I've never let anyone dominate me and I've never told anyone what I want to try in bed."

Mila looks at me with big blue eyes, full of understanding and pity, but I don't need her pity. My hackles rise and I narrow my gaze at her in anger before I stand up from the bed, find my briefs and throw them on. I don't need this. I don't need this girl to look at me with pity.

I reach the door and rip it open. I need some air.

"Wait, Cillian!" Mila stands up, wrapping the top blanket around her naked body and following after me.

"No," I growl, stomping into the kitchen to get water.

"I don't know why you're having this reaction to me asking you questions about it. I want to know what you want in order to be that person for you," she says, her voice calm and collected. The opposite of mine. "Can you tell me why you left? Why you're angry?" Her warm hand wraps around my bicep as she tries to turn me to look at her.

I pull my arm free from her grasp without saying anything. Because I don't know. I can't answer her questions because I don't know why I'm so... whatever I'm feeling. Embarrassed? Frustrated? Jealous, even?

"Cillian?" she says softly, moving to put her hip on the counter. I can feel her close to me, but definitely giving me space. She's not forcing herself into my space like others do when they want something from me.

"How do you do that? How do you know?" I whisper, dragging my eyes from the counter, to her.

"Do what?"

"Know what I need."

"Because I care for you and I watch how you respond." She smiles softly.

"And that, that right there, is more than anyone else has done for me."

She doesn't look at me with pity anymore, if that's what she was even before. Now that I'm a little calmer, I can see that I let my emotions and my own perceptions influence things.

"The only reason I asked you that is because I want to be that for you. The same way that you want to be what I want and what I need, I want to be the same for you. This thing, this dynamic, can't happen without us talking about it. In order to really enjoy it, really be *vulnerable*, we have to be honest and open with each other." She steps into my space, still not touching me yet, letting me choose when I feel comfortable enough to have us touch. "Why did you leave? What did I say?"

"You didn't say anything." I sigh. "It was how you looked at me. You had this look in your eye. Pity. You were feeling sorry for me because I'd never been able to explore this."

"You're right." She shrugs her shoulders. "But let me explain. I haven't had anyone that I could explore my likes and dislikes with either. My knowledge about this is from research that I've done. Things I've scraped together that I enjoy. I don't know everything, but I want to learn… with you."

I take her hands in mine and look at how well we fit together, in and out of the bedroom.

"I want that, too."

"Whew, good." She feigns worry, wiping her forehead with the back of her hand. "So, tell me. Tell me what you want. Is it everything that you said you couldn't tell others?"

I nod, and one of my hands goes to the back of my neck uncomfortably. I don't know why the fuck this is so hard for me. Mila's asking me, she's actually *asking me* how I want this to go.

"I do. I want us to continue to fuck like we just did. It was… it was everything that I've fantasized about, everything that I've wanted, for as long as I can remember. Everything I've wished for. And you're telling me that you like and want it to? The girl of my fucking dreams?" I groan in pleasure. "There's no way that this is happening to me." I chuckle, turning to the cabinet and grabbing two glasses to fill with water.

"Oh big guy, it's happening." She smirks, taking the one glass that's filled in my hand while I hold the other under the tap. After taking a long drink, she looks at me seriously.

"That sounds perfect." I bite my lower lip.

"I really liked it," she says softly.

"What?"

"When you called me Ma'am."

It makes sense because as much as she watched me, I watched her just as closely. She turned nearly feral when I said, 'Yes, Ma'am'. I noticed. I want to have her feel like that, over and over again.

I smile and put my hands on either side of her face, and barely hold back from kissing her deeply. "Then Ma'am it is."

I smirk. "We will figure it out as we go along. I trust you."

She smiles, holding my hands on her face.

"You're mine now, and I'm not giving you up, do you understand?" I look her straight in the eye, my brown ones meeting her blue orbs.

"I do." She smiles, leaning into my body even more, like she's relieved. "Kiss me."

She doesn't have to tell me twice. I lean down and take her lips in a deep kiss, sealing our conversation, our agreement in the kiss. It's getting heated faster than I can control and my hands move toward the back of her neck and her waist, pulling her closer to me.

Both of Mila's hands wrap around my hips, pressing us close together. I can feel my cock start to harden against her belly. When her hands leave the sheet, it slips from her body, only being held up by the points where our bodies touch. Her skin is so soft, her curves are so luscious but her muscles are pulled taunt from use and strength. I reach down and grip her thighs, lifting her up and placing her on the counter so her exposed core is pressing against me, letting me feel the wetness that's building between her legs.

I can't believe that she wants me. That she's making the *choice* to be mine. Because that's what it is. A choice.

There's no space between us.

Mila pulls my head back with a tight grip on my short hair. I wince, and move where she wants me. "You're mine, Cillian. Mine. And when I claim something, it's mine for life. So, get good with it," she says pointedly.

"You say that as if I didn't just tell you the same thing." I smirk, my head still cocked slightly from her intense grip.

I can't say I hate it. I like the slight sting of pain, the intense attention she's giving me, the feeling of being held. Combine that with her legs wrapped around my waist, ensuring that I feel every throb and clench she has and that she can feel every time I twitch for her…. It's fucking heaven.

"Cillian! Where are you?" Bryan's voice booms through the apartment as he rips open my front door, and Mila shrinks in my arms. I immediately spread my back as wide as I can to cover her body and she curls into me.

"What the fuck, man?! Get out of here!" I yell at him over my shoulder. His jaw drops and for a moment he looks shattered. There's a sadness in his eyes, but I don't know why. But within a blink, the broken expression vanished and was replaced with anger.

"Are you kidding me? Cillian, you can't be this stupid," Bryan nearly growls, his voice deep and daunting like I'd done something wrong. But this thing with Mila is without a doubt the most right thing I've ever started.

"Get. The. Fuck. Out," I snap.

"Cillian, the sheet," Mila whispers, like she's almost afraid to say anything and draw attention to herself. The sheet is still caught on my knee so I'm able to bend and lift it higher, pulling it over her shoulders and wrapping it tightly around her.

I can see her putting up her walls, safety guards between us. Fuck Bryan. Fuck him. I'm sure she's fucking traumatized all over again with someone, another man at that, seeing her naked against her wishes. And of course he goes and makes it worse by spewing shit. I cup her cheek with my hand and kiss her forehead, letting her know I'm here and I understand.

"Why are you still here?" I turn myself around so Mila's front is to my back and I'm in between her and him.

"What are *you* doing? She's part of the Bratva, an assasian for fuck's sake. You don't know her well enough to trust her yet, and you're letting her emotionally compromise you. This isn't something that you are usually dumb enough to fall for. I'd thought you'd grown up." He scoffs at me and with each word, my anger grows.

How dare he say that shit to me? How dare he say that shit about her?

"I'm only going to say this one more time, you mother-fucker." I seethe, looking at Bryan through my eyelashes. "Get out of my house before I break your jaw."

"Kieron will be hearing about this." He points an accusing finger at me.

"Is that supposed to scare me?" I smirk angrily. Who gives a fuck if Kieron finds out? I'm sure he's not going to be surprised.

"It should."

"It doesn't. So take your cheap-ass threat and leave!" I wave my arm out wishing I could push him out the door, but if I move, I'll leave Mila exposed.

Bryan's jaw juts out and his nostrils flare, but he turns his back and slams the door closed.

I release a deep breath, and turn to hold Mila.

"Are you okay?" I whisper, knowing it's a stupid question because how could she be?

She's strong, stronger than most people I've met, but to go through all that trauma, then to be intimate again only for some brute to walk in and ogle at her, while saying terrible things… It makes me murderous. Even if the brute in question is one of my best friends.

"Did he see me?" She keeps her head down, her eyes closed,

blocking off any ability for me to connect that way. So, I'll connect another. I hold her hands, making sure to keep the sheet wrapped tightly around her shoulders.

"For a moment, but I covered you mostly."

"He didn't see… all of me?" she asks worriedly.

"No, doll. I don't think so. Probably just your arms and shoulders, maybe your legs. But everything else, everything that's just for you to show to who you want, that was covered. I made sure of it." I really fucking tried to.

"Okay," she whispers, gazing up at me with her big blue eyes. "I'm sorry."

I lean back from her even though it pains me to do so while she's this fragile. "Why the hell are you sorry?"

"Because, once again, you're in a mess because of me."

"Not because of you." I hold her face gently. "Because of him. Bryan's obviously going through something and it's causing him to lash out. Don't listen to him. I'm not."

"You're not worried about Kieron saying something?"

I laugh, throwing my head back. "No, no, I'm not. He can say anything he wants, it's not going to change my mind. And if anyone will understand how I feel, it's Kieron. Bryan just wants to stir shit."

"But what if—"

"What if nothing. Mila." I kiss her forehead, breathing her in. She smells like my laundry detergent; clean and warm. The scent is blended with her own unrecognizable sweetness. "Nothing will happen. Did you see Kieron watching us last night? Did you see him taking everything in? I made no effort to hide my feelings or my intentions." I smile down at her. "Nothing bad is going to happen. I promise."

"I don't want to be taken from you," she says, and her breath hiccups a beat.

My heart stutters. I want to kill Bryan. I vow to protect her and keep her at all costs. "You won't be. I won't let that happen."

"Ever?" She smiles, but it doesn't quite reach her eyes.

"Ever."

***

"I need to talk to you," Kieron calls into the phone, over the sound of an infant screaming.

"I think you have something a little more pressing to worry about at the moment." I put the phone between my ear and my shoulder, and dig into the bag from the bakery down the street. I pull out a few different pastries, and a croissant for myself. After Bryan interrupted us earlier, I ran down to the shop while Mila showered. I think she needed a little bit of a break away from everyone, including me. Not that I could blame her.

"She's just hungry and the bottle is warming," Keiron responds, dismissing my redirection. "Sweetie, you need to be patient for Daddy. I'm trying here," he says to his newborn daughter as if she would be able to understand him and stop her wailing.

"What do you need to talk to me about, especially right now?" I ask, reaching for the silverware drawer and pulling out a knife to cut the croissant and put some butter on it. At the same time, I put the pastries in the microwave for a few seconds for Mila and I to share.

"Bryan called me."

The cries quiet down and liquid sloshes on the other end of the line.

"And?"

"So, do you have anything you want to talk to me about before I call a meeting to go over the information Bryan found? Something that might be good for me to know? Something that might change how we do things going forward?" he prods, as his daughter sighs with contentment.

"Thank god. She's got a set of lungs on her, huh?" I say with a smile. My newest little cousin is adorable and I love her, but I don't know how he can hear that loud screaming all the time.

"Only when she's hungry. Just like her mom." He chuckles. "But really, tell me what I need to know, Cillian. It will change some things."

"Mila's mine," I say simply, shrugging my shoulders.

"Just like that?"

"Just like that. She's not going back and I won't let anyone suggest that she is. Fuck that. Does that answer your question?" I pull the plate out of the microwave and put it on the counter. I don't mean to sound confrontational, but I'm not going to let him have any doubt in his mind where I stand.

"It does. The road forward will be hard, man. But not impossible. There are things we can do to protect her more, but we will cross that bridge when we get to it. Okay, so I'm going to call the guys and we will be meeting after dinner, say 7:30? Us only."

"Got it."

"Meet in my office in HQ. Be prepared to fight for this."

"I will. I am. See you then."

He hangs up the phone so I let mine slip from my shoulder. Picking up the warm pastry, I eat half of it in one bite. But now all I can think about is what Kieron meant when he said that there are more things I can do to protect her, but we have to wait to 'cross that bridge when we get to it'. If anyone knows about protecting their girl by any means necessary, it's Kieron. He freaking married Talia a few days, if not a week or so, after they reunited just so she was officially a Tavish. And all the protection that… Fuck.

Would Mila do that? Would having my last name, the name of the Clan, provide Mila with more protection? Smirnova is a pretty heavyweight name itself.

I can feel my heart speed up, sweat starting to form down my spine. Am I ready for marriage, even if it would just be for her protection? Is she scared enough to want that? Would she even want me to suggest this?

"Hey," Mila says behind me.

I jump and whip around to face her. "Hey, how was the shower?"

"Good, warm and relaxing. Why are you so jumpy?"

Her long hair is damp and she has it pulled to the side. There's one droplet that's hanging from a tendril of black hair, right over her pebbled nipple that's very visible through her white shirt. My shirt. She's wearing another one of my shirts and she looks so fucking good it's distracting.

"I'm…" I shake my head and place the plate of pastries in front of her as she sits at the kitchen island. "Kieron called. He knows about us, officially, and he's supportive."

"He is?" she asks, her voice carefully level. But her eyebrows raise a fraction, just enough to tell me that she's surprised, before her expression goes neutral again. Maybe she really was that concerned about him kicking her out.

"My sweet girl." I pull her to me by her shoulder, wrapping her into my embrace. I can't help but smile. "Who would've thought that the master assassin of the Bratva would be so kind and hopeful?"

"Oh, shut up." She smacks me lightly in the stomach, but I can hear the smile in her voice.

"I told you that he would understand. And even if he didn't, it wouldn't change a damn thing for me."

Mila leans back, and there's still some hesitance in her eyes. I know she wants this; we just talked about it, but so much has happened, even since that conversation.

"You can tell me, you know. Whatever it is that is worrying you." I lift her face with my index finger under her chin. "I can help you. I *want* to."

She takes a deep breath and closes her eyes like she's in pain. "Even if we get Kieron and the rest of them on board, I'll never be really accepted."

"We will figure it out." I kiss her forehead. "I just got you, I'm not going to let anything stand in our way. And I'll kill any motherfucker who tries to take you from me."

The Protection Detail

Cillian

7:30 in the evening rolls around and I'm nervously pacing outside of Kieron's office door. I think I got here at least fifteen minutes early. Mila's concern about what would happen if her family found out that we were harboring her keeps tumbling around my mind, mixing and intertwining with what Kieron had to do to keep Talia safe.

"Hey man." Trent rounds the corner with Bryan right behind him. They're both dressed similarly to me: leather jacket with dark jeans. I know for sure that if they took their jackets off, I'd be able to see the glock tucked into their waistbands. Just like mine is.

"Hey, what's up?" I nod back to him, but wait for Bryan to acknowledge me. Which he doesn't. So he's still pissed off.

Well, so am I. Fuck him.

"Nothing much. Trying to get Auggie to move in with me, but she's stubborn as hell." Trent shakes his head, huffing in frustration. "I want to get her name changed and a baby in her belly soon, but she needs more time. Which *I know* I have to respect. But damn, I swear she's just stringing me along at this point because she thinks it's funny."

"So, she's a perfect match for you then." I chuckle.

"Without a fucking doubt." He smiles proudly. "And I hear that you might've found yours? Or… is it just a moment?"

Kieron pulls the keys out of his pocket, waiting to see what happens. If I'll rage or if I'll keep my feelings bottled inside.

The smile drops. Anger and frustration fill my chest as I glare at Bryan. Fucker. It's clear that he's gossiped about my business to the others and put his own spin on it.

"No, it was not just a moment," I snap, answering Trent's question but for Bryan's sake.. "She's *mine*, understand?"

I feel, more than see, Trent move to the side, but my eyes never leave Bryan. I want him to see how serious I am. How he can make up whatever shit he wants to spew at me, but it won't change the fact that Mila and I are together. His hands ball into fists at his side and he takes a deep breath. His eyes narrow and darken, the brown looking nearly as black as the jacket he's wearing.

"You can't be—" Bryan starts to growl more nonsense, but Kieron cuts him off.

"He's made his choice, Bryan. Apparently so has she, so let's move on and figure out how to make peace with the Bratva without handing her over to them," Kieron snaps, his tone telling the three of us that he gave an official order, not a friendly suggestion.

"Kieron, man, we don't know that she wants that," Bryan says almost desperately, like he's grasping at straws.

I see fucking red.

"What the fuck does that mean?" I push him into the wall.

A heavy *thunk* sounds through the room. I may have a good couple inches on Bryan in height, but he's like a bulldog. Short and packed with muscle.

Bryan pushes me back and I put all my energy into blocking him.

"I just mean fucking her doesn't mean that she wants to stay here with you."

"But she might want to stay with you? Is that it?" I crowd him, yelling at the top of my lungs.

"Oh shit," Trent whispers, and in the corner of my eye I see Kieron stand by me and Trent stand by Bryan. They're ready to pull us apart.

"Maybe! Maybe she just feels she owes you something. What kind of asshole are you for making her feel like she has to fuck you in exchange for our protection?"

Those words feel like he punched me in the face with brass knuckles. Jesus christ.

"That's how you think of me, huh?"

"That's how it looks," Bryan sneers, squaring his shoulders like I'm going to hit him, but the fight has left me. The understanding that someone I think of as my brother, my best friend, thinking I'm a piece of shit that would force a woman…. It's pretty devastating.

"Then you don't actually know me at all," I say, looking to Kieron to try and see if he feels the same way as Bryan.

Kieron, my older and sometimes wiser, cousin, shakes his head. He's not looking at me straight-on though, instead assessing the situation and trying to keep everyone safe.

"Back down, Bryan," he orders, his hands up in between us. "Shut your goddamn mouth before you say something else you'll regret just because of some misguided feelings."

Bryan grits his teeth, his nostrils flare, and he finally steps back. I don't know what the hell is happening anymore. Why he's not being supportive. Why his attitude has changed on a dime.

Kieron nods, and unlocks his office door, holding it open. "Get in, you fuckers."

The three of us barrel inside and I make sure to keep my distance from Bryan. His words, his actions hurt, but deeper than that, I'm angry as hell. My chest is on fire from fury at his suggestion that I don't actually feel anything for Mila. That I'm no better than the rapists in Los Muertos or the power-users in the Bratva.

Trent plops into one of the leather chairs, a small smirk on his face as he stares between Bryan and I.

"Get that smirk off your face before I knock it off," Bryan says, taking the other chair in front of the desk.

I move to the other side of Trent, leaning heavily on the window ledge with my arms crossed.

"Trent, behave," Kieron says, taking his own seat behind the desk in the pristine dark brown leather chair that he rarely uses. "Bryan, report what you've found."

Bryan takes a deep breath, crossing his leg, holding his ankle at the knee. "I was able to recover some communication on the dark web from someone who calls themselves 'The Haunted'. From what I can tell, this user is a singular person with a vendetta against the ghost story of *The Prizak*. Their communication is all about how to track them down, how to use their own weaknesses against them. There is some very precise insider information on the Bratva that I can only assume is coming from someone inside of the organization."

"Like what?" Kieron asks, folding his hands under his chin.

"Routines, processes, things to look for. No names have been mentioned outright, but there are work-arounds. Nicknames. It's information dumping, but all centered around the idea that 'The Ghost' is more than a story."

"Shit," Trent says, putting his hands behind his head and looking up at the ceiling.

"Okay, so we have someone leaking information on the Bratva. Can we use this to our advantage?" Kieron asks. His eyes are focused forward, not looking at any of us, but like if he stares hard enough the answer will come to him. "Is there anything in the communication that makes you think it's Aleksander?"

"Aside from the insanely well-written code and the usage of a few Russian words instead of English, not really." Bryan runs a hand through his hair.

"Were you able to find anything about the 'proof' that Mila said the Bratva required in these communications?" I stand up.

"Yes, actually. It was one of their 'tips' for people who want to track *The Prizak*." Bryan shakes his head and sighs.

"It has to be him," I say, looking to Kieron. "It has to be Aleksander. He's leaking information to people he knows will go after 'The Ghost'. He's setting her up in the best way he knows." We'd already had an inkling that it was Aleksander behind this, but to hear it just makes me want to hunt him down.

"We don't know that for sure yet. It could be another rat," Kieron says.

I can tell that he doesn't believe it.

"He put her in the path of Los Muertos! He knew what they would do to her and he did it anyway! He hurt her, he's not done hurting her, and I'll be damned if I'm going to let it happen again. I promised her, and I intend to keep that promise no matter what."

Losing control of my feelings and words isn't a great thing for me to do, but Kieron understands. I know he does. My rage flows freely through my body, feeling like fire burning its way through my veins. If I don't do something, if I don't punch something, release this energy in some way… I don't know what I'll do.

I start to pace the length of the room, pushing shit out of my way like a toddler having a tantrum, but I can't stop.

"Cillian, calm down," Kieron snaps.

"No! This is her family doing this to her, Kieron. *Her family*," I emphasize, unnecessarily.

"I get it. It's not something that we would do, but that's the Bratva."

"Oh, 'that's the Bratva?' And so I should just accept it?" I flare my nostrils, squaring up to Kieron from across the room.

"Killer, wait a minute." Trent stands up with both hands out to me in a calming motion that pisses me off more.

"Of course not, Cillian. Don't be stupid." Bryan stands up, pulling his jacket off and nodding to Trent.

"Now I'm being stupid? What the fuck is wrong with all of you?" I snap, throwing a random book within my grasp across the room.

"You're throwing a fit like a fucking baby. Maybe listen to what they're saying and act like a grown man. Get your head on straight," Bryan growls at me, and him even speaking to me enrages me more.

"Back off, Bryan. Shut your damn mouth before I hurt you," I threaten, pointing a finger. The fact that I'm able to give him a warning before smacking the shit out of him is impressive for how enraged I am right now. Not just at him, but at everything.

"Oh, come on. Don't be a bitch."

"Oh, fuck you!" I charge for him, my fist begging to meet his face.

"Shit!" Kieron comes around the desk, but Bryan puts a hand up to stop them both.

"She's in trouble, her family is trying to hurt her. Not only to *kill* her, but kill her spirit! I gave my word and I need your help to do that. But instead, you're telling me I took advantage of her like they did! Some fucking help you are!" I'm yelling now.

The three of them are looking at me; Kieron's looking at me with understanding and hesitance, while Trent looks somewhat chastised at my words, but Bryan, it seems like he's egging me on like a dick.

"What a fucking joke. I've been there for each of you, willing to do whatever it took to help you. And you,"—I point accusingly to Bryan—"you have the fucking gall to tell me I'm taking advantage of the girl I think I'm meant to be with. She's it for me, and instead of supporting me and helping me, you're being a goddamn asshole! For no reason!"

"You're right! You're right! But right now, Cillian, this is not about us! This is about her, and about what she needs! She doesn't need us pissing on her to claim her!" Bryan steps forward and I clench my jaw.

"You don't think I know that?" I sneer.

"You're not acting like it. How do we even know she wants you? It didn't seem like it when I walked in on you both," Bryan says, his gravelly voice low and taunting.

I fucking lose it.

My fist flies, knocking Bryan's head back as it lands across his cheekbone. He stumbles, and I hit him again. His cheek is already bloodied and bruised, and it makes me feel better.

"That's enough, Cillian," Kieron says loudly, ordering me.

My fist is still cocked, ready for the next hit, but I step back.

"Do you feel better now?" Bryan touches his cheek, bringing his fingers back bloody, and winces.

"Do you?" I snap, still breathing heavily.

"I think you're a good guy, Killer. One of the best guys I know. I have my own issues that I'm working through, but I shouldn't have said what I did." He puts his hand on my shoulder in a comforting gesture. "I'm here for you and will do whatever I can to help. I'm in your corner, Cillian. If Mila is it, I'll respect it." He nods, and looks down.

"What is happening?" I say softly between us.

"We'll talk about it at a later time, okay?" He pats my shoulder. Stepping back to where Kieron has gotten and is offering a fresh washcloth, Bryan takes it and holds it to his cheek.

"Now that that bullshit is all settled, can we make a plan to protect your girl?" Trent says, smiling at me in a knowing, accepting way.

The anger has dissipated, the fire leaving my body, as I take the three of them in without the emotion clouding my judgment. Kieron nods, agreeing with Trent. Bryan holds the rag to his cheek and nods as well. And I realize that he pushed me to fight so that I could feel better as well as a punishment for himself, an apology of sorts.

Like a brother might do.

They've got my back. They're telling me they'll be there no

matter what.

I take a shuddering breath. "Okay."

* * *

"We need more information. We need to know for sure that we are dealing with Aleksander before trying to meet with The Haunted," Trent says. We are all huddling around Kieron's computer watching Bryan as he types away on a dark screen with a crazy amount of numerals and letters in random-looking configurations. Kieron is standing behind us, his arms crossed and his hand over his mouth as he paces.

"What are you looking at?" I ask Bryan, the only one of us that knows what we are watching unfold on the screen.

He points to part of the screen that is constantly refreshing with new code. "This one there, this is him updating his information sector, I guess that's what you'd call it, he's saying that the last people who went after 'The Ghost' held it in their arms, but were weak and it slipped through their fingers. He's basically calling out Los Muertos, but not giving enough information for people to know who it is."

"Is that different from how they've talked before?" I'm staring at the small part of the screen that's constantly moving with code. Maybe if I keep watching it, I'll understand what's going on.

"It's definitely becoming more unhinged. They're pissed that The Ghost wasn't captured and broken," Bryan says, his fingers flying across the keyboard.

"What if we set up a meeting?" Trent asks offhandedly.

"That would be the best way to determine if it is, in fact, Aleksander," Kieron interjects.

"That's if The Haunted is just one person. That's *if* Aleksander is convinced that he's safe enough to come to the meeting himself," Bryan says distractedly, his eyes never leaving the screen.

"That's not a bad idea." Kieron nods, walking over to stand in front of us on the other side of the desk. "How long do you think it would take you to build a relationship, or at least get to a point where he'd meet you?"

It's a valid question. We're all on a time-crunch here and my main priority is keeping Mila safe and with me.

I cross my arms and wait while Bryan considers. He may have pissed me off, but he's still our best chance at catching this guy on the dark web. He's the best one with technology and intel gathering. He's the one that would be able to communicate to The Haunted in a way that doesn't look amateurish and essentially blow our cover.

The rest of us are decent at gathering information and going undercover, but tend to be more old school: stake-outs, torture for information, etcetera, etcetera. We're not well-versed in the art of the dark web and gathering info through a screen. Damn, I should get better at it though. Bryan is always in the know with a few clicks of his keyboard.

Speaking of Bryan, he clicks his tongue against his teeth, looking at the computer screen and rubbing his neck as he thinks on Kieron's question. "If I were to give him what he might want in return... a week, maybe? But I can't promise what information he'd want in exchange for a meeting... Maybe..."

He looks at me, and I know what he's asking.

"Absolutely-fucking-not," I growl through clenched teeth.

"Killer, it might help," Trent says from the side.

My fury turns to him. "Oh yeah? Giving information about Mila to the man that is *hunting* her seems like a good idea? No, hell no. How would you feel if we had done that with Auggie? Fuck you all for suggesting it," I snap, my words flowing through my mouth before I can stop them. Not that I think I would.

I take a deep breath, moving to stand on the opposite of the three. Their gazes feel like pins and needles as they watch me shift uncomfortably, and I rub the back of my neck in frustration.

"Okay, okay. I… I understand that this is different. That we're dealing with another Mafia, like with Talia. I get that this situation is more in-depth because of Mila being 'The Ghost'. She's a bit better prepared for danger and has lived this life. But guys, I promised her."

"Oh fuck." Kieron stands up and runs a hand down his face.

They all know me, they know what a promise means to me. So if I promised her I wouldn't put her in danger, I'm not breaking that promise for anything. And Kieron knows that better than anyone.

"What did you promise, Cillian?" Trent asks. I appreciate that he's not cold or short with me and just rolling with the emotional punches. There are too many emotions going through me right now.

"That she'd never be in danger again. In any way. That I'd do everything in my power to protect her."

Trent nods, understanding and respectful. It's silent for a moment as they think through what I said and I know that Kieron's thinking through what we need to do.

"She's been through too much, guys. Too much for any one person to handle. I can't play around with her safety, her mental health, her emotions, regardless of the potential safety it may bring. The cons far outweigh the potential pros." I drop my head, looking down at my boots.

"I can see what information he's peddling in. I might be able to feed him some outdated Clan info that will suffice. Let me talk to him and start building rapport." Bryan steps in, pulling me from my thoughts.

"That will be a starting point. Talk to The Haunted, see what they're working with and what they require. Do not give them anything until you talk with me, understood?" Kieron puts a finger on the table in front of Bryan. Bryan nods, typing code into the computer before shutting it down.

"I need to meet with Kellan. We all know how my father can get if he isn't involved in each of our operations. I think it's also a good idea to try to get a meeting with Sergei. If The Haunted wants information about the Clan, and they're working for Sergei, it might be a carrot to dangle in front of them. He might be more willing to trade information to Bryan."

"And me, boss?" Trent stands up, rolling his shoulders back.

"How do you feel about being the one to hold the meeting with The Haunted?" Kieron asks.

All three of us turn to Tent, watching with hesitation. The last time he was undercover was really bad for him. It twisted Trent up in a way I've never seen him before. He wasn't bubbly or jovial. He didn't joke or laugh about anything. He didn't insert himself into things or comment. It was like he was a shell of himself. Lost in booze. Until Kieron had him guard Talia's sister, Auggie. Only she was able to pull him back.

"How long?" He tips his chin up, and it's impossible not to see the immediate tension that enters his shoulders.

"Just the meeting itself. Bryan will be the one to do the tech, find the information and feed it to you. You'll be the one in person to make sure it is, in fact, Aleksander," Kieron says.

I keep quiet, but I won't let Trent do this if it will send him back to a bad place. I can't. I won't let him harm himself for me.

"I can—"

I start to step in, but Trent cuts me off.

"If it's just the meeting, I've got this."

"Two hours, max," Kieron says, nodding.

I take a deep breath, knowing that he's made his mind up and all I'll do is offend him if I push it.

Besides, Trent's the best at undercover work. I know he'll be safe and get what we need.

"And you..." Kieron looks at me. "You and Mila need to get out of here. Out of Boston. Out of Massachusetts."

"Oh, hell yeah!" Trent says with a big smile.

"I'll set you up in Maine," Kieron says, pulling his phone out and sending an order off to someone to get the safehouse set up.

"Maine?"

"Yes. We have a safehouse set up in Little John Island." Kieron puts the phone back in his pocket and smirks. "Go get packed, tell Mila to go fully in disguise and not take any tech. You'll be picked up in two hours."

The Old-School Spy

Mila

I can't help but pace.

Pace the hallway, pace the living room, pace the kitchen.

Wringing my hands together, I flip my braid over my shoulder as I reach the end of the hallway and turn around. I can't help but feel that something is coming. Something big. Something dangerous.

I turn into the living room and bite my thumbnail nervously. I hate this.

I hate just sitting here and not being in the middle of everything. Knowing every bit and piece of plan A, and then the three additional plans in case the first plan goes to shit. I feel like a stupid damsel in distress and that's not me. I'm a fighter. I'm an assassin. I am in control.

"Fuck," I whisper, shaking both of my hands out. Trying to shake the anxiety from my fingers.

A loud screeching comes from the TV, making me jump as the screen turns on, the static overtaking the room. My instincts kick in and I spin around, taking inventory, looking for an intruder.

My hands ball into fists and I stand in a defensive stance, waiting for the attack.

I've been well trained, I know not to call out to whomever is coming for me and give my location away. So, I stay quiet. I wait.

The static is overwhelmingly loud, but I tune it out.

Focus, Mila.

I can feel my heart pumping with adrenaline, making my senses sharper and more alert.

Out of nowhere, the TV screen turns black, and the static stops. After it being so loud, the silence is deafening. I take a tentative step toward the TV, but quickly move back as a green blinking cursor appears in the corner of the screen.

Someone found me. Someone's here. They know I'm here. I move slowly against the wall, inching my way toward the kitchen while keeping my eye on the screen. Waiting.

My fingers move as slowly to the knives as I can. I need something, anything, to protect myself. And Cillian didn't tell me where his weapon stash is, nor do I have the time to search for them now.

But a kitchen knife would work.

I've killed with less.

The dot starts to blink faster just as my fingertips touch the cool handle of the cleaver in the knife block.

"You won't stay out of reach much longer," is slowly spelled out threateningly, in the green neon block text across the black screen. My eyes dart around, looking for any clue as to who is watching me.

"I have you now. Not everyone around you is your

friend," is typed on the screen next.

"Who the hell are you?" I snap, stepping forward once.

"You tell him about this, he dies," pops up on the screen, and before I can ask any other questions, the TV goes black and the lights all through the apartment black out.

Breathe, Mila. Breathe, I remind myself. *You're not there. You're not back there.* I struggle against my initial reactions to cover my eyes and ears, to curl into a ball in a corner to protect myself. Everything bad always happens in the dark.

My training, that's so ingrained in me it's like a reflex, takes control and I snap to focus. I lean down, moving into a crouch and push myself into a stealth position against the wall. I move slowly, re-canvassing every spot that could potentially hold a threat that wasn't there before this happened. The darkness sharpens my senses as I move through the room.

Scraaaaape. It sounds like nails on a chalkboard against the front door. I slip into the kitchen quickly and silently, holding my breath. My fingers rip open the first drawer I can reach and I grab the first thing I touch. Flattening my back against the small wall separating the kitchen and the front door, I wait and listen.

If Aleksander thinks he's getting past me, getting in my head, he's going to meet his maker. Fuck feeling guilty. He's waged a war on me, on those who I consider mine. This won't end well for him and whatever lackey he's sent for me.

The front door creaks open, barely allowing any light to slip through, but it's enough to backlight the tall figure that enters Cillian's apartment. The heavy footsteps make it obvious the intruder is wearing biker boots.

I hold my breath.

A hand slips around the wall, reaching for the light, but I

raise my makeshift weapon – still not completely sure what it is – and hit the hand hard. My eyes have adjusted to the darkness and I know the layout of the apartment blindfolded. If I keep the lights off, the intruder is handicapped. Giving me the upper hand.

"What the *fuck?!*" A deep baritone voice cries out, and the hand recoils.

Shit. Cillian.

"Mila? What?" he breathes out, reaching with his other hand for the light again.

"Oh my god," I whisper. "I'm so sorry, I'm sorry. Are you okay? Fuck, is your hand broken?" I reach for him, looking at the hand I smashed. With a wooden meat tenderizer, apparently. I guess if I had to protect myself with a random object, a meat tenderizer would definitely be the way to go.

Cillian's cradling his hand to his chest, and it looks gnarly. Bright red and sore-looking, but what makes it worse is the tiny dark purple dots from the spikes on the tenderizer. If it isn't broken it's definitely going to bruise.

"Why do you even have that?" he asks.

I throw it on the floor and take his hand in mine, inspecting it closer.

"Why did you hit me with it?" He tries again when I don't answer, the pain he's feeling lacing his tone.

"Long story." I pull him toward the kitchen and push him lightly to one of the stools at the island. "Where is your med kit?"

"There's one under the sink." He tips his chin in a jerking motion, then turns his attention to his hand. "It's not that bad." He wiggles his fingers. "I can still move them, so I think we're in the clear."

"Just let me patch you up." Where is it? I reach under the sink, into the dark cupboard and blindly search around for anything that resembles the shape of a first aid/ medical kit.

Ah, ha! Found it, it was pushed behind the bottles of cleaner.

"It's not that bad," Cillian grumbles, but I turn around and stand up just in time to see him wince as he sets his hand flat on the marble.

"Oh yeah, it's not that bad." I roll my eyes. The big, strong, mafia man can't let any weaknesses show.

It's been trained into him, for sure. Just like it's been trained, painfully, into me. The Ghost shows no weakness. Ever.

"Please, let me do this for you. I fucked up and hit you when I didn't mean to." I cup his cheek, hoping he can see how sincere I am. I can feel the guilt creeping up my spine, at both keeping the secret that someone found me, but also that I hurt him.

Fuck, I hurt him.

"God, I'm so sorry, Cillian." Opening the kit, I pull out the different things I'll need. The only sound in the room is my heart beating so hard I think it's going to beat right out of my chest.

Instead of saying anything to acknowledge my apology right away, Cillian just takes a deep breath and runs his uninjured hair through his cropped hair. Just when I think the tension can't rise anymore, he lets out a deep breath.

"Why did you feel the need to hit me?"

"Obviously, I didn't know it was you."

Cillian winces again as I wipe an alcohol swab over his hand. The spikes on the tenderizer must have opened skin. Shit.

"Okay then. Why did you feel so unsafe in my apartment that you turned all the lights off and found yourself a weapon?"

Fuck. I school my features, reigning in the anxiety.

"The lights went out unexpectedly, and you didn't tell me where you store the weapons. The meat tenderizer mallet was the closest thing to me when I heard you start to come in. It was better than nothing."

"I'm sure The Ghost could've taken anyone down, bare-handed." The smirk on his gorgeous face is contagious.

"I'm sure I could've. But I wanted the upper hand." I unravel one of the ace bandages and tenderly wrap his palm.

"You could have definitely fucked someone up with that." He chuckles.

"That was the plan." I laugh along with him, but my smile drops quickly. "I'm incredibly sorry that you got caught in the crossfire between me and my imaginary intruder."

Cillian lets me finish wrapping his palm before he grabs my hand in his, holding it gently against his chest.

"You're safe. I promise you now, just like I promised you before," Cillian says deeply, his voice low and soft.

I can hear just how sincere he is. How much power is in that statement.

"How?" I didn't think that the Irish Mob's headquarters could be infiltrated in any way, but I was wrong. Aleks has found me and he's not forgiving me or being understanding at all. I don't know if I'd be understanding either if the roles were reversed.

Cillian stands up, his smile bright and his eyes shining as he looks down at me.

"Go pack a bag, babydoll. We're getting out of here."

The Safehouse

Cillian

Kieron made it clear that I wasn't able to bring my car or my bike to Maine. Instead, I get to drive a boring, beat-up old Toyota that blends in everywhere. As much as I'd rather be driving my own vehicle, the Toyota has a good radio so we'll make due.

I have my window cracked enough that I can feel the cool breeze as we fly down the interstate. Looking over to the passenger seat, I watch as Mila sleeps soundly. Her black hair is pulled back and tucked under a ballcap as much as possible, but a few wisps fly in the breeze as she rests her head against the cool glass. Oversized sunglasses cover her eyes as she sleeps.

She's so naturally beautiful, so effortlessly peaceful-looking that it makes me feel calmer just being near her. I don't know what happens for us next, but I'm here for whatever life, or our families, throw our way.

I slide my hand over the console, resting it gently on her legging-clad knee selfishly, while she's sleeping, to connect us. I don't know exactly what happened earlier in the apartment, but I know her. Something happened, but she doesn't want to tell me what.

It's killing me not knowing. I don't know if I need to kick someone's ass, if I need to tighten up my security at HQ, if I need to let someone know. I don't know what to do, but what I have come to terms with in the last few hours as we've been driving and she fell asleep, is that she must have a good reason. I know that something else went down, so what I'm going to do is tighten the security and her protection as much as possible. While she was packing, I got the go-bag ready, complete with wigs, colored contacts, and a few prosthetics. Just enough to change our appearances on the rare instances we have to go out.

I've heard every single story possible from Trent about his time guarding Auggie and the biggest takeaway I got was that he should've changed their appearances in some way.

Before they went around the town. *Before* people saw their true faces. If Trent'd had Auggie wear a hat and sunglasses every single time they were out, they might not have been tracked down.

I'd never tell him that to his face though, I'm pretty sure he knows it and beats himself up about it, to this day.

I'm going to have to wake Mila up soon so we can stop at a gas station and put on disguises. We only have another forty minutes until we reach Little John. But I hate to wake her, she seemed so scared earlier and she obviously hadn't rested while I was talking with Kieron and the guys.

"Mila?" I whisper, squeezing her knee softly.

Her eyes shoot open and she rights her posture. "How long was I asleep?"

"Not long." I lie, she's been asleep for at least two hours. She needed to rest.

"How much farther do we have?" Mila asks while she rubs her eyes, and runs her hands over her face to try and get rid of the sleepiness she's probably still feeling.

"We have about forty minutes, but I want to stop soon and change our appearance."

"Do you really think that's necessary?"

My eyes dart to hers and I try to keep the scowl off my face. "Yes, I think it's necessary. I'm not taking any chances. If we need to put on wigs to keep you safe, we're going to put on wigs."

I don't mean to snap, but this isn't the time for her to question me. I'm not going to take no for an answer.

"I know how to get around undetected." She looks at me out of the side of her eye, a slight smirk on her face.

"I understand that, but I'm in charge of your security from now on. Therefore, you're going to listen to me and we're going to not be easily recognizable as we roll into our new town to stay *hidden*. It will literally take you ten minutes. You know this."

"Yes, yes. Okay, Boss Man." She waves her hand at me in a dismissive gesture, but then rolls her head to the side to stare right at me. "I'll let you be in charge for now, but as soon as we get set up in the safe house, it's my turn." She bites her lower lip seductively.

My dick immediately jumps to attention, pushing hard against the denim of my pants.

"I like when you call me Boss Man," I say softly, but it's like all my fucking cool has left my body because the words squeak out of me.

"More than when I call you my good boy?" Mila reaches over the console and trails her fingers down the arm closest to her.

My fist tightens at her touch, and my muscles clench unconsciously. "Well, no."

"Good. Because if we hurry, we can be naked with my mouth on your cock in less than an hour." Her fingers slip over to my quickly hardening dick, tracing the outline of it and making me shiver. Without saying another word, I push down on the accelerator.

* * *

"Blonde? Really?" Mila calls over the bathroom stall. I stopped at the smallest, sketchiest gas station I could find along the highway. Even though Mila complained, I can tell she approves of my choice. The building looks like it's about to fall over; the owner was sitting at the register with his eyes glazed over and glued to the staticky TV in the corner. There wasn't even a bell over the door so I'm not totally sure he even knows we're there.

"Everyone knows you've got raven-black hair. The opposite of that is blonde, bright- white blonde. When they're looking for a black-haired beauty, and all they see is another blonde, they'll skip right over you."

Mila closed herself into the only stall to change into the outfit I brought her. Even if it wasn't necessary, I like that she's not arguing with me about the lengths I'm going to keep her safe anymore.

"Okay." She lets the word trail off, and I can hear the mental eyeroll in her tone.

"Don't get sassy with me, doll. I told you I'm not taking any chances." I slide a black baseball cap on my head, because there's not much I can do with my short hair anyway.

I hear an overly dramatic sigh from the stall. After changing my shirt into a dusty-red flannel, I put my leather jacket back on. In the reflection of the dingy, dirty mirror, I see her exit the stall.

"You look…" I start to say, but let the sentence hang in the air between us.

She doesn't have the wig on yet, but her eyes are no longer the piercing blue I crave looking at. She's put on dark-green contacts that look odd on her, but definitely change her appearance. Instead of my shirt and her leggings, she's in a very… ill-fitting outfit that drowns out her figure. A boxy brown shirt that meets some big blousy pants that look like they'll fall off of her at any moment, but are staying up with a tightly cinched belt at her waist.

Mila looks at me expectantly, waiting for me to finish my sentence, but I don't know what to say. She looks over my shoulder to see herself in the mirror.

"Uncomfortable."

"It is." She nods, walking closer to me and the mirror, handing the wig to me. She starts swiftly braiding her hair into a tight braid around her head into a crown like she's done this many times. "I've donned many disguises, I've gotten used to being someone else, but I haven't had to in a while. I haven't had to at all with you. So, us being here together and changing into new people… it is uncomfortable." Mila bends at the waist with a dramatic flourish, holding the blonde bobbed wig to her forehead before flipping back up and securing it in place.

I take a deep breath and pull her into my chest, holding her close. The fake blonde strands mask her sweet smelling shampoo I've grown so accustomed to. When she leans in, wrapping her arms tightly around my torso, I feel the tension in her body melt away.

"It's only for a moment. Once we're inside the safehouse, we can get back to just us." I kiss the side of her head before cupping her chin and turning those fake green eyes to mine. "This isn't you turning back into The Ghost. It's protecting Mila so that The Ghost doesn't have to be who you are anymore. So, you don't have to look over your shoulder forever, so we can just be us. It's a momentary discomfort for a lifetime of security. For us, doll."

Her smile is most definitely forced. Her lips curl up just a bit, and it doesn't reach her eyes. I want to keep holding her, to keep whispering my promises until she feels better. But this isn't something I can fix. This isn't something that I can push. I just have to be there for her.

Mila pulls out of my arms, clears her throat and turns to the mirror, fixing the odd-looking wig. I watch her roll her shoulders back, and take a deep breath. She stretches her neck from side to side like she's putting on a new skin.

It's like watching her transform into a new person; this blonde-haired, green-eyed woman who I don't know.

"Where are we going?" She turns to me, with a sassy, yet seductive smirk and crosses her arms confidently.

There's my girl.

* * *

The safehouse is a shoebox.

That's putting it nicely.

It's taking everything in me not to call Kieron and strangle him through the phone. Little John is a small island town, so it's mostly vacation rentals and hotels. The houses for residents that live on the island aren't always the best. They're too expensive to upkeep, so people just let them go to shit. The wooden planks that are holding up the siding are covered in sea salt from the beach.

At least it has that going for it. It's right on the beach.

It's standing on raisers in case of flooding, and the lattice on the outside is cracked, even missing in whole chunks. There's palm leaves and dirt covering everything. It looks as if it's just been forgotten.

Which I guess is what we are going for. But it's not very impressive.

"Is this it?" Mila asks, looking out the window.

I just nod, my hands clenching the steering wheel tightly.

"It's not bad. Maybe it'll be nicer inside?" She shrugs, and reaches over the console, placing her hand on mine.

I do my best not to roll my eyes. Especially since I know just how many safehouses Kieron and Kellan have. And just how many of them are freaking mansions.

"It's really not bad at all, Cillian. It has a roof, it looks clean, it's just for a little bit. But best of all, it's ours."

"Knowing Kieron, and well, Kellan, it's clean but bare. I'm just pissed off they sent us here. They could've at least sent us to a penthouse. Not this shack that looks like it's going to fall over with one rainstorm." I take her hand and thread our fingers together, bringing the back of her hand to my mouth. Kissing it softly, I hold our hands to my chest.

"It's a safehouse, big guy. It's not meant to be luxurious or a holiday." She chuckles. "It's meant to not draw attention and be a place to lay low."

"It could be both," I grumble. I'm annoyed but aware how childish I'm being. It's just because I want to show off for Mila, to have her be comfortable. It's difficult for me to remember that she's been in this life like I have. She's had it all; barely any of the good, most of the bad, plenty of the ugly. She's used to this.

Mila throws her head back and laughs, opening her door quickly. "Come on, you big baby."

Groaning, I roll my eyes and follow her out of the car.

Kieron will be hearing about this.

* * *

"It's not bad at all," Mila says, standing in the middle of the living room, clutching the small black duffel she'd packed.

I have a lot to do to get this place ready to be comfortable. As far as crappy safehouses go, it *is* better on the inside. It's clean, there's running water and electricity. The kitchen is small, but we don't need much. The one armchair and couch in the living room, an unmatched set, look to be at least a decade old. Even with all the dirt and decrepitness, there are endearing touches that make the place a bit more cozy-feeling. Hardwood floors, big storm windows that,while covered with

153

dirt, will be a great place to watch the sunrise over the water, an enclosed porch with a table and chairs.

"We'll go shopping and get some things to make it a little more..." I drop my bag and gesture around the room before taking my ball-cap off, tossing it onto the chair. "Homey?"

"Let's at least see the rest of the place first." She rolls her eyes, pulling me through the small space. There's two doors off to the side, and an open arched doorway that shows a small kitchenette.

"What's behind door number one?" She smiles, lighting up the room as she opens the door to a small, but functional, bathroom.

At least I can rest easy knowing that at first glance, I don't have to replace any bathroom necessities.

"There's a bathtub, nice." Mila smiles, inspecting the small tub that looks big enough for only one, but two if we squish in there tightly.

"I didn't take you as a bath kinda girl."

"You never know." She smirks, running a hand over my chest. "I like being able to get wet all over."

Instant boner. Fuck, what this girl does to me.

And she knows it.

I shift my weight from side to side, trying to conceal the semi she gave me.

"Let's go look at door number two, and maybe there's a bed where I can get you all kinds of wet in another way." I pull her closer to me, holding her tightly by the waist.

"That's what I'm counting on." She leans up just as I lean down and we meet in the middle for an explosive kiss.

That's when it hits me, we're alone. All alone.

No one knows where we are except for the necessary few

and they won't bother us. I have uninterrupted access to her.

I move my fingers to her wig, carefully locating the two pins I watched her place at either side of her head, and pull them out, letting them fall to the floor. I push the blonde wig off her head and let it fall to the floor, joining the pins. Her tongue slips between my lips, tasting me and deepening the kiss. I pull the elastic from the end of her braid, and carefully unweave her black hair letting it fall in waves around us. "There. That's better."

"Don't like the blonde?" she says in a teasing tone, her fingers going to my flannel buttons and pulling them open, one by one.

"I like *you*," I say huskily, breathing her in before I kiss her again.

"Bed. Now," she says against my lips, pushing against me so much that I stumble backward. She walks me backward, guiding me into the next room.

I'm so caught up in her touches, her lips, her soft moans, that I barely hear her open the door. Her hands are everywhere; sliding up the back of my shirt, pulling off my jacket and my flannel, pulling me down so she has more access to my upper body. All while I let her move me where she wants.

The back of my calves hit something and Mila pulls back. Her kiss-reddened lips twist up into a sexy smile before she shoves me down. I bounce on a surprisingly soft mattress, but my girl wastes no time in crawling over me, straddling my torso.

"In case it wasn't clear, I like you too, Cillian."

"Thank fuck," I say, bringing her mouth back to mine by threading my fingers through the hair at the back of her head. Without waiting for another word, I pull her shirt over her head, leaving her in her bra. The tops of her breasts push against the cups as she breathes deeply. The look in her eye is predatory, and I can't get enough. She and I both know that I'll let her do whatever she wants. She's caught me and I'm gladly held by her.

Mila rocks her body against mine causing fire to erupt where we touch. I try to shrug out of my t-shirt, and instead of letting me sit up to pull it off, Mila just rips it up the middle.

It's like she's thrown gasoline on the fire. I can't get enough. My cock is harder than ever, and I need to be inside her. My fingers grip her thighs, the energy radiating through me, practically vibrating with need to bury my cock in her as deep as possible. I watch in delight as Mila's eyes widen while she stares at my naked chest.

"Is this how the next couple of weeks are going to be?" she asks breathlessly, grinding down on my dick.

Fuck. Me.

"What do you mean?" I'm barely holding on. With each twist of her hips, I get closer to coming in my pants.

"This"—she waves a hand between us—"magnetic. I want to be with you all the time. I need you all the time."

"I fucking hope so," I whisper against her lips, bringing her chest to mine so she's laying on me. Flipping us over, I slide my hips between her thighs and let her feel just what she does to me.

"God, you feel so good." She moans in my ear, sliding her hand up the back of my neck.

I slip one of my hands down to her cunt, the much-too-big pants she's wearing make it easy for me to meet her heat immediately. Mila cries out at the first swipe of my fingers, and I shiver at the wetness I find between her legs.

"You're ready for me, babydoll." I slip one finger through her folds, gathering the wetness at her opening and bringing it to her clit.

"I've *been* ready for you."

I can feel her clench down around nothing, empty, wanting to be filled. So, I feed her my middle finger, slowly.

"That's it, you just needed something. Something to hold onto, huh?" I whisper into her neck, holding her in place with my weight. She moans and shivers, as I keep my finger still. It stays curled inside her, stationary, bringing barely any relief to the bonfire between us that she started.

She grinds against my hand, trying to get me to move. "More, please," she whines.

The sound is like an orgasmic melody in my ears. I pull my hand from her pants, savoring the whine of loss as I slip my finger from her heat, and with one hand, unbutton my jeans, pulling them down just enough to free my cock and thrust inside her. She's so wet and I'm so hard that one thrust is all it takes.

Heaven.

"Yes, *yes*," she moans, wrapping her arms around my shoulders.

The movement brings us tighter together and I move my mouth from hers to her neck. If we have to be in this hellhole, I'm going to take advantage of the fact that she can have hickeys all over her body. Proof that I've tasted every single bit of her.

I bite down, sucking in the skin of her neck hard enough that I feel her go limp. Surrendering to me.

A shiver runs down my spine. Goddamnit, I like it a lot.

"More," she demands, holding my head to her neck tightly.

Her wish is my command. I bite down harder, letting myself get lost in the moment. For once, I'm not holding myself back.

Mila lifts her hips to meet my thrusts and when we come together it's aggressive and needy. I pull my hands from her waist to grab at the back of her thighs, forcing her legs to wrap around my hips. Her heels dig into the small of my back, the pressure pushing me deeper into her cunt.

"Any deeper and you're going to be able to see me through your stomach," I groan, pulling out a few inches just to push back into her heat slowly. She's tight and wet, warm and pulsing, and each movement, each breath, each sound she makes, pushes me closer and closer to coming.

"Do it," she moans, throwing her head back, exposing her neck and the mark I've left. "I want to see it. You. Us."

My breathing kicks up, coming in shallow as I can barely stop myself from fucking her faster and faster. I kiss her deeply as I pull my body from hers just enough that we can both see between us.

I spread my hand over her stomach, stretching my fingers wide and marveling at how small she is compared to me. My whole hand spans her waist, covering her skin from hip to hip. Locking eyes with her, I can see her excitement and desire.

"Do it."

I pull out all the way, savoring the feeling of her clenching around my cock, before thrusting into her as hard and as deeply as I can. She's so slight that when I slide into the hilt, there's a very prominent bulge that appears. *No fucking way.*

If that isn't the sexiest, dirtiest, raunchiest thing I've seen.

"Well, look at that," I mutter, my hand going to where the tip of my dick is trying to poke through her.

"Oh my god." She moans gutturally.

It's a sound I swear I'll do anything to hear again and again for the rest of my life. I can feel the sweat bead down my spine.

"That's it." I repeat the motion, over and over, bringing us together as much as I can. I have the best view and keep my eyes wide open. Not going to miss a single moment to blink.

Mila's hair is falling out of her braid, wisps of black hair sticking to her damp face and neck. Her skin is flushed and reddened from our kisses and my fingertips. Her mouth is falling open with the sounds she's making and with each push, her tits bounce in the bra. Thrusting into her faster, I rip the cups of her bra down and twist one of her nipples.

A scream of pleasure is pulled from her lips and her eyes scrunch closed as her back bows. My abs tighten, my spine tingles, and I finally let myself go. The feeling of her coming around my cock is too much for me, and I know I'm a breath away from coming. My hips snap into hers, fucking her roughly through her orgasm.

"Cillian! Oh fuck, Cillian!" she cries out, her fingernails digging into my back so hard I'm sure I'm going to have marks on my skin to match hers.

With a deep moan of release, I come so fucking hard I swear I see stars.

Mila pulls me closer, whispering sweet nothings and dirty words to me as I fill her up completely. "I... That..." she says breathlessly, never finding her words.

With great effort, I push up onto my forearms. Brushing strands of hair out of her face, I cup her jaw and stare into her crisp blue eyes.

With a slow-growing smile, I say, "We're going to have such a great time here."

* * *

A bony elbow nudges between my rib cage painfully, and I jolt awake. After we'd finished, I was going to go get us settled, put some of our things away, but Mila wanted to stay in bed and talk. Get to know each other better. Cuddle. And I wasn't going to say no to that, especially when we both stayed naked. Besides, we've already talked about all the bad and awful stuff, so now, we get to focus on the light stuff, the fun stuff.

Like how her favorite color is green. How she could eat blinis—thin Russian pancakes—by the pound. She claims she needs at least two cups of coffee in the morning to feel human. What surprised me was that she said if she had had the chance, she would have been a gym teacher because she likes being active and wanted to pass that onto kids. Her favorite movie is, surprisingly, *When Harry Met Sally*. I wouldn't have guessed she was a rom-com girl, but that was the whole point. We started off playing twenty questions, but for each question she answered, I had at least ten follow-up questions.

I want to know all about her. What makes her tick. What makes her smile. What makes her *happy*.

After a few hours of us going back and forth with questions and laughter, of me holding her against my chest and breathing in her scent, her eyes start to flutter closed. And a nap where I get to hold her close the whole time doesn't sound so bad.

It's one of the best naps of my life, until she freaking nudges me in the ribs.

"What? What is it?" I jump up, my eyes tracking the space around us to make sure there isn't any threat or imminent danger. There's nothing. No one but us. No weird noises, except for a random, insistent buzzing sound.

"Your phone's ringing." Mila smirks, tipping her head in the direction of my discarded jeans.

"Fuck." Throwing the blanket off, I grab it and hit the green button before Kieron can hang up the phone or get pissed that I didn't answer. I *am* supposed to be on high alert and answer each and every call from him. "Hello?"

"Took you fucking long enough. Already broke in the safehouse, I take it?" Trent's voice is the first one I hear, then his stupid fucking chuckle, a thud, and then a soft 'ow'.

"Thanks to whomever just smacked the shit out of him."

"You're welcome," Kieron says through the phone.

Obviously, I'm on speaker and the three of them are there.

I can hear Trent complaining to Bryan in the background.

"Guys, shut up!" Keiron hollers. "I'm trying to tell Cillian what's going on. Jesus. You're like toddlers, all of you. It's hard enough that I have an infant that refuses to sleep at home, but then I have to come to work and babysit my best friends as they hit and snap at each other? Fuck."

I do my best not to roll my eyes or make a snide comment about how he just couldn't wait to knock up his wife, and then about how he spent the whole pregnancy whining about how much he wanted the baby to be here and he couldn't wait for the sleepless nights holding her.

I guess theory and practice are different.

Trent and Bryan mumble their apologies,sounding exactly like two toddlers who just got scolded and don't actually think they did anything wrong. I start to laugh at them, but then I hear Kieron take a deep breath like he's gearing up to yell again and I start coughing.

Maybe they'll buy that.

"I'm going to ignore the fake-as-fuck cough because I don't have the energy for you three today," Kieron says.

"How much coffee have you had, man?" Bryan chimes in.

"Only one pot. I need to start on my second," Kieron mumbles, "Anyway, the reason I'm calling you, Cillian, is that I wanted to let you know the meeting with Sergei and Kellan has been set."

"When is it?" I ask.

Mila is sitting up on the bed, looking at me intently as she takes in each and every word I say.

Giving her a small smile, I walk out into the living room, slipping my boxers on, and peeking out the curtains.

"Three days."

"I want to be there."

"Absolutely not," Kieron snaps. "I understand this is personal for you, it's personal for us as well. Sergei agreed to the meeting to potentially discuss adding a new tariff between our lands. And before you get annoyed, it's a cover, of course. We can't go in guns hot and ready; we might need to go back and push for information later."

Sighing, I rub my hand over my face. "Yeah, I get it. But it doesn't change that I still want to be there for that meeting."

"Cillian…" Kieron grumbles.

"No, seriously, Kieron. I want to be there to make sure, for myself, that Mila isn't in danger." And put a face to the people I'm—we're —going to destroy, come hell or high water.

"What about Mila's safety at the safehouse? If you leave, she'll be exposed," Bryan pipes in.

I really do roll my eyes then. Of course, Bryan's concerned about how well I'm protecting *my* girl.

"I'm going to talk to her about it, but I think she'll agree I should be there." I grind my teeth together, trying to keep my annoyed, protective, and offended feelings out of my tone. "You seem to forget that she is one of the most feared assassins in the world. I'm sure she will be okay for 12 hours." 12 hours is the absolute max I'm willing to leave her alone up here.

There's silence on the other end of the phone, but I can tell that Kieron's thinking about it.

"God, fine. Fine! You're not going to fucking listen to me anyway, are you?" he snaps. "It's at noon, at Magnolia's. Be at HQ by 11:00 am and we'll go together. You'll be my bodyguard, if anyone asks. That means you're to be seen and *not* heard, understood?"

"Yes, sir." I keep my mouth shut, not willing to say anything that might make Kieron change his mind.

"Kellan's going to be pissed," he mumbles.

I can hear Trent say, "It'll be fine, man. You each are expected to show up with protection. Cillian looks like a beast, no one will blink an eye at him being at your side."

I laugh boisterously. It's true, I do look like a beast. I'm tall and intimidating, covered in tattoos and have a buzz-cut that might suggest prison time. Being tough and scary is part of my job, after all.

"You better wear a disguise. A good one too." He sighs. "I can already see this ending badly for me," Kieron mumbles again, more to himself than the group.

I can see how he would think that, but I'm not promising anything one way or another.

Mila cracks the bedroom door open, pointing at herself and then at the front room with a look that asks if it's okay for her to come in.

I nod. She smiles and my jaw drops as she walks toward me. She looks satisfied; her hair falling from the braid that she's made no move to redo, her lips still slightly red from my bruising kisses. She's wearing my shirt, and only my shirt. She's ditched the bra though, because I can see her hard nipples through the white fabric. It barely covers her front, and the sight is driving me wild.

I'm sure that the sight of her will forever drive me crazy with want.

"I'll be there. 11:00 am, Wednesday, Headquarters," I confirm, distractedly.

"Seen, not heard," he reminds me. "Keep your head down and change up your looks. Don't be stupid." And with that, my fearless leader hangs up on me.

"Goodbye to you, too," I say to the dead line before putting my phone down on the small side table next to the couch.

"What did they say?" Mila asks, wringing her hands nervously in front of her.

"I'm sure you can piece it together, super-spy." I smirk, taking her hands, squeezing them softly before pulling her against my chest and dropping us to the couch with her on my lap.

"I can, but I'd rather you tell me." Mila rubs the back of my neck, releasing the tension held there from the phone call. Her warm breath on my neck, her naked thighs on my lap, her clothed chest pressed against my bare one, all of her is turning me on again.

I put my hand over hers on my chest and take a deep breath. I don't know how she's going to react. I'm hoping she'll understand why I need to do this.

"I'm going to meet your family."

The Meeting

Cillian

"What?" Mila whispers. Her blue eyes widen and all the humor leaves her face.

"I'm going to go with Kieron and Kellan as their bodyguard and meet Sergei and his men," I say with a shrug.

"Why would you…"

"Because I want to know who hurt you. I want to make sure, without any kind of doubt, that you're safe. There's a lot that can be left up to tone and innuendo that I don't want to rely on Kieron to focus on that. They need to focus on their roles, and I need to focus on mine."

"Cillian, you don't have to go. You aren't going to find out anything new just from being in the same room as them. My Uncle is a steel-trap and devious. He's not going to give any sort of information, verbally or otherwise, about me." She, unfortunately, pushes off my lap and starts to pace the small room.

"You don't know that," I say roughly.

"I do, though. You don't know them, Cillian. I should be going if you're trying to get information."

"Absolutely-fucking-not." There's no way I'm letting her within twenty feet of those people. Jumping up from the couch, I physically have to restrain myself from pointing a finger and going all possessive male on her. "There's no way you're going."

Her eyes narrow at me and she crosses her arms over her chest, mirroring my stance. Her jaw clenches and I know I'm in for a fight. A fight I'm not going to lose.

"I can be in and out before you guys without being seen at all."

"No. No!" I snap. Sure, it makes sense, but there's no way that it's happening.

"Cillian..." Mila starts to step forward, her hands out in front of her, reaching for me, but I step back.

"Putting aside the fact that I barely got clearance for me to go, there's no way I would send you into the lion's den again. Could you imagine if they caught you? Fuck that. There's no way. I'll get what I can and that's it." I turn my back to her, trying to hide my anger and fear. Fear that she might actually go through with following us. It's not as if I ask her to stay here and take the truck, she won't find a way to get there.

"I don't want..." Mila starts to say something, but she stops.

I turn around slowly and see that she's covering her mouth, the sad expression she had before morphing slowly.

"You don't want what?"

Her eyes dart to mine, and she reaches out to me. Her hand rests on my forearm covering my chest, and she looks at me seriously.

"I don't want what they might say, what they might do,

to influence your feelings. I've done a lot of really bad shit, Cillian. I've killed, maimed, tortured, hurt plenty of people, some that weren't bad at all. Some I hurt simply because I was told to." Her eyes line with tears, the guilt and agony that she's been carrying around forever clear on her face. "I know that's selfish of me to worry about, but I'd be lying to you if I said it wasn't a fear."

Taking a deep breath, I step up to her. Mila stays silent; waiting for me to say something, do something.

Instead of saying anything, I cup her cheek and look into her eyes. "I thought we talked about this already," I whisper against her lips.

"We did, but things can change. You might think it's fine, but I don't know what spin Sergei will put on it. He'll say and do anything to get what he wants. *Anything.*"

"I can't promise a lot, but what I can promise is that my feelings for you won't be affected by the words of a madman. Of a man with fucked-up morals and complete disregard for human life, let alone a member of his family."

"Promise me?" She looks hopeful.

"I'll promise you, doll, if you make me a promise of your own."

My words immediately put Mila on the offense. Her head leans back, out of the way of mine, and her eyes are very guarded. "What do you want me to promise?"

"That you won't go to the meeting. That you'll stay here where it's safe and where I can know with certainty that you're far, far away from those people." I fully recognize that both promises work in my favor, but if I have to promise something, she does too.

She drops her forehead to my chest with a groan. "I really

want to, though."

I chuckle and kiss her head. "I really don't want you to, though."

"If I remind you one more time that you, yourself, called me a super-spy, would it help my case?" she mumbles into my chest.

"Not even a little bit." The fact that she attempted to joke means that she's going to do what I asked, I realize with a smile.

"Fine," she mumbles again, so softly that I almost miss it.

"*Yes.*" I smirk, pumping my fist in the air.

She smacks my shoulder, playfully. "Shut up. Fine, I won't sneak out and go. Because you asked so nicely."

"But do you promise?" I press her, asking as seriously as I can. We both know how important promises are.

"I do. I promise," she says.

Relief courses through my chest. That's one issue solved. Mila will be here, far away from trouble and as safe as possible. I can focus on my task without constantly looking for clues that she's found her way to Boston.

Taking her mouth in a deep kiss, I feel her smile against my lips and decide that the rest of the conversation can wait.

—————-

Wednesday comes quicker than I thought it would. All my other undercover or protective detail jobs have dragged on like time moving through molasses. But not with Mila.

With Mila, it's fun. We read, we play games, we talk, we fuck, we eat, we play. It's been like a true vacation. Like a boyfriend and a girlfriend taking their first trip away, save for going out on actual dates.

This morning, the morning of the meeting with Kellan and Sergei, I had to leave her all alone in our bed bright and early in order to make it to Boston in time. I also had to stop by my apartment and grab a suit. Typically, we can wear whatever we want and the four of us have our own unofficial uniform of jeans, ass-kicking boots, and our leather jackets. But today, that's not going to work. I know for a fact that Kellan's security guards wear all-black suits. Kieron will probably wear a suit today as well, since they're meeting with a rival gang, but I don't know. He could say 'fuck it' and come dressed like he's going to the garage.

If I'm meant to be security, I need to look the part. I fucking hate wearing a tie though. The only things worse are the green contacts in my eyes and the blonde wig that I have pulled into a low bun. The plastic strands feel like I'm constantly being tickled as I push a lock behind my ear, again.

This shit is going to get old really fast. I don't know how Kieron stands the long hair he has.

I adjust my tie because it thing keeps cutting into my Adam's apple. I'm just in for a day of being uncomfortable, itchy, and having to stand across the room from a man that I can't let know I'm there, even though I want to take an ice pick and stick it between his eyes.

I'm enjoying my bloody fantasy of murdering my girl's uncle as I wait for the elevator to reach the top floor where Kellan's offices are.

Ding. The door opens, and I'm greeted with the sight of Kellan and Kieron locked in a argument; both men standing toe-to-toe and screaming 'fuck-yous' and 'fuck-offs' left and right. It's a sight I've seen many times before, growing up with the two of them.

Trent and Bryan hover in the background, as Trent stands there smirking while Bryan looks bored. I've never been more jealous that they get to be in their jeans and leathers.

"The decision hasn't been made yet, but when it is, I will let you know," Kieron snaps off to his father, his tone condescending as hell.

"There's no decision, Kieron. If he wants to keep her, he's going to need to prove that she's part of the Clan now. There's only one way to do that." Kellan points his finger at Kieron menacingly.

"Whoa, whoa, whoa. What's going on?" I say, putting my hands in between them. Trent and Bryan wouldn't dare, but being Kellan's nephew, I get away with a little more. When neither man looks at me, I turn my attention to Kellan. "Uncle?"

"Ask your cousin. He should've already briefed you," Kellan snaps, his eyes never leaving Kieron.

"Kieron?" I ask.

Kieron's pissed. Livid. His eyes narrow further, his nostrils flare, and his jaw clenches so hard that I can see his beard move with the muscle. "Marriage, Cillian. He's demanding a marriage between you and Mila if you want to keep her under the Clan's protection," Kieron says, clearly enunciating each word so there's no way I misheard him.

"Excuse me?" I ask, not because I didn't hear him, but because I can't fucking believe that Kellan is pushing this.

"It's the same thing you had to do, Kieron, and look at how that worked out for you. You're married to the 'love of your life.'" Kellan has the audacity to do air quotes around that, as if he doesn't believe the depth of Kieron's feelings, or in love itself. "And you've got a beautiful daughter. You wanted to protect Talia, and you knew it was the best way to do it. Cillian's situation is different."

With that, my Uncle turns and speaks directly to me. "You say you want to protect Mila Smirnova. That she needs our protection from her family, The Bratva. In doing so, that means that she will naturally become more exposed to Clan secrets, locations, regimes. I can't take the chance that she's a double agent. Only you guys would be able to actually find 'The Ghost'. Jesus," he mumbles exasperatedly. "I can't chance the Clan for a girl."

"She isn't, Uncle. She's—" I start to defend Mila, but Kieron chimes in.

"She's been vetted thoroughly, Father. Cillian has proven to me that their relationship is real, true, and that she's to be trusted. She's being hunted and we need to help her. Think about the information she'll be able to give to us on The Bratva. The technique and expertise she'll be able to give our spies to help them be more effective." Kieron raises his eyebrows.

I want to step in but Trent catches my eye and shakes his head, ever so slightly. So, I keep my mouth shut.

Kellan nods, his mouth twisting into a devious smile. "We could finally acquire the territory The Bratva took from us years ago."

"Exactly." Kieron nods.

"Then, the wedding needs to happen to prove that she's with us. With the Clan. A wedding will prove her dedication," Kellan reiterates.

I can't say I didn't see this coming. Kellan is all about people proving themselves to him, to his cause. He prefers permanent ties and methods, unions and death, to deal with anything. Kieron warned me ahead of time that this was a possibility, so I should've expected this conversation to happen.

"She's given us valuable information. Is that not proof enough?" I ask.

"No. She accepts the union, and gives her allegiance to the Clan, or she goes back to the Bratva and can take her chances with them," Kellan booms.

Fuck, *fuck*.

"I understand, Uncle," I say through my clenched teeth. "I will discuss it with Mila and let you know what she decides."

"That's not how it goes, Cillian. She accepts and marries you, or she's gone." Kellan leans into me menacingly. "One way or another. You have until tomorrow morning."

My uncle is nearly as tall as I am and when he chooses to, he can turn from the charming, charismatic guy that I've seen make every woman in a room flock to, to a guy that can make even his enemies begrudgingly agree with him. A natural-born leader, to your worst nightmare. A demon in a human disguise waiting to skin you alive.

I know what he's done, I know what he made me do to prove my allegiance to the Clan when I came of age, but I also know it was nothing compared to what he made Kieron do.

Kellan Tavish isn't a man to be messed with. Kieron is the only one I've seen him give leniency to. So as much as I want to snap and defend my girl, I know that I can't.

"Understood." Kieron steps behind me, taking control of the conversation.

"Good." Kellan nods to Kieron, but points his finger at me.

"Understood." I nod to him, and put my clenched fists in my pockets.

"Don't let a wolf in sheep's clothing come into my home. Don't think with your dick," he snaps at me, fire burning behind his eyes.

The amount of self-control I have to exert over myself to keep my fist from snapping out and punching my uncle in the face is astounding. My teeth grind together, hard enough that I'm pretty sure I feel a filling crack. I'll be the good little soldier he expects me to be. I have to be. For Mila.

Not trusting myself to speak, I nod tightly. Looking over to the guys, I see that Trent is uncharacteristically silent and without any humor in his gaze, Bryan... Well, I think Bryan looks how I feel. His dark gaze is narrowed and his arms are crossed tightly against his chest, the leather straining to contain his muscles.

"Let's go. The meeting begins soon and it wouldn't be good to start off our faux business relationship with the Bratva by being late," Kellan says with a smirk forming at the corner of his mouth. We watch as he transitions into the charming devil who isn't going to take no for an answer.

* * *

We arrive to the restaurant with typical Mafia style; in three blacked-out SUVs, one for both men; our Skipper, Kellan, and the Second-In-Command, Kieron, and an extra for the rest of our security detail as well as if we need to confuse anyone that might be following us.

I follow them into the little Italian place that serves as neutral ground for meetings. It's not run by the Italian mob, but instead paid off by each and every Don in the city to keep the restaurant neutral. It's one of the strongest unspoken rules that all the heads of power in the city abide by.

The whole place is empty, except for Sergei and his men. He's seated in the middle of the room at one of the tables, eating his fill of spaghetti with his men standing behind him with their hands behind their backs, clocking every step we take.

Kellan and Kieron stride into the room with four of us security guards surrounding them without encroaching on their space. Marcus, Jamie, and Spencer join me in their protective detail, the four of us walking in sync and ready for anything.

"Well, well, well," Sergei says with a mouth full before he dabs a napkin to the corner of his mouth and lays the white cloth back on his lap. "If it isn't Kellan Tavish and his protégé. You still need to have him shadow you to learn the business? That's a shame."

What the fuck? We haven't even talked yet and he's being a condescending son of a bitch. My fist clenches and I grind my jaw to keep from reacting.

Normal security does not jump in on these matters and I need to remember the role I'm playing.

Kieron reacts the same way I do, but puts on a cocky smile. "What a way to greet someone that might potentially bring you millions."

"Yes, I agree. Maybe we should go talk to Pavel, he will at least be cordial," Kellan says, buttoning his suit jacket and standing tall.

Sergei's amused smile drops and he puts his fork down. "Fine. Down to business, then." He dismisses his men with a wave of his hand, looking at them out of the corner of their eye, before turning back to us.

"Agreed." Kellan nods, pulling the chair out and sitting down. A waitress—the poor girl looks like she's going to break down in front of us—sets down a glass of water and a glass of red wine for both Kellan and Kieron.

Kieron sits down next to his dad, crossing his arms over his chest and leaning back. If I didn't know better, I'd say he was a biker rather than a mobster. Kellan waves off the other three, but Kieron looks at me pointedly before gesturing to the side of him with his head.

I guess that's how he's going to make sure I can stay and hear what this fucker has to say.

"We have some questions before we get wrapped into business together," Kieron says.

"Naturally." Sergei picks up his wine glass and takes a sip.

The three of them discuss opening in a new trafficking input for gun sales, discussing how they'd remove the serial numbers and make them completely untraceable, who'd they'd sell them to, how they'd share the profits.

As they talk, I listen intently for anything that might be helpful.

"Now, as you know," Kellan turns the conversation, "Kieron will be taking point on this. If you are going to give this to any of your heirs, then I want to meet them and determine if they're to be trusted."

Here we go.

"If you're going to have your son be in charge of this, then it is only fair for one of mine to be. Marek is older, but has no head for business. Ivan, it is."

"Very well." Kieron jumps in, leaning forward to put his

elbows on the table. "Now, my sister will also be helping me with this. The point of contact, in fact."

Sergei's eyes widen and he gapes at Kellan with a look akin to shock and horror laced with amusement. "Are you kidding me?" he gasps.

Kellan remains still, letting it play out. As per usual in our world, the old-school guys think that women can't do anything. Or that they'll fuck up business.

They couldn't be more wrong.

"Is that a problem, Sergei?" Kellan raises his eyebrows. This is going to be such a fucking treat to watch the two of them school Sergei.

"Women do not belong in business. They're bad luck. To be seen, to be easy on the eyes, to open their legs when we need an heir, but that's it. You're going to let your daughter step in? Lunacy." Sergei speaks animatedly, talking with his hands and shaking his head like he can't believe it.

"That's where you're wrong," Kieron presses. "But in any case, Augustine will be joining us. She, and I, would feel better if one of your daughters is also involved. As a sign of good faith."

Shit, they're pulling in Auggie? Trent will not be okay with that. I'm not okay with that. Fuck, Mila will really not be okay with that. Shifting my weight from side to side, I keep my eyes forward.

"You know that I have no daughters. Just one niece. And unfortunately, she's... unavailable," Sergei says, clearing his throat.

"Why?" Kellan asks, looking at his watch. I know this is a ruse, the whole reason we are here is to get information about Mila and Aleksander, but he's really playing this up.

"She's out of town at the moment."

"Visiting family, visiting a suitor, or...?"

"Family," Sergei says quickly, lying his ass off.

"Right. Well, when will she return?" Kellan asks, shaking his head. "If you're wasting our time..."

"If you're not interested in how we are planning on accomplishing this new venture, then we're going to walk. You may not understand this, you fucking dinosaur, but the next generation is the future. We don't sit here, turning our noses up at women because we have some backwards ideas about gender equality. Women can do, and will do, everything men can and probably do it better. So tell us about your niece, and set up a goddamn meeting, since she's apparently your next female in line," Kieron bellows, rising higher from his chair with each sentence and pounding his fist on the table in anger.

I'm impressed.

Very fucking impressed.

Sergei clears his throat again, looking from Kellan to Kieran, before lifting his wine glass and gulping it down. I've always known that the Tavish men were intimidating, myself included, and I've seen them take people and work them down until they get what they want, but I've never seen someone this high up fold so quickly. Or be so nervous.

Something's up.

"Mila is not one to be involved in this life. In all honesty, she's gotten into some trouble recently and is not..." Sighing, he covers his fat chin and leans back in his chair. "She was taken."

"How embarrassing." Kellan smirks, using the same tone that Sergei did when we arrived.

"You don't think I know that?" Sergei barks at us. "I've been trying to find her ever since we lost contact. I have my best people on it, but she's well-equipped in getting in contact with us in many ways. Or avoiding our detection." He shakes his head and rubs his eye exasperatedly.

As he should. He's treated her terribly, cruelly, used her, and now he's shitting himself because he lost her. In more ways than one. But right now, he's just concerned about covering his ass.

"How would she know how to do that?" Kieron asks innocently, bringing attention to the stupid viewpoint he has of the fairer gender.

Sergei's eyes snap to Kieron's, nervous yet again. We caught him.

"As you've probably prepared your daughters, your wives, your sisters…" Sergei's head twitches slightly, cocking to the side. It's so subtle, but it's exactly what I was watching for. A tell. "We taught her how to use morse code and leave a digital trail for one of us to find."

"Are you telling me you don't have foot soldiers out looking for her?" Kieron scoffs.

"Of course I do. That was one of the first things I did. I'm not an idiot, youngling," Sergei snaps, his face turning red with frustration. He looks like a bowling ball with a balding head and red face, all dressed up in a cheap suit. "I have some people doing surveillance as well as one of the best hackers searching."

"Aleksander Smirnov, by chance?" Kieron asks, innocently.

Sergei's eyes widen slightly.

"Do you think we wouldn't do our research before we go into business? I'm not an idiot, old man."

Sergei laughs boisterously, annoyingly, frustratingly loudly. Too loudly. "Obviously you are. Aleksander has been dead for years."

"Are you sure about that?" Kellan cocks his head to the side. "Very sure."

"Well then, whomever you have scouring the web for her is leaving a very similar digital signature all over." Kellan puts one hand on the table, showing his Clan ring as the gold glints in the overhead lighting.

Sergei's head twitches again, slightly cocking to the side. "What are you trying to say, Tavish?" he asks through clenched teeth.

"I'm saying either you have Aleksander alive, working for you and for some reason you're telling everyone that he's dead. Or, he's your cover-up for your niece somehow. Either way, business is going to be tricky if we can't trust each other."

Sergei raises one eyebrow, leaning back and placing his arm across the empty chair beside him. Something's changed. And I don't think it's in our favor.

Shit's going to go down. It's turning into a stand-off between the three of them.

"And what about this 'sister' you have, hm?" Sergei says, confidence returning to his tone. "Do you really take me for a fool? How long have you and I been head of our families, Kellan? I know this is your only son. Unless you stepped out on Maylen back th—"

Kellan stands abruptly, reaching across the table and grabbing Sergei's tie, ripping the man from his seat. In that split second, all of Sergei's men pull their guns on us, and we respond in kind. I draw my gun from my waistband and aim it right at the man closest to Sergei. Kieron has jumped up as well and pulled his own gun, but I play his bodyguard and stand in front of him.

"What the fuck do you think you're doing?" he whispers angrily, stepping to the side so he can see and aim at Sergei.

"I can't let you get hurt, sir."

"You don't talk about Maylen. Ever," Kellan seethes.

It's not often that we hear Kieron's mother's name. It's even less often that someone is using it to get under Kellan's skin. Everyone, and I do mean *everyone*, knows how in love Kellan and Maylen were. Until she was killed brutally, right after Kieron was born. My mom was devastated, still is, if I'm being honest. Kieron was too young to remember anything about Maylen and I never met her myself, but while Kellan refused to tell Kieron anything about her, my mom wouldn't stop.

"Let go of me. Before we leave, the neutrality of this place is void." Sergei rips Kellan's hands from his tie and Kellan lets him.

I keep my sight trained on the pitbull of a man with his gun pointing at my Skipper, until both leaders signal to their respective teams to stand down. Slowly, as slowly as they do, I lower my gun, ready and hot for any inkling that they won't listen and open fire.

"Before you so rudely interrupted," Sergei starts over, sitting down and fixing his tie, "I was saying that I very well know that you have no more legitimate children, Kellan. And your nephew isn't involved with business, well, *your* business. He works pretty exclusively for you, Kieron, right?"

Kieron clenches his jaw and I struggle not to try and hide my face or shift in any way.

"That being said, the only other heirs you have are your wife, Talia—and I really don't think that you're going to let your wife, a brand-new mother at that—be in the line of fire. So that just leaves your infant daughter."

Kieron jumps up and smacks the table so hard it shakes. I jump forward, physically pulling him back. I feel him lunge forward under my fingers, and I so badly want to let him go. This fucker has it coming. How dare he bring up not only Kieron's mom, but his wife and daughter, too? For all they know, we're the one bringing them the multi-million-dollar favor, not the other way around.

As angry as I am, as much as I want to pulverize this asshole's disgusting face so that no one ever has to deal with him again, and make sure he knows it's *me* that's bringing him to his death, I dip my head and hold Keiron back. My index finger itches to move to the trigger of the gun in my hand— it would be so easy since both hands are also trying to hold Kieron back —but I can't. Not yet.

"Let him go, Kieron," Kellan booms.

My fingers grip Kieron a little tighter. If I can give him some strength, I will. He's huffing his breath through his nostrils, obviously not able to make a decision yet on what he wants to do. But I know without a doubt that whatever he chooses, I'll back him up.

"Kieron!" Kellan snaps, and instead of starting a brawl like I secretly hoped would happen, Kieron is responsible and lets go, standing up, all while never taking his eyes off of Sergei.

Kellan buttons the top button on his jacket and smooths his hair back. "I think we've derailed from the main reason why we're here. The merger. The money. We came into this meeting demanding respect and we pushed it too far. My apologies, Sergei."

Sergei nods, straightening out his too-small jacket. "My

apologies for the… ill-spoken words. My anger got the best of me."

Kieron and I step back, and Kellan nods ever so subtly. I know that if I was in their position, I wouldn't be as… polite. If I wasn't undercover, I wouldn't be as fucking quiet as I am.

"Understand this though, Sergei, if you talk about my wife, my daughter in-law, or my granddaughter with such disrespect again, I will not stop my son from protecting his family," Kellan says lowly.

I can hear the *gulp* Sergei takes as he nods and am, yet again, blown away by the ability to intimidate that my uncle has.

I shouldn't be. It's a trait he taught both Keiron and myself..

Kieron stands with his hands balled into fists. The tension in his shoulders is as clear as day, visible to the naked eye.

I'm taller than Kieron, broader and typically more willing to let my emotions get me into trouble in situations like this. But hell, the moment his girls are threatened, his body morphs and he somehow becomes taller, bigger, more intimidating and scary than ever. A bad-ass fucker.

Sergei's eyes flit from Kellan to Kieron and the fear in them is clear as crystal. If only for a moment.

"Understood. As I was saying…" Sergei sits back down, making a fist to his side, signaling his men something. "By process of elimination, that only leaves one other woman close to you. Your sister-in-law, Augustine."

If he knows about Auggie, that means he knows who took her and why.

Kellan cocks his head to the side slightly and Kieron and I hold our breath to see how he will respond.

"Well, in the Clan, family is family. Yes, Augustine is Kieron's sister-in-law, but she shows promise and has expertise in business. The issue remains, if you're wanting to go into business with us then you will need to follow our rules and requests. I feel as if the potential benefit will outweigh the inconvenience. Don't you?" Kellan pulls the meeting back together.

"Fine. What do you expect me to do? My intel for my niece is limited, my sons are unmarried. Perhaps we can have another person's daughter brought up from the trenches to join this… group," Sergei says with an attitude.

"Let us help," Kieron chimes in. It's clear from his tone that he's still very pissed-off but following through with the mission. "Our IT department is superior."

Sergei clenches his teeth and the action makes the fat roll under his double chin jiggle. "Fine."

"The sooner we find her, the sooner we can get started making money. Is there anything specific that would help us find Mila? Any information or maybe the name of the person who has already been looking for her?" Kellan asks.

"Just one of our techs. No one important," Sergei says uncharacteristically fast. "I'll get the file sent over. Are we done here?"

"Yes," Kellan says, starting to stand, at the same time Kieron says, "Almost."

They look at each other and Kellan sits back in his chair, letting his son take over.

"One more thing." Keiron leans forward, putting one leather-covered elbow on the table. "What do you know about The Ghost? I believe in Russian they're called *Prizrak*."

Sergei's head drops back as far as he can and a laugh erupts from him. "The *Prizrak*? The ghost tale we all tell the kids to get them to fall in line? You can't honestly be asking about some story."

"I really am," Kieron presses. "We have information that 'The Ghost' may not just be a scary story that's told. There are some disturbing trends in the murders within our city, clearly linked to a mob. The problem is, we don't know which and we don't know who is behind it. It's as if they disappear without a trace. As if they're *a ghost*. It got me thinking that maybe those stories… weren't just stories."

My eyes are trained on Sergei, taking in each and every glance, each movement, every muscle twitch.

"That's ridiculous, Kieron," he scoffs, the only one in the room making Keiron out to be a fool. "There must be just some other serial killer running in our circles. Not *the Prizrak*."

"And of the trophies they take?"

Sergei rolls his eyes in an over-the-top way, but he puts one of his hands on the table and starts to innocently tap his finger on the tablecloth. "Trophies? It can be anyone, any mundane person-turned-serial killer. It is not necessarily mafia related."

What an odd fucking thing to say.

"You're right. I was just trying to figure it out. Rafael in the Spanish mob had mentioned something that happened and how this weird patch of hair was taken."

"Hair? That can't be right."

"A very specific patch and amount, still connected to skin. We can't figure out, the significance, just yet." Kieron plays the part perfectly, letting his words echo around the room without anything more.

Kellan stays quiet, letting the silence deafen us all.

Sergei swallows, his chin jiggling with the action. "I really don't know what to tell you. It's an odd thing, but I don't see how a serial killer, even if they seem to be an organized-crime-obsessed one, is our main concern."

"You're right. I just wanted to see if you knew any deeper meaning to The Ghost in the stories." Kieron shrugs his shoulders, and looks to Kellan.

He nods, and stands. With Kellan standing with intent to leave, his security detail comes close, surrounding them once again.

"It's been a very successful meeting, Sergei. At our next meeting, hopefully, we will have all the kids join us," Kellan says with a charismatic smile.

Sergei stands and his security team comes close, each one of them with their fingers on their handgun's triggers. Like they're just waiting for the signal to take us all out, forgetting the neutral ground.

"Perhaps. I will wait to hear news about my dear niece. I appreciate your help finding Mila. If we could keep her disappearance between us, I'd appreciate it. Maybe I'd even delete the research on Talia and her daughter, keeping her out of our information database, available for any soldier to see, if I knew that news of Mila not being able to be found wouldn't be shared." Sergei purses his lips and raises his eyebrows.

And damn, that's a good deal.

"Of course. Not a problem. A sign of good faith." Kellan nods before holding his hand out for Sergei to take.

"Yes, good faith," he repeats, shaking Kellan's hand firmly.

They drop hands and Kellan walks away, Kieron following him closely. I take one last look at Sergei.

He's smirking like he thinks he's won something.

And that means we've been deceived in some way. This

isn't fucking good.

The Homecoming

Cillian

I roll up to our little beach house at dinnertime. I'd called Mila before I left to make sure everything was still okay and to let her know I was on my way back. The drive was… well, I spent most of it thinking about how to tell Mila that her Uncle definitely knows something.

That and other things.

The house is dark as I turn the engine off and get out. The beach is empty now, making it so I can actually hear the relaxing sound of waves crashing ashore as the sun dips closer to the horizon.

"Mila?" I call out, shutting the door behind me.

"Cillian!" Mila jumps off the futon and hugs me, breathing me in. I wrap my arms around her body, pulling her in closer, and I let myself be held for a moment before I turn the tables. "Are you okay?" she asks, pulling back to look me in the eye.

"Your family… they're really fucking shitty. But Sergei, he's definitely up to something. I just don't know what."

Mila sighs. "Are you glad you went?" she asks after a moment.

"I am. I know what we need to do next, but for right now, I just want to get out of this monkey suit, get some food, and make out. Not necessarily in that order." I smirk, dipping down to kiss her quickly before I go to change.

She must have the same desires I do because she grabs the end of my tie and pulls me in close. "I missed you today."

"I missed you too, babydoll." I lean down and kiss her again, lingering this time.

"Prove it," she says against my lips.

She wants me to prove it, huh? I can do that.

The corner of her mouth tips up in a sultry smirk, a challenge, and that's what does it. I let myself go and push forward, hard, kissing her passionately. It's sloppy and messy, needy and desperate. It's a great kiss with the promise of more depravity to come.

I rip away from her as she leans in for more, and sternly say, "Go lay on your back. No peeking."

Mila's eyes turn excited again, the arousal pooling in them as she turns and runs to the bedroom.

I throw the wig to the side, happy to be rid of the damn thing, and unknot the tie around my neck, but let it lay loose, hanging down my chest. If I was nicer, I'd insist on a shower, but right now I need to fuck her so hard that she doesn't have a care in the world except getting more pleasure from me.

Walking into the bedroom, I bite my lip at the sight that greets me.

Mila did what I asked, and is laying completely naked on the bed, her eyes closed as her fingers fidget with the covers. I know her well enough to know that she doesn't necessarily like to be kept waiting and she really doesn't like not knowing what's going on.

But the fact that she's done this, it means she trusts me and she wants this.

Pulling off my suit jacket, I fold it and set it to the side before I unbutton my cuffs and the top few buttons. She must hear me because I see Mila's legs shift, sliding across the bed and clenching together. I grant her this small reprieve, as I'm sure the pressure from her thighs pushing against each other is satisfying, if just a small bit.

"Here's what is going to happen, babydoll. Eyes on me." I speak slowly, huskily, and just over a whisper, watching in delight as her blue eyes lock onto mine. "You're going to watch me get naked and then you're going to ride my face. If you don't want that to happen, tell me now."

Mila nods, and I watch as her nipples pebble up with the cool air, and watch her breasts jiggle with every quickened breath.

"Good." I run a hand up her leg, over her knee, further up her thigh. "You're going to ride my face," I say, letting my words resonate in the room before I work on unbuckling my belt. "You're going to let me lick and suck on your cunt and worship you from underneath. You're going to enjoy every moment until you squirt all over my face."

Her breathing deepens and she looks as if she's going to eat me alive. My words set her off in a feral way, and I know she's going to give me all she's got.

If I die under her pussy, I will not be upset about it. There are worse ways to go.

Unbuckling my belt, I whip it out quickly from my belt loops and it snaps like a whip at the end.

"Fuck, yes," Mila says breathlessly. I can see how much strain she's under, trying to keep herself from moving.

"You like that?" I smirk.

"I do. Are you going to spank me?"

If I wasn't hard before, I'm definitely hard now. *Yes, yes, I'm going to spank you.*

"Oh babydoll, now that I know you want to be spanked, I'm going to make your ass red with my handprint. You'll have my hand on your ass for days." I unbutton my pants and let them sit low so my Adonis muscles are on display.

Mila squeezes her thighs together again.

"Flip over."

She does what I ask instantly, lifting her hips slightly so her peachy ass looks perfect. I smack her lightly, but hard enough that she yelps. I keep my hand there, squeezing the soft globe of her cheek. The tip of my middle finger sits close, dangerously close, to the warm, tight heat of her cunt.

"Hands and knees," I order, smacking her ass once more.

Mila quickly clambers to her hands and knees like I asked and my cheeky girl shakes her ass at me in a tantalizing way that makes me groan.

"Tease." I spank her harder, and her body shifts forward from the force of it. When I pull my hand away, there's a perfect print spanning her cheek.

It's beautiful.

She doesn't say anything, but she does look back at me and smirk.Then she bites her bottom lip and keeps her eyes on me the whole time I unzip my pants and let my boxers fall with them, leaving me stark naked at the end of the bed, watching her watch me.

Without saying a thing, I grab her thighs and use them as

anchors as I dive face first into her wet cunt. Mila cries out, and drops her head to the bed, pushing back into me so I get a much better angle and a mouth full of her. I seal my lips over her pussy and suck, lick and tease her as much as I can before pulling away. She tastes fantastic, I can't get enough.

I want more.

I lay down beside where she's propped up. With one movement, I lift her up and put her on top of me. She responds in kind and grabs my face, kissing me fiercely. She has to taste herself on my lips and that's so fucking sexy.

"Sit on my face," I whisper when she pulls back slightly.

Mila wastes no time in sliding herself up my body, leaving a wet trail in her wake. I fucking love it.

She slips her thighs on either side of my head and shifts forward so she's right above my mouth. I can see everything when I look up, and she looks like an absolute goddess. So fucking sensual and hot. She looks down at me and when we make eye contact, my eyes roll back.

I lick her clit, slipping my tongue back and forth against her folds until she's writhing. But then I notice she's not actually putting any weight down. She's fucking *hovering*.

I wrap my hands around her thighs and *pull*. She fights me for a moment before giving in and when she does, her pussy envelopes me. She's everywhere. Her thighs cover my ears, her cunt in my mouth, her clit on my nose, and all I can see is her.

Nirvana.

I put my hands on her hips and try to encourage her to move. I feel her thread her fingers through my hair and she uses it as a holding post while she grinds against me. I'm so fucking turned on that I bet if she blew on my dick, I'd come.

"Grab my ass. Now," she says urgently, her voice breathless with need.

Without hesitation, I reach up under her thighs and grab her ass with both hands. One globe in each hand perfectly. My fingers are gripping her so tightly, I'm sure there will be indents. Little marks that she'll wear every day and think of me.

I hold her closer, keeping her against my mouth like she's a meal I'm devouring without any mind for manners.

And it's exactly what she needs.

She rocks forward, and her clit rubs my nose in such a way that makes her shake. I arch my hips a bit, thrusting into the air unconsciously. Mila starts to rock back and forth on my face, keeping a rhythm that makes her shiver under my hands. I feel her arousal drip into my mouth and I lap it up sloppily. The noises that I hear myself making are wet and dirty. So much so that I'm debating whether or not to reach around and start stroking my dick, just for some relief. I know my cockhead is leaking.

The muscles of her thighs quiver under my hands from holding back. She tries to lift herself off me, but I double down, pulling her thighs downward so her heat meets my lips completely. I don't let up, and I'm getting more and more desperate to feel her cream on my tongue with each roll of her hips.

She pulls my head closer, and my mouth floods with her orgasm.She seems to both push me away so I can breathe and keep me close. I lick and suck to make sure to catch every drop.

And I do.

I catch every single drop of her sweet nectar on my tongue. I keep her locked to my face as she writhes and moans, sucking down every single thing she gives me greedily.

She starts to push me away as my nose bumps against her clit over and over again, and I let her go slightly. Her chest is heaving as she moves off me, and I take a soft breath as she shimmies down my body until she's laying on top of me. Mila tucks her face into my neck, and breathes me in. I smack her ass and hold her closer to me. Her body rests against my erection and I can't help but thrust against her.

I wrap my arm around her waist and she says softly in my ear, "Did you like it?"

"You did so good, doll. *So* good. Did I like being smothered in your pussy?" I scoff. "You riding my face like that is my new favorite activity. I could have you seated there all day, every day, and not get tired of your taste and the sexy fucking sounds you make. So yes, I *fucking loved it,*" I growl in her ear, smiling when I feel the goosebumps rise on her shoulder and arm.

Instead of saying anything, Mila sits up and smiles darkly. She reaches down and runs her hand up and down my hard cock teasingly.

I watch her hand, desperation probably clear to see on my face. I can feel myself clench my teeth, and my hands are balled into fists at my side.

Mila hums, pumping me faster, but somehow still barely touching me.

"Babydoll," I moan softly through my clenched teeth.

"I want you to come," she taunts, pulling her hand away slowly.

"No, don't stop."

She smirks, leaning over so fucking seductively, and takes

my dick deep in her mouth, swallowing me down. My thighs clench and shift under her palms, I pant and moan, and I'm desperately fighting between reaching out for her or keeping my hands on the sheet and balling them into fists. I'm so fucking wound up, I'm sure it's not going to take much to make me come.

I shout and thrust deeper into her mouth, and she gags. Fucking hell, she gags and it's the best sound ever.

"Oh, I like that. I like that sound a lot." I groan, and drop my head back against the pillow. But I don't want to miss a moment of this beautiful fucking view. She hollows out her cheeks and drags her lips tauntingly up my dick before pulling off with a pop.

Mila plunges down onto me suddenly and without any extra warning. It's like coming home, warm and welcoming. I groan, long and pained. My head arches back, I swallow hard in an effort to calm myself down. I don't want this to end too soon. Fucking her bare is life-changing.

She doesn't give me any time to adjust. Instead, she starts fucking me hard and fast, bouncing up and down on me, clenching her pussy and rolling back onto me like a goddamn pornstar.

"Wait, wait. Please," I start to mumble.

"Do you need to stop?" she asks, her voice breathless.

"No! Fuck no."

"Then no, I'm not stopping, or slowing down. You're going to come, hard. Tell me when you're close."

Well, damn. I like it when she talks like that. A dirty mouth to rival my own.

"I'm close, I'm so fucking close." I groan, and move my hands to her hips, helping her bounce on me.

This goddess on top of me suddenly stops.

"What? Why?" My eyes snap to hers, staring at her in agony. I was so fucking close, maybe one or two more thrusts and I'd be coming inside her.

I wait because as much as this is my show, it's hers too. If she wants to stop, we stop. No questions asked.

But the way she's looking at me, teasingly and seductively… She wants more. I can feel myself start to shake from keeping still. She smirks, staring at me with hooded eyes and kiss-abused lips and wraps her foot under my hip, and pushes us up and over with the other leg so that I land on top of her. All without ever slipping out of her. Her skill is impressive.

"Come for me, use me and come," she whispers in my ear, nibbling on my earlobe.

Permission given, I don't miss a beat, thrusting into her as hard and as fast as I can. I swear I'm hitting her cervix, making me see stars. Underneath me, I feel her brace her hips up and meet me thrust for thrust.

"Oh fuck, oh fuck," I groan, tucking my head into her neck this time, and bite down.

The moment I do, I push into her one more time with such force we hit the headboard, and I shout her name into the pillow by her head.

We don't move. We stay in the same spot, as close as fucking possible. I thrust my hips slower as my cum fills her up completely. I push in once more, shallowly, and the tension leaves my body. I collapse on top of her, letting her have my full weight, and I feel her stroke my back lovingly as I come down.

I can't begin to describe how much I love being with Mila, she's perfect for me, but this, this moment where we're both as satisfied as we can be, where we are both vulnerable and holding onto each other while we're still as close as two people can be, this is what I crave.

She runs her hand over my head, down my neck and back up to repeat the calming motion. Letting me know that I can take my time coming back to the world of the living, that I can enjoy this pleasure. That she has me.

The Proposal

Cillian

I savor this moment, holding her as tightly as I can before I know we'll have to get back to reality. I don't want to leave her body, or move away from the bubble of fantastic sex and mind-numbing pleasure we'd made together. I move to shift us, pushing off of her body, but Mila wraps her arms around my waist, keeping me there.

Her bright blue eyes are so full of love and warmth that I've never experienced before, that I can't look away. She seems to understand because she just smiles at me softly before moving her hand up to cup my face.

"I'll be right back, I promise." I press my lips to hers, giving her the softest, gentlest kiss that I hope conveys how much I'm feeling for her.

Mila nods, and I pull out of her, running to the small bathroom to take care of business. I leave the bed quickly, already desperate to get back to her, and I can't help finding myself awestruck by how intense that was.

I think this thing we have will only get better with time. I can't fucking wait.

Mila is sitting up, unbraiding her hair, when I walk back in.

I lean my shoulder against the doorframe and watch her. "You're breathtaking."

She smiles at me brightly and pulls the covers back. "Come join me."

"Yes, Ma'am." I smirk, jumping into the bed. Wrapping my arms around her, she rests her head on my chest. I feel Mila's fingers trailing along my chest, her touch sending sparks of electricity coursing through my veins. We sit quietly, just enjoying each other's company.

"Thank you," she whispers, her words charged with emotion, and I know she's not just talking about the sex.

I smile. "No, thank you," I reply, my voice barely more than a breath. "For being here, for sharing this with me. For giving me you, for not judging me, and for loving me."

At this moment, everything seems to fall into place for me. The doubts and insecurities that plagued me before are washed away, replaced by a profound sense of gratitude for the woman lying in my arms. Whatever I need to do, I'll do for her. For us. For this.

We lie together in silence, our bodies entwined as we savor each other. It's a moment of pure bliss, where nothing else matters except the warmth of her skin against mine.

I know we have a lot to talk about and discuss, some of which I don't know if she'll like. But right now, I just hold her as she falls asleep.

* * *

"You know how good you looked in that suit?" Mila smiles shyly and pretends to fan herself. "I wouldn't mind seeing you in that again."

"Hopefully not with that hair and those contacts." I squeeze her around the middle back into my chest.

Mila slept for a couple hours, and I know I napped for at least one. It's past dinner time now, and I've heard her stomach grumble once or twice, but she's made it clear she doesn't want to leave this bed yet. To my delight, that means she still hasn't put a stitch of clothing on.

"I think it was more you in the suit than anything else." She rolls her eyes. " You looked mouthwatering. The pants hugged your ass perfectly and the jacket made you look even more ripped if possible. You, Cillian Tavish, wore that suit well."

Well, when she puts it that way…. Maybe the monkey suits aren't so bad.

"I'll have to wear it more. Just for you." I kiss her forehead, and lean back again against the soft mattress that's beckoning to pull me back in for another nap. I'm just so tired. And yes, it's probably from all the fucking, the stress from the meeting, but I know it's also because I can really and truly relax around her unlike ever before.

"Just for me," she repeats sternly.

As if I'd wear that suit for anyone else's benefit except hers. Silly girl.

"How was the meeting?"

Sighing, I put my hand on my forehead and cover my eyes to block out the annoying memory.

"Well, it started promising. Both Dons and Kieron sat down to discuss the venture and Sergei was acting like a little field mouse. Ready to kiss ass at whatever Kellan said. But, somewhere along the way, he grew a pair and pissed off everyone."

"What pissed him off?" Mila sits up on her elbow, her raven hair falling across her shoulder.

"What do you mean?"

"You said something changed in his persona. What pissed him off?"

"It's hard to say, babydoll. It was like a dick-measuring contest. Kieron was getting so annoyed I'm pretty sure he was pretty close to suggesting they lay out them and measure them, and whoever has the biggest one gets to lead everything."

Mila's face screws into a grimace. "What a disgusting thing to imagine, thank you."

"It was like tit-for-tat. But then Kellan mentioned how he wanted the next female heir, you, to help them with the takeover. And that ruffled Sergei's chins because he turned around and insulted Kieron's mother. Not to mention, he threatened Kieron's wife and daughter." I try my best to keep a straight face, but the memory makes me angry. They shouldn't have been thought about, let alone discussed.

"Oh god." Her hand covers her mouth that's fallen open in horror.

"Yeah, that's when shit really seemed to go downhill. Kieron barely kept it together."

"What did Sergei say about where I was?"

"He just said that you weren't cut out for this life, or that you had decided it wasn't for you and when Kellan pressed, he said that you were taken." I know telling her this is going to upset her. We'd always just assumed that he knew she was taken by Los Muertos, but I know there was some small part of Mila that thought maybe he hadn't and that's why no one came after her. I don't want to be the one that has to ruin her thoughts and feelings about her family, but I'm not going to lie to her.

"That son of a bitch."

As I watch, I see a storm brewing within her, every emotion swirling like dark clouds ready to burst. Her once gentle eyes now blaze with an intensity that could set the world on fire. Each word she speaks crackles like lightning, sharp and cutting. I notice her fists clenching the sheet, knuckles turning white with the force of her anger, as if she's ready to unleash it upon anything that crosses her path. In this moment, she's a force of nature, unyielding and untamed, and I can't help but feel a shiver down my spine as I witness the sheer power of her rage. I almost feel bad for Sergei, because I know she's going to use every tool he forced her to have, to take him down.

"He has some kind of plan though. He's hiding something."

"Why do you say that?"

"When we left, after Kellan and Sergei called a weak truce, he was acting weak. Like he was scared of everything and would bow to Kellan's command. That itself is off for the leader of the Bratva. But then as we were leaving, after basically sniveling and when he thought that no one was watching, he stood up straighter and smirked."

Mila's eyebrows raise and she takes a deep breath. "Fuck."

"Exactly."

"This is bad."

"I know." I nod.

"No, Cillian. This is really bad. Fuck, I thought they'd drop it. I thought they'd leave it alone…"

"What?" I sit up quickly in alarm. "What is it? What aren't you telling me?" As I watch her, there's a heaviness in her eyes that I can't ignore, a weight that seems to make her shoulders tighten.

"Don't… don't be angry with me," she says, pulling the covers off and throwing the shirt of mine that she was wearing before back on.

"I won't be." I follow her lead, never taking my eyes off of her and pull my boxers on. "What's going on?"

Mila stops talking and starts searching the room frantically. She's running her hands over the walls, checking the corners, under the bed, running her fingers along the edges before getting on her belly and checking underneath the bed as well.

She's checking for bugs. For someone listening in.

What the fuck? Why does she even think that someone is listening to us at a *safehouse*?

I know the drill though, I've been bugged and bugged enough people to know to shut the fuck up until the person searching has deemed it safe to speak freely.

After a few more moments of searching, she stands up quickly and looks at me nervously.

"Aleksander, or I think it was Aleksander, contacted me while we were still in Boston. You… you had gone to a meeting with the guys and he "reached out"." She speaks quickly and steps closer to me with her hands out in front. Like she's worried I'm going to explode.

And she should be worried. I'm livid. As I feel the anger rising within me, it's like a wildfire igniting in my chest, consuming every rational thought in its path. My jaw clenches as I try desperately to think before I speak.

The world around me blurs as adrenaline courses through

my veins, heightening my senses to a razor's edge. My fists ball up, nails digging into the flesh of my palms, a primal need for me to lash out.

"What?" I snap. "Are you fucking kidding me? That was days ago! You weren't going to say anything? Not a goddamn thing?" I walk to where my pants and shirt were discarded, and hastily throw them back on. I'm angry for so many fucking reasons: she put herself in danger, she kept herself in danger, she let me bring her here when she was being tailed and I didn't know it, but the main reason, the one that hurts, is that she didn't tell me because she doesn't trust me or my family. "Why don't you trust me?"

"I do! Cillian, I do." She rushes to me as I step back, the hurt and anger still coursing through my body. "He told me he'd kill you if I said anything! Please, believe me."

"What else did he say? How do you know it's him?" I ask, putting aside my feelings for a moment to break down what happened. Someone has access to my girl, and has been making her feel unsafe. I need to fix this. Immediately.

"We were at headquarters and you had the meeting with the guys, and I was hanging out in your apartment when the lights went out. The room went black and then the TV screen turned on, but instead of a show, just static started to play." Mila swallows, bites her lip nervously and looks at me. "Someone typed over the static that they knew where I was, that you couldn't keep me safe and that if I told you about it that you'd die."

"This was at headquarters?" I snap.

"Yes." She looks down at her fingers, twisting them together nervously.

"I need to call Kieron and tell him. Someone was able to

infiltrate the internet and computer systems. We need to go on the offense and take the fight to them. I'm not going to let you be in danger." Walking out of the room, I grab my phone and start to dial Kieron's number, but my phone is kicked out of my hand.

"What was that?"

"I can't let you do that," she says, standing tall with her hands balled into fists.

"Why?"

"Aleksander doesn't want anyone but me, the Bratva just wants their weapon back, and from what you've told me, it sounds like my Uncle knows exactly where I am. This ruse of a partnership, pretending that they don't know where I am, that Aleksander isn't behind everything… it's all to get closer to you guys before they strike."

"Haven't we already talked about this? I won't let anything happen to either of us."

"You're right, because I'm not going to take the chance." She shifts her weight back into her fighting stance. Something I've seen before.

Fuck.

Fuck. Fuck, Fuck.

"Mila, wait a minute. We've been through this before, we've…. I thought we decided that this wasn't how we would handle things. That we were in this together and would make choices together." I don't want to fight her, but I can't let her go back to them.

"This is the only way. Don't you see? It's not like before when we didn't have information. We know now. Aleksander is hunting me and knows exactly where I am. He's proven that he can get into the Clan headquarters, he can find me anywhere. He can easily find where we are. We think we're a step ahead of him, but really we're already three behind." Tears line her eyes, the bright blue of them looking even more azure.

"So what's your plan here, doll? Knock me out and then run back to the Bratva, hoping they'll take you back? Shift back into the shadows like The Ghost? You know as well as I do that they'll kill you on sight. If you're lucky." I can't let that happen. I won't.

"It's better than the alternative."

"It's not."

"I won't let you die!" Mila screams at me, tears falling from her lashes and dripping down her face. She raises her fist, throwing her body weight into a punch that I know would knock me flat out if I let it hit me. I grab her wrist and twist her so that her back hits my chest with a thud.

"You promised me last time that we'd work through all this shit together," I snarl in her ear. "That you would stop making decisions to fight against them on your own."

"That was before. You saw with your own eyes that Sergei is planning something."

"So giving yourself up is the answer?" I shake my head roughly. "It's not and you know it. Take a breath and let's think this through."

"Until Aleksander has his pound of flesh, my flesh, he'll never stop. And he's got Uncle working with him? No chance. What happened with Auggie will just happen again and again. I can't... I can't let that happen. To you. To your family. To anyone. I'm not worth it!" She cries each word.

Her sobs are like echoes in a cavern, haunting and filled with a raw, visceral agony that tears at my heart. I hold her even tighter as the fight leaves her body and she collapses, letting me hold her weight.

"Think about it, Cillian. Your life with me will be looking over your shoulder, always running. I know too much, I know how they work and who they are going to hit. Being *the Prizrak*, I know *everything*. Things they want to kill me for and things they'll do anything to keep silent. We don't know what they're going to do, but I know Sergei's playing a fool and will come down on Kellan twice as hard." Mila turns in my arms, pulling at the collar of my shirt. Her eyes, once bright and full of life, are now dull and clouded with desperation.

"Then we tell Kellan. We get everyone included on this. You come completely clean. Kellan already said he wants to meet with you, let's set that up and then… then everything will be okay."

Mila's head rests against my chest, the sobs making her body shake but I just hold her tighter.

"Mila, look at me."

Her sad eyes meet mine.

I take a deep breath because I want my words to resonate and for her to believe every single word I say. Cupping her soft cheek, I run my thumb over her cheekbone softly. "You are absolutely worth it. You're worth everything. You're so amazing and so fucking strong. I would go to the ends of the earth for you. I'd take on everyone; The Bratva, The Italians, The Polish… I'd take on every single mob for you. I'd take them all on, and I'd fucking win, because you make me stronger. We make each other stronger. You're worth more than you know and it kills me to think that you don't see it. But I'll work every single day for the rest of our lives to prove to you just how fucking worthy you are. I'll work to prove that *I'm* worthy of you." I lean down and kiss her lips; it's sweet and kind, full of understanding and hope. I take it as a good sign that she doesn't push me away. Or sucker-punch me and run off.

I hold her and stay silent, letting her work through my words, hopefully letting them sink in. I don't need her to say anything, I just don't want her to leave.

"I love you," she whispers.

My eyes widen in shock. Happiness fills my body. And I choke.

I fucking choke. On air. On nothing!

What a joke.

"Are you okay?" I hear her ask through my embarrassing coughing fit. I nod and cough a few more times, trying desperately to get myself under control.

"Fuck, I'm sorry. It's too soon, I'm sorry," she mumbles, holding my hands as I hit my chest to clear the last of the coughs.

Mila turns to go into the small kitchen area, but I grab her hand and pull her close.

"I love you, too." I lift her effortlessly off the ground, fitting her body perfectly against mine. I can feel her heart beating rapidly against my chest, the rhythm matching my own as I draw her nearer, closing the distance between us until our lips are mere inches apart. "I love you and want us to be together. You're mine, I'm yours. Your problems are my problems, and my problems are yours. I'll burn the world for you as long as you promise to do the same for me. You said I was yours, babydoll, and that you were mine. That means that we go through everything together. No more of this 'turning yourself over' bullshit, do you understand?"

She nods and I can tell that we've turned a new page. Hell, we've started a new chapter.

"Besides, even if you did, I'd follow you," I say softly, my voice low as I bring our lips closer together until finally, they meet in a kiss that sets my soul ablaze.

It's soft, yet passionate, a dance of longing and desire that leaves us breathless. Nothing else exists but her and I. Her arms wrap around my neck, pulling me closer as our kiss deepens. I savor the taste of her lips, the feel of her body pressed against mine, committing every detail to memory as if I never want this moment to end.

But even as the world spins around us, I know that eventually we'll have to come up for air. I have to call Kellan, I have to call Kieron. We need to scrub this safehouse from any electronic file. Bryan should be able to do that, no problem.

Reluctantly, I lower her back to the ground, but the connection between us remains unbroken. And as we look into each other's eyes, I know that this is just the beginning of our journey together.

That we're in this, no matter what.

And for the first time in my life, I'm so fucking excited.

"You know that it's us against them now," I say softly. "It has been since I got you."

"I know that."

A shiver runs through my spine.

"You're lumping yourself in with us, are you?" As excitement bubbles up inside me, a true smile spreads across my face like wildfire. It starts small, a flicker of anticipation at what she'll say, in the corners of my mouth, but then it grows, spreading wider and wider until it feels like my entire face is lit up with joy.

"I'm one of you now. If you'll have me." She smiles softly, shyness clear in her blue eyes, but after everything, she should know that I want everything she will give me.

"This might be easier than I thought," I mumble, and drop down to one knee. "Mila, will you marry me?"

The Marriage

Mila

"What?"

I'm sure I've heard him wrong.

"Marry me."

I look down at Cillian, and my heart flutters in my chest. This can't be real. I never thought it would happen for me. I never thought I'd get the choice to get married to who I want, not for total political gain to some seventy-year-old asshole.

I smile, and tears line my eyes once again but for a better reason this time. There he kneels; this perfect man, who for some reason chose me, with his eyes locked on mine, filled with a vulnerability that takes my breath away. I know that he's probably doing this for the protection that being his wife will bring me, but there's an overarching feeling that this is how we should have happened anyway. I can feel it in the air, in the way his gaze pierces through me, laying bare the depths of his love.

The tears prick at the corners of my eyes threatening to

fall, but I blink them away, unwilling to let them cloud this moment of pure, unadulterated joy.

"Yes," I say simply, smiling brightly.

Cillian jumps up and our mouths meet in a kiss, a fiery display of passion that would make anyone watching us blush. Luckily, we're completely alone. And I intend on taking advantage of it.

"Are you sure?" he asks, each word interrupted by a kiss.

"More than anything. When can I become your wife?" I ask. Holding him close with my arms around his shoulders, I tuck my head into his neck. I can't stop smiling. How can life go from such a high, to such shit, then back to being perfect?

"Tomorrow? I need to get the clearance from Kellan, but I'm very sure he'll be okay with it. Hell, Kieron will give me the name of the person that married him and Talia in a day. Unless you want something specific? Do you want a church wedding or something like that?" He goes from excited to nervous, as if he'd misspoken and I'd change my mind.

"I'd marry you anywhere. In the middle of a fight, or now, during a calm part of our lives. It doesn't matter to me when or where we get married. What matters to me is why. I just want to make sure that you're choosing to marry me for the right reasons, not because you're being forced to. You've mentioned that your cousin had to marry his wife for protection, and while I think it's admirable, I'll take my chances without it." I'm not giving him an ultimatum, or accusing him of anything, but just trying to gently show him that I understand that there may have been some demands put on him.

"Why would you think that?"

"Because I'm an operative, a spy trained to know how to read between the lines better than most. I'm so good at it because my life depended on it. When you said, 'I'm very sure Kellan will be okay with it', then mentioned Kieron, I put it together from the story you told me about Talia and Kieron before. You're not the heir, but you are Kellan's nephew who he genuinely cares about, so if you've had everyone bust their asses to help me, I'm sure Kellan made you do everything within your power to help me too. That includes marriage. Plus, what is the ultimate way to show that I'm not going to be running back to the Bratva?"

Cillian shakes his head with a smile of disbelief and sighs.

"Do you have to be so observant about everything?" he mumbles. "Yes, okay. Kellan did want me to lock you down and make you my wife. He wants to have you prove yourself and to him that means marriage. Divorce happens, sure, but not in the Clan. If one of us Tavish men marry, it's for life and well into eternity. If you agreed to marry me, then you would be agreeing to being a Tavish, to putting the Clan above everything, even your own flesh and blood. Do you understand? Once we get married, you'll be expected to tell Kellan everything you know about The Bratva, about Sergei, about their plans, and anything else he asks. So yes, I want to be married to you, I want you, and I want you to want me, but I need you to think about this. Think about betraying your family because there's a difference between wanting to be free from them, and turning your back on them in totality." Cillian sighs. There's a heaviness in his shoulders that wasn't there before, a pressure he now feels.

And as much as I know that my answer and decision won't change, he has a point. Going against the Bratva, it's a huge undertaking. But deep within, there's a clarity I can't deny. My heart beats with a fierce determination, pulsing with the certainty that I will, I want to, I *need* to choose love over the ties that bind me to my family. They've done nothing for me, whereas Cillian and his family...

They've chosen me. They've chosen to protect me. To treat me as an equal. And that means everything to me. Especially when no one else in my life ever has.

Though it's a daunting prospect, the thought of a life without Cillian is dark, too dark. And so, with unwavering resolve, I take a decisive step forward, and leave behind Mila Smirnova. I'm ready to embrace a future where my life, my feelings and my love reigns supreme. I know that in choosing Cillian and the Clan, I'm choosing the path my soul was meant to follow.

"I don't want to wait. I want to marry you tomorrow. Set it up."

***

Cillian

"Good work, Cillian. I expect that when I call and ask for information, your new bride will be forthcoming," Kellan says, calm and collected through my phone speaker. I love my uncle, he's a great guy and has been kind to me through the years, but he's no-fucking-nonsense.

After Mila demanded we get married tomorrow, she walked off to make us a late-night dinner, and I got to work setting everything up. The first call was to Kellan and I explained what Mila had decided. I would normally feel guilty that she had to marry me much sooner than planned—because let's be honest, I knew from the moment that she fought me in my apartment to try and protect me that I wanted her to be my wife—but I told her everything. I haven't hidden anything from her and was as honest as possible. She knows that I love her, that I'll protect her until my last breath. She knows what my Skipper expects.

And she still chooses to marry me.

"Yes, Kellan. Understood." I roll my eyes. "I trust you'll take all the information and start preparing for the war against Sergei and Aleksander. There's absolutely no doubt in my mind that Aleksander is behind everything and they're not going to stop until Mila's dead. We can't let that happen."

"I hear you, son. You and your cousin, both head over heels for your women." He chuckles. "I can't say I'm upset about it. You're good men. Don't worry about Mila. We take care of our own, and the moment that she's Mila Tavish, she'll be completely protected. Even more so than she is now."

To hear that praise from my uncle, that I'm a good man, fills me with a sense of validation unlike anything I've ever felt before. It's not just the pride in his voice that makes me pause, but the understanding that I've earned some of his respect and he takes what I say at my word. I say Mila is with us, and he extends his hand.

I mean, I'm not happy that he gave me an ultimatum about proposing, but I can understand why he did.

"Thank you, Uncle." I clear my throat, suddenly uncomfortable with the silence following his praise. "I'll call Kieron now and get the ceremony set up. Do you need me to do anything going forward with the Bratva?"

"No, your main objective is protection now. Once we drop the pretenses of the merger, the Russians will be gunning for her even harder. I don't need to tell you to make sure there are no gaps in your protection detail. From now on Kieron will be your point of contact unless absolutely needed."

"Yes, sir." I nod and clench my teeth. This was it; the safehouse would be subtly scrubbed from the system, hopefully before Aleksander notices, and Mila and I will be on our own.

"Keep her safe, Cillian. We will handle the rest," Kellan says, and before I can reply he hangs up.

I'll keep her safe. With every fiber of my being, every part of my body, every bit of strength of my name, I'll keep her safe.

* * *

The moment I get off the phone with Kellan, I immediately go into the warzone mentality. I know we're at a safehouse and no one but the specific people at headquarters know we're here, but there's a shit-ton of other things I can do to keep it that way and to keep us anonymous while we're here.

I just need to find that fucking notepad I saw the other day. I need to list everything out so I don't forget.

My phone starts to vibrate in my pocket and I see Kieron's name flash on the screen. Perfect, just who I need to speak to.

"Kieron, I need the name and number of the guy who got you your wedding license on the down-low, and quick. Mila and I are getting married, as soon as I can get the license." I tuck the phone in between my ear and shoulder as I pull a notepad and pen out from one of the drawers in the sparse living room.

"Hello to you too, little cousin. And congratulations! We're happy for you." Kieron chuckles. "I'll forward you the info to your phone."

"Speaking of that, we need to set up a secure connection and talk through that only from now on, if neither of us can meet in person. Actually, no, don't come here. That will also bring too much attention." I start writing down all that I need to do, everything I can think of to keep our safehouse safe and secure. We have a secured line through our cell phones, we've always made sure to keep this direct line between us as ironclad as possible, but that's just for auditory. If we send emails or texts, there's a small chance someone can get it, but it's very small. I'm not willing to take any chances though.

'Create a secure network connection' is the first thing on the list. Frankly, we should've done that the day we had the meeting with the Russians. I just hadn't known yet about Aleksander reaching out to her.

"Yes, okay," Kieron says, and I can hear him stifle a laugh.

"Why are you laughing at me?"

"I'm not!"

"Fucker, I've known you your whole life. I know when you're laughing."

"It's just funny how worried you are about her. How much you're second-guessing yourself as if you haven't been on protection detail in one way or another for a decade."

What the hell?

"Kieron!" I start to snap, but his boisterous laughter cuts me off.

"Cillian! You know what to do. You don't need a list or to overthink it. Follow your training and what you believe is best, learn from Trent's and my mistakes." I can hear a thud and then Kieron groans and tells off someone else, before adding, "and enjoy this alone time with your new wife."

I drop the pad and run a hand over my face. There's so much to do and I'm starting to get worried that I'll forget something and it will be the reason why they find her.

"If they find her, and I can't protect her…" I say softly.

"They won't. And if they do, you'll be ready. I have complete faith in you, brother." Kieron shuts down any more talk of this, and if I take a look at myself, I know I've been overthinking this whole situation. But honestly, every single thing that could go wrong has been playing in my head. Every scenario, every possible outcome, has played out in my mind a hundred times over, leaving me tangled in a web of nerves.

"First and foremost, you two need to get married."

I feel my phone vibrate on my shoulder.

"I just sent the information of the guy on our payroll in your area through the dark web link. It will pop up as a message, but it's going to be pinging around to different phones and servers as if it went to others as well. Once you get the information, delete it off your phone and delete the message chain. Bryan will scrub that data, too. Do not go anywhere else. They'll have to use your real names to make it legal, but he's going to go to a different state to file the paperwork, hopefully sending anyone sniffing around on a wild goose chase. Get the house locked down, use the petty cash that was sent with you to get it set up the way that works for you, and I'll have a bank account with your undercover name set up."

"Got it." I nod, pacing back and forth in the small front room.

"Bryan has had some progress on the dark web. He's building a good rapport with the guy we think is Aleksander. Tomorrow I'll suggest that he go ahead and set up the meeting."

"But he knows us, so he's going to know it's Trent right away."

"Would you calm down? I know how to send a man undercover. Trent infiltrated the Italian mob for a long time and no one suspected him. This will be for an hour, maybe two, tops." Kieron's voice gets low and he stops for a moment. "He will be fine, we're taking all precautions this time. For his sake and ours."

"Okay, okay. When the meeting happens, let me know."

"Of course."

"Thank you,"

"Not a problem. Keep your heads down, trust no one, and enjoy the honeymoon." He chuckles and hangs up the phone.

This is it then. We're cut off. By ourselves. Alone. And we don't know for how long. If it's a day, a month, a year. My job, and my pleasure, is to keep Mila safe. Although the thought of being cut off from the familiar voices of the guys weighs on me, there is a flicker of relief. It's just us now. And if we do our jobs right, it will just be us until we take down her family.

With a determined stride, I move to join her in the kitchen, mindful of the responsibility that rests on my shoulders. Standing behind her and wrapping my arms around her, I rest my chin on her shoulder. She reaches up and cups my head, holding me as I settle with the new identity of responsibility. As we embrace, I silently vow to shield her from harm, cherishing the quiet moments we share as a beacon of light in the shadows.

The Wedding

Mila

All through the night, Cillian was setting things up. His phone was in his hand non-stop as he paced through the whole house.

Around four in the morning he finally called it quits and laid down, his eyes barely open with his clothes still on. He just fell onto the bed and wrapped his arms around me, his face in my hair as he spooned me.

When I open my eyes, I turn over and am greeted by the sight of him, my husband-to-be, peacefully asleep beside me.

There's a gentle calmness in the air, a sense of peace that envelopes us both in this quiet moment. I watch him sleep for just a moment longer, as a tender smile tugs at my lips. My heart swells with love for this man who was placed in my life serendipitously.

Every detail of his face, softened and peaceful, fills me with happiness. The steady rise and fall of his chest, the faint lines etched around his eyes from laughter and from stress, all spoke of the life we both had lived apart, and hope for the future we were so desperately building together.

I realize how much gratitude I have for him being unwaveringly by my side. It could've been anyone who found me and the universe sent Cillian. His presence is a constant source of strength and reassurance, grounding me amidst this fucked-up, crazy life we live.

As I reach out to gently brush a stray lock of hair from his forehead, I silently marvel at the depth of emotion he's stirred within me. Emotion I haven't ever felt before, and that I thought would never happen for me. In his arms, I've found solace, companionship, and unwavering support—a love that filled every corner of my being with joy.

With a happy sigh, I nestle in closer to him—coffee and starting the day could wait for a few more minutes—savoring the simple, yet immense happiness of waking up beside the man I love, knowing that regardless of whatever is thrown our way, we can and will handle it together.

Cillian sighs deeply, a small smile curving his lips, and I can't help but kiss his cheek softly. I don't want to wake him yet.

I slide out of the small bed, and make my way to the kitchen to start breakfast. We're getting married today. That means we'll have to head out of the safehouse, which means Cillian's going to want us to change our appearance.

I can't let that trip me up today. It doesn't matter what I look like, it matters that I'm genuinely *me*. I'm Mila under whatever disguise I can make up here. Cillian has proven to me that it's not my looks, it's who I am that he wants and loves. So, I just need to keep that in mind and not let my own past issues and fears stand in the way.

I head to the restroom, and after doing my business, I stand before the mirror. My hair is pulled into a side braid that's gotten messy with sleep. Dark tendrils fall around my face. My eyes are puffy with sleep and the bright blue is a welcome sight. The color of my eyes is very telling, a distinct feature. It's always been the first thing I change when I put on a disguise. I'll need color-changing contacts, and I'll have to do something different with my hair. Normally, I'd choose a wig. But I think it's time for a change. A scary one for me, but a change nonetheless.

Undoing the braid, I turn my thoughts to a more positive event. Our wedding. Yes, it's going to be two signatures, not even five minutes, but that doesn't matter to me.

The anticipation bubbles in me, and I can't contain the flutter of excitement dancing in my chest. Today is special, a day filled with promises and possibilities, and the smile on my face reflects that.

Gazing into the mirror, I take in every detail. My reflection smiles back at me now, a twinkle of excitement illuminating my gaze. I trace the curve of my cheekbones, the slope of my nose, and the sparkle in my eyes, each feature becoming a canvas for the happiness and excitement radiating from me.

With each passing moment, the anticipation grows, a rush of exhilaration coursing through my veins. Today is a day of new beginnings, of stepping into the unknown with confidence and grace. And as I stand here, bathed in the soft glow of morning light, I can't help but feel a surge of empowerment wash over me. This is my life, my choice, my future. I'm done with Mila Smirnova, and I can't wait to meet Mila Tavish.

In that fleeting moment, I embrace the thrill of who I was

and who I am becoming. I take one final glance in the mirror. With a determined nod, I reach for some scissors in the small drawer under the sink.

It's just hair. It'll grow back. It's a moment in time, but marrying Cillian, that's forever. That's my future. It's time for me to embrace it.

I pull a chunk of hair from the side of my face and hold the scissors at my chin. And I cut.

And cut. And cut.

Black locks fall around me, landing in a pile on the floor. My waist-length hair becomes chin-length in mere moments. I spend some time inspecting the ends, making sure that the cut is as straight as can be.

I feel lighter. Like tons of weight has been lifted from my shoulders. I twist my head from side to side, and the ends flare out a bit. It's flattering, at least.

"Woah," a deep, sleep-filled voice says from the doorway.

"What do you think?" I ask with a smile, pulling at the ends for any loose pieces.

"Well…" Cillian walks in, shirtless , and leans against the doorframe with his arms crossed and his hands under his rounded biceps. Like a book-lover's dream. I barely contain the drool that forms in my mouth. "I think it suits you. It's beautiful and striking."

My mouth turns up in a small smile, and I roll my eyes teasingly.

"No really." Cillian pushes off the doorframe, wraps his arms around my waist and makes eye contact with me in the mirror as we both look at each other. "It looks amazing. You look amazing."

"Thank you," I say softly, covering his hands with mine and

curving into his body.

He turns his face into the side of my head and whispers with a big smile, "We're getting married today."

"We are. When?"

"Getting anxious?"

"I'm just ready for our future to start."

Watching him in the mirror, I see his eyes soften and his smile brighten even more.

"Me too." He hugs me tighter before stepping back and twisting me around to face him. "We have to leave to meet the guy Kieron sent in forty-five minutes. We have a few things we need to do before then."

I wrap my arms around his shoulders and jump into his arms. "Is fucking me against the sink one of them?" I lean over and bite his neck lightly before licking and blowing the spot.

Cillian shivers, his fingertips dig into my hips.

I love how I can make him react with just a few movements. A carefully placed kiss, a slide of my hand, a whisper in his ear. I barely touch him and I can elicit a visceral reaction.

"It can be. If that's what you want, doll," he says in a smoky, husky tone.

I pull my shoulders back, sitting straighter in his hold and bite my lower lip. "Take me against the edge of the sink, Killer. Please."

His breath catches at my use of his nickname and he moves forward, lowering me until my ass hits the cold porcelain.

I reach up and push his short hair back, it's grown out just a bit from the tight buzz-cut that he had when we first met, and it looks really, really good on him. I jerk his head back so he's making eye contact with me.

Without saying a word, Cillian drops to his knees and looks to me for permission. His gaze is like a magnet, pulling me in with its need and intensity. I find myself drawn to the way his eyes sparkle with mischief, a playful glint that promises trouble and unbelievable pleasure.

Nodding, I shimmy my way out of my underwear and let them drop to the floor next to him. I see him shift with excitement. Raising my leg, I move it over his head so I'm spread open in front of him like a feast.

Cillian licks his lips, his gaze locked on my exposed pussy mere inches from his face.

"Do you like this?" I taunt, clenching my muscles and letting them relax, pulsing my cunt in front of him.

"Yes," he says breathlessly, mesmerized.

I feel his breath on me, and I shiver with need. "Taste me."

He dives in eagerly, pulling me closer to him by my ass, holding onto my globes with his huge hands. Each cheek fills his hand as he grabs me like a man possessed. My head drops back and hits the mirror as I breathe deeply to control my responses.

Fuck, he's good at this.

So, so good at it.

"Baby, oh fuck," I moan, setting my feet on his broad back, and grip the sink with my fingers.

Cillian looks up at me and I can tell from his eyes he's smiling. His tongue snakes inside my heat and he licks me from bottom to top, over and over, while he brings his hand up to my clit, thumbing it quickly. He's going to make me come within minutes.

"Someone's not playing around today." I groan, eyes glued to where he is. It's so fucking hot to watch him work.

Cillian pulls back and his face is wet. From nose to chin, he's covered in me. He opens his mouth to say something, but fuck me, the sight is so erotic, I snap. Bending over, I hold his face with both of my hands and kiss him deeply, licking into his mouth to taste as much of us together as I can.

"Please," I groan, pulling my—his—shirt over my head, and turning around. "Like this. Fuck me from behind where I can watch you in the mirror."

"You're filthy." He doesn't pull his pants off all the way, just enough to get his cock out, and he pushes into my greedy, wet hole in one thrust.

Goddamn it.

I moan loudly. The feeling of him fucking me from behind is so much more intense. He hits my g-spot so easily like this. I grip the sink edge and hold on, crying out in ecstasy when he pulls out and I feel his cockhead push back in harder, hitting my g-spot again.

"Oh god, right there. Keep going! Cillian, keep going!" I yell, my words echoing in the sink. I'm not going to be able to keep up with him, I'm completely taken over by the sensations and explosive feelings that are happening. I can feel myself letting go, and Cillian effortlessly picking me up.

Give and take.

I don't know when my head dropped down into the sink, but I pull it up and look at Cillian in the mirror. As I catch his gaze, a shiver runs down my spine. His torso, so lined with tattoos and muscle, flexes with each movement. His arms are tight and bulging as he holds my hips while he thrusts upward into me. He's so fucking hot, I get even more turned on just from looking at him. But what really gets me dripping even more is the look on his face. He has a possessed look on his face as he pounds into me. Sweat beads forming on his forehead, his eyes wild with lust, but his smile.

His smile is feral.

The way his lips curve into a filthy grin sends my heart racing, awakening a hunger for him. For his cum and his pleasure.

His smile, equal parts captivating and primal, sends a rush of heat through me, bringing me that much closer to my peak. There's an intensity in his eyes, a raw energy that's terrifying and electric. I'm drawn to him like a moth to a flame, unable to tear my eyes away from the magnetic pull of the image in the mirror, knowing that we are driving each other mad.

I reach down to the space between us, spreading my fingers to lightly caress his cock with each thrust inside me. The way I can hold him, as well as grind down on my own palm, is exquisite.

"That's right, babydoll. Ride your hand. I want to feel you come around me. I want to feel you soak me." Cillian groans, his thrusts quickening and I feel one of his hands on my shoulder, holding me in place against him.

"Cillian, I—"

I'm cut off when he uses his hips to pin mine to the sink and his other hand goes to my back, sliding over my ass before he reaches down and wets his fingers. I'm leaking like a faucet, pretty sure that my wetness is leaking down my legs. Leaving a wet trail around my leg and hip, he brings his fingers to my ass. "Oh, yes. Yes, yes, yes, please," I mumble, pushing back onto his dick to bring his fingers closer to my ass.

"Are you sure?" he asks.

"Oh fuck yes, please. Please."

"Good." He spits on my asshole before slipping his thumb

inside me.

"Cillian!" I cry out, throwing my head back, my body shaking all over.

"That's right, scream my name."

He doesn't let up his thrusting, in fact, he speeds up and I feel his thumb disappear into my asshole completely. It's so naughty and taboo, just knowing that he's filling two holes at once, makes me come. His cock hits my g-spot with such force as he grinds into me, that I feel my wetness push around his cock as I come. My cum covers his cock, dripping down his thighs and mine. I'm shivering and shaking with the force of my orgasm, and Cillian keeps fucking into me. My wetness sticks to both of us, making the space between us slick. The sound of his wet thighs slapping the backs of mine, along with my cries and his moans, fill the room.

"Yes! Mila, oh fuck, fuck, fuck. Yes!" Cillian cries out.

I feel the warmth of his cum fill me.

Cillian folds his torso over mine, my sweaty back sliding against his sweaty front, as he shallowly thrusts while his orgasm slows. Just our breathing fills the small room now as we try to catch our breath.

"That was…"

"Explosive," he says, looking at me in the mirror, sweat dripping down one side of his face.

"Amazing." I smile at him. He smiles back fondly before pulling out of me, his softening cock leaving my body and with it, gobs of his cum that mixed with mine follow. The white liquid slips down my legs slowly and we both watch, transfixed. Without saying a word, Cillian puts his finger on my middle thigh, and slowly pushes everything back in.

"Keep it there, keep me stuffed inside you," he whispers, his voice low and dangerous.

"Yes," I whisper back, the pressure of his finger in my abused pussy making me clench down.

Now that we're facing each other again, I lunge forward and kiss his lips, glad to have access to them again.

"Did you like that?" I whisper against him.

"I really, *really* liked it." He smirks, holding me close.

Noticing he's still wearing his now-ruined sweats, I push them down to his feet. "Come on, let's shower and get ready to get married."

"Showering together? You know that's never not ended with us having sex, right?" he says, but leans over and starts the shower anyway.

"Are you complaining?" I tease, stepping under the hot spray. It's a small shower, small and outdated, so the both of us barely fit in it together. Showering together does always lead to us touching and sensually cleaning one another, and then comes the kissing, and once we start kissing there's no stopping.

"Not even a little bit." He jumps in with me. "Let's get dirty again before we get clean."

I know then that we are going to be late meeting Kieron's contact to sign the papers.

* * *

"We're going to be late!" I grab my shoes, and slug the last bits of coffee in my cup.

"Relax, doll. It'll be okay." Cillian smirks, pulling his leather jacket over one of his plain black t-shirts. He looks so fucking good. Mouthwatering, like he always does in his black-on-black-on-black ensemble.

Calm down, Mila. You guys literally just got done fucking like bunnies. You're sore, get a grip.

But he looks so good.

I bend over and start to tie my converse. "It won't! We're getting our marriage license. I'm excited." I look up and smile at him. It's so weird to not have to flip my hair over my shoulder or tie it up for my hair to not get in my eyes.

"Me too." He smiles at me, and holds his hand out for me to take. "So let's go. It should only be a few minutes' drive." He pulls me closer, both hands resting on the top part of my hips. "Once we're there, we're going to sign the papers, become husband and wife, and then I'm going to take you to lunch to celebrate. Somewhere big and fancy."

"Oooh, where are you going to take me?" I know he's just teasing, it's not safe for us to be out and about longer than necessary, but it feels nice to pretend.

"I was thinking somewhere super nice. Somewhere we could sit down and have wine." He smirks, and wraps his arm around my shoulders, and swings his keys on his index finger, guiding us out the door.

"Oh, fancy-fancy, then." I smirk.

"Definitely fancy-fancy. Like driving through McDonald's and then, I run inside a liquor store and pick up a bottle of wine. What do you think?"

We step outside as I laugh, and Cillian locks the front door as I enjoy the sun on my face.

"McDonald's sounds so good."

"Then McDonald's you shall have, my Queen." Cillian

smiles. As we saunter toward the car, there's the excitement and lightness that's enveloping us, infectious and thrilling. His grin widens mischievously as he gestures grandly, like a chauffeur for royalty. With a dramatic flourish I feign a regal poise when he opens the door.

"Your chariot awaits, milady," he quips, his tone dripping with playful theatrics. I can't suppress a giggle as I fasten my seatbelt, playfully rolling my eyes at him. His laughter echoes mine as he settles into the driver's seat.

With a wink and a nudge, Cillian starts the car and threads his fingers through mine.

He takes a deep breath, smiling softly as he looks at me. The sun reflecting off the hood of the car reflects on his face, highlighting his strong jaw, his dark eyes that look like honey in the sun, and the rosy pinkness of his lips still bruised from earlier.

"Are you ready?" he asks.

"So ready." I squeeze his hand, bringing the back of his hand to my lips and kissing it softly. "Come on, Mr. Tavish."

———––-

"Brad! Hey man, how is it going?" A bald man with a giant neck tattoo, thick, black- rimmed glasses, a baggy sweatshirt, and a gold tooth that shines in the light when he smiles, stands up as we walk into the busy coffeeshop. He looks like a gangster, but as I look around I realize that the thick glasses and the sweatshirt make him somewhat invisible in the sea of hipsters that frequent this place.

"Mark, good to see you." Cillian shakes his hand and gestures to me at the same time that he pulls me tightly to his side. "This is my girl, Nina." He smiles at me.

With the colored contacts he'd slipped in before we walked inside, and the black baseball hat he added, Cillian Tavish wasn't recognizable if someone was indeed following us. He'd handed me a gray beanie and now I see that it helps me blend in here, as do the black aviators hanging from my shirt.

"Nice to meet you." I wave at the guy and sit down in the closest chair. Cillian sits down next to me, and drapes his arm over the back of my chair. His fingertips graze my shoulder and it hits me. He is keeping a hand on me at all times.

As an independent woman, I want to scoff and push his arm off. And as his girl, I love the display of possessiveness.

"So, I hear that congratulations are in order. I just need you both to sign here." Mark, if that's really his name, slides a stack of papers over to us with a random one in the middle tabbed for us to sign without other people being able to see what it was we were signing.

Cillian pulls the stack to him, flipping until he gets to the tabbed page and looks it over quickly before signing 'Cillian Tavish' in a flourish.

"Your turn, babydoll." He smirks, giving me the pen. His hand rests on my thigh, but then he turns to Mark to chat about the weather, giving me a moment of privacy to do this myself.

I click the pen and sign my name, quickly and precisely.
That's it.
We're married.
We don't need vows or nice words, we've already vowed ourselves to each other. Promised our futures. The commitment and love Cillian's shown me daily is more than enough.

Quickly, I scan the document, my eyes darting over every line, every word, ensuring that every detail is perfect, just as we'd planned. A small, shy smile crawls its way onto my face as I trace our names intertwined on the paper, a tangible symbol of the love we shared and the future we are embracing together.

Mark reaches over and flips the paper underneath it up, and I scan that document too. They brought a form for me to legally change my name. Smart. I sign that one quickly too.

"I know, I hope it stays this nice. The heat isn't terrible, but the sun feels amazing," Mark says, never breaking from their conversation as he pulls the stack from me and slides it into the messenger bag next to him. "Next time you guys visit, we should do dinner. I'm so sorry I have to run. But next time, right?" Mark stands up and shakes Cillian's hand, then waves at me.

"No problem, man. It was good to see you." Cillian stands also, and I follow their lead.

"No, stay and have a coffee. Here, on me." Mark pulls out a twenty and hands it to Cillian. It's impossibly straight and stiff-looking to me, but to someone that wasn't actually paying attention, it wouldn't seem weird at all.

"Thanks, that's very kind of you," I say, and Cillian stuffs the bill in his jacket pocket.

"Congratulations again!" Mark says with a golden smile that's super friendly.

Weird.

"What would you like? I can't do fancy-fancy, but I hear this place has a good iced latte." Cillian says, smiling brightly at me.

I smile right back, and wrap my arms around his waist. "An iced latte sounds perfect."

He tucks a lock of my hair back into my beanie, trailing his finger down my cheek, then tipping my face up to his.

"I love you," he whispers against my lips, and kisses me. It's our first kiss as husband and wife and it feels significant, like the entire universe narrows down to just the two of us. It's an intimate moment, surrounded with love and promise. Our kiss speaks volumes, expressing a lifetime of devotion and commitment. With each heated press of our lips, we seal our unspoken vows, affirming our undying love for one another. The world around us seems to fade away, leaving only the warmth of our embrace and the promise of a future filled with endless love and happiness.

The Routine

Cillian

3 months later...

In the months since our non-wedding wedding, we've created a nice little routine here in Maine. We stay inside mostly, but after a few weeks my beard has grown nicely. It changes my look completely, covering a lot of recognizable tattoos on my neck and any that peek out from the top of my t-shirt. My hair is longer, too, falling over my forehead and into my eyes. Luckily, if I put on a long-sleeve shirt to cover all my tattoos, stay away from my black jeans, leather jacket and boots, instead wearing blue jeans and converse, I look like any of the other hipsters here. I can move around our small town without drawing any attention.

I logged into the built-in security system and boosted the security as much as I could. And then I asked Bryan to enforce it. I was able to adjust the miniscule front room so that our security screens are in the corner, always up and visible. All the security systems and routines that I had been trained on, and some that I'd layered on, were in place.

I'm thankful that Mila doesn't seem to be stir-crazy, so keeping her inside hasn't been a fight. It's like a dance we've perfected. She'll ask for something every week or so when I go to get groceries with the card Mark slipped me under the twenty he gave me at the café, and I'll get it. Sometimes it's a stack of books, or a few DVDs, sometimes it's baking supplies or coloring books, or other activities to keep her busy.

It's easy to see that she's been trained and spent a lot of time in safehouses or away from others. She has a strict routine. Mila wakes up at 7:30 am on the dot. She does a yoga-pilates routine for thirty minutes, then takes a fifteen-minute shower before starting the coffee and making breakfast. She never wakes me up or pushes me to help with anything in the house, but I always try to do anything before she has to ask me. Thankfully, I like to keep my home tidy and neat anyway, so it's not that much of a stretch for me.

Now for Bryan, this would be damn hard. That man's apartment is a shit-hole. Trent, well I would've said it would be hard for Trent too, but he had to go undercover for months, then also had to stay in a safehouse with his girl for months. All without driving her away. So, he must be able to keep his space clean.

Kieron has always been a clean freak, except for during his college days.

After breakfast, Mila sits in the chair by the window and reads or writes in a journal. Sometimes, she sits outside with a blonde wig and sunglasses on. Sometimes, she takes her burner phone that I put a tracer in, just in case, and walks along the beach. Each time she leaves the safety of the house

I get incredibly stressed and watch her like a creepy asshole with binoculars and catalog each person around her. Just in case.

I try my best not to be too… controlling. She's trained and she's able to protect herself, but still, every time she walks out that door, there's an increased risk of someone seeing her and attacking. Thankfully, she limits it so my heart doesn't explode from stress.

Throughout the day, Mila and I bounce around each other with soft touches and small kisses. It's domestic bliss.

And I never want it to stop. I don't think I want to go back to Boston. I like the slow- paced routine we've set, but with the freedom to go wherever we want.

"I'm going to go for a short walk today. Okay?" Mila says, interrupting my train of thought, as she gives me a kiss on the cheek and hands me a full cup of coffee.

"Just be careful, okay?" I remind her, not that I need to.

"I know. Trust me, I know." She smirks and rolls her eyes.

———-

Mila slips my black baseball cap on her head, and pushes loose hair into the sides before walking back into the bathroom to put in the contacts that cover up those beautiful blue eyes. I kick my feet up on the too-small couch and cross my arms behind my head, just watching her and getting completely lost in the memory of fucking her from behind, up against that sink.

"Are you just going to watch me?" She smirks, looking at me with one brown eye and one blue eye in the mirror.

"Every day for the rest of my life."

Mila smiles and drops my gaze shyly. "Smooth talker."

She slips the other contact in and my wife's face somehow changes drastically when the blue is absent from her eyes. After drying her hands, she walks over to the small table she'd put by the door in the first few weeks that holds keys, coins, our burner phones, etc. She tucks her phone in her back pocket of the jeans she's wearing, then comes over to bend over me, holding the back of the couch to brace herself.

"I'll be back in thirty minutes and I'll stay within viewpoint of this window. If there is any funny business or anyone new, then I'll readjust my hat. If something happens, then I'll dispatch the person and meet you a mile away at the small restaurant and sit in the back booth with my back to the wall." She repeats the plan we came up with together. I lean up and kiss her soundly.

There's always a risk when we go out, even for necessities. But knowing that I will be able to see her every moment she's gone makes me feel a bit better.

"I'll be here. Watching you. Not like a creeper."

Mila squints her eyes and the corner of her mouth tips up as she hums. "Maybe a little bit like a creeper."

"You like it." I smirk, kissing her again.

"From you, I do." She pushes off the couch and walks to the door, blowing me a kiss before walking out the door with a smile.

Sighing, I feel my smile fade and I immediately jump up to watch her through the blinds on the window. A knot of worry tightens in my chest as I watch her step onto the sand and look up at the sun. She smiles, letting the sun warm her skin and I'm transfixed. Her eyes are closed, a serene smile on her lips, as if she's communicating with the very essence of nature. In this moment, she is a goddess, an embodiment of grace and tranquility, and I'm completely spellbound by her radiance.

I sit at the small computer area and cycle through the security screens. I lean forward, studying each of the grainy images with a sense of vigilance, scanning for any sign of anomaly or difference. My eyes shift between tasks, and I see Mila getting closer to the shore.

She walks in the water, the waves crashing over feet, and she's got a guarded smile on her face. I watch her turn around, taking a cursory glance toward the house before her body fills with tension and her gaze sharpens as she looks at me worriedly.

Something's wrong.

I jump up, getting closer to the window and opening the blinds more. Regardless of whatever it is that's making her stall, I'm not going to just wait around until something happens to her. I grab my gun from under the couch and stride with purpose toward the door, tucking the gun into the waistband of my jeans. Without knowing what's going on, I don't want to blow our cover.

I reach the doorknob, just as it shakes from a fist pounding on the outside.

Fuck.

"Brad, it's me. Open up!" Bryan's deep voice booms.

Son of a bitch.

Opening the door, I snap, "Did you have to knock like a fucking policeman about to break down the door?"

"I wanted to make sure you heard me," Bryan says with a smile that tells me he knows he's being a smug ass. "Are you going to invite me in?"

"Come on in, you fucker." I chuckle, shaking his hand and pulling him in for a hug. It's so good to see him. I usher us into the room, and he closes the door behind him. The already small space seems even smaller with him here.

His dark eyes look around, and he nods awkwardly.

"What are you doing here?"

"I'm here to update you on all the shit that's going on at home," Bryan says simply, pulling off his leather jacket and sitting down gently on the small chair we have to the side of the couch.

"Ah, okay. Well, you're more than welcome to talk, but I need to keep eyes on Mila," I say, and move back to the window. She's still standing in the same spot, waiting to hear from me to know what to do. I grab a small flashlight and flash it twice at her, a sign that everything is fine. After that, I can see the relief in her body language as she starts to walk the shore again.

"I'm glad to see you guys have figured out a system," Bryan says softly.

"We have." The air turns awkward between us, and I'm thankful I don't have to look at him. I know why he's upset. But, I can't let his feelings affect how mine and Mila's life will be. I can't.

"I heard about the marriage."

My head drops down as I sigh. I knew he would.

"Yeah," I say softly. "And?"

I don't turn from my post. I want to make sure that Mila's safe, but also, I don't want to see the hurt look on his face. It's obvious he likes Mila. Maybe more. And all that bullshit from before... I don't want that to come back.

"Congratulations, man. Are you happy?" Bryan says,

shocking me.

I turn to him and inspect him for any signs or tells of insincerity.

But I see none.

"I am. I'm very happy."

"Is she?" His eyes, dark and stoic, break contact with mine.

"I hope so. I try to make her as happy as I can." I answer him sincerely.

"That's all that matters. That you both are happy." He stands up and joins me at the window. "I know I was an asshole, but I don't know, man." He looks between the blinds at Mila. "She's just something else."

"I know." There's a vulnerability in his words that resonates deep within me, a vulnerability I didn't anticipate from someone I've always seen as strong and dependable. Someone that hasn't let anyone, or anything, trip him up in any way. I'm not angry or hurt, I'm just worried about what this means going forward for the two of us.

"I know you know." He smirks, mirth flowing through his eyes. "You locked her down, as you should've." He claps me on the shoulder in congratulations before turning and going back to sit in the chair. "I'm not staying long, I just wanted to tell you that I like Mila. Romantically."

I know this, but it still pisses me off. Possessiveness and rage duel within me, and I open my mouth to smart off, but he waves his hand to cut me off.

"I know you know that. But I needed to say it out loud. I like her and it kills me that she doesn't return the feelings. It's plain as day to see how much she loves you. How much you love her. So, I wanted to say that just because I like her, I will always respect your marriage and you as my brother.

It's... it's gotta just be a crush, so I might have to stay away until my feelings fade because I'm tired of being an asshole to you when you've done nothing wrong."

As happy as I was that he'd come to this conclusion, it did nothing to make my anxiety better.

"I'm still going to be working on this whole Bratva bullshit. I'm still going to be working with you guys, but I can't be around you or talk to you guys while you're so happy. It just... it hurts," he says softly, and I can see the pain lacing his face.

"I'm sorry." What else can I say?

"Don't be sorry." His dark eyes meet mine again. "Don't be sorry at all. You two are meant to be and that's great. Wonderful. It just hurts for the moment until I, hopefully, find the one meant for me. Okay?"

I nod, and turn back to check on Mila. She's stopped, just her back visible from here. I smile as I watch her tip her head back again to let the rays absorb into her skin, little pieces of her hair that can't be contained under the hat are flowing around her.

"Now, on to official business." Bryan claps his hands together. "Lots of shit has gone down, and I'm going to go through it quickly. I was able to make contact with 'The Haunted' on the dark web and set up a meeting. He wanted to get intel on the Clan's secured servers in exchange for a meet-up."

"Secured servers, that's where personnel and safehouses are located."

"Exactly."

"Then what the fuck did you guys do?" My eyes widen as I turn to face him. They wouldn't be that stupid. There's no way that Kellan or Kieron would endanger anyone like that, even if it was for me. It's too much and too risky.

"I made a duplicate. Compromised the code enough that they weren't able to see that it had been copied, and it gave them false information. Trent made contact at a park and met with a man that meets Aleksander's description."

"Fuck." I run a rand through my hair.

"You're copying my look there, man," Bryan teases me, running a hand through his beard.

"It's called 'trying to stay inconspicuous and cover any telling features'. I now see why you refuse to shave."

"It does come in handy in times like this." He smirks.

"So, what's the plan? We know it's Aleksander, that he's alive and gunning for Mila. We know that Sergei is going behind our backs to get to Mila. Did you guys reach out about the 'information' you had on her?"

"All communication has pretty much stopped since that meeting. It's painfully obvious that both sides are using each other and have dropped the pretenses. Their main goal is to get Mila and to take us down for harboring her."

"Just what she was scared of." Shaking my head, I see Mila start heading back toward the house. "Do not tell her that. I'm serious, Bryan. Don't mention it."

He holds both hands up and shrugs in acceptance.

"Is there a plan in place?" I ask him quickly.

"There is. But we need to draw him out into the open." Bryan finishes speaking just as the door opens and my girl's smiling face greets us.

"Bryan, hi!" she says brightly, bending down to hug him.

"Hi, Mila. How are you?" He returns her hug, and I can see how he's trying to hide the pain in his dark eyes as she holds him.

"I'm great. How are you?" She stands up straight and crosses her arms over her chest.

"Can't complain." He purses his lips and looks at me.

I nod, understandingly. "Bryan was just stopping by to let me know how everything is going back in Boston. It's Aleksander, like we thought."

Mila's smile drops, she holds her stomach and swallows like she is going to be sick. "Oh, god."

"It's okay. The guys made sure he doesn't know where you are, and Bryan was able to erase any mention of this safehouse."

"But what does that mean we need to do? If Aleksander is working with our Uncle…" She shakes her head. "I've been thinking. I think Aleksander is the new *Prizark* of the Bratva. Think about it, it makes sense."

Bryan and I nod, and I sigh.

"Aleksander is already considered dead among a lot of the other mobs. He has the same physical training, spy training and on top of that, he's a skilled hacker." She counts off the reasons why her theory is probable.

"You're right," I say, and look to Bryan. "You need to tell Kellan and Kieron to treat this as if Aleksander is the new Ghost. That means he now has access to everything that Mila did before. Our information might be outdated."

"Got it."

"What is the plan? How do we make it so that Cillian and I can come home?" she asks Bryan intently.

I kind of hope they don't figure out a way. Mila and I could stay here, or move somewhere else and make a simple life together, away from everything.

But if she wants to stay in Boston, we will do whatever makes her happy. She deserves to be free and I'll do whatever I can to support her.

"We need to get Aleksander to come to the surface. We need to take him out, and then I'll replicate his dark web presence. From what I could tell, Sergei and Aleksander only communicate through emails so it shouldn't be hard." Bryan shrugs "We need to take Aleksander out, then once I'm into his system I can see how deep this all actually goes. War isn't what we want, but if we have to get Sergei to stop coming after…"

I shake my head once and widen my eyes, but Bryan continues.

"After Mila, then we will. Once I know how far it goes, Kellan will take over."

"So, we will never know what comes of it."

When Kellan 'takes over' the matter is handled and never talked about again. We are usually told what they moved onto, but never what happened once the mission left our hands.

"Have you guys discussed how you're going to draw Aleksander out?" Mila asks. She puts her hands in the back pockets of her jean shorts and shifts her stance.

I sigh, knowing what's going to come next. "Not yet."

"We have some ideas." Bryan cocks his head to the side, looking right at me sheepishly just as I shoot him a glare. "I'm not going to lie to her."

"You son of a bitch." I swear at him under my breath.

"What are they?" Mila shifts again, crossing her arms over her chest and leaning back. Her eyes shine with determination through the colored contacts, her jaw set to the side, and she raises an eyebrow at me.

"Nothing that you need to worry about." I say, trying to stay calm. I don't want to snap at her.

I look to Bryan for help, because I know as well as he does that any plans that have any shot of actually working, include Mila. He looks at me with pity or frustration, I don't know which one, but at the moment, I don't have time to determine or care, really. I can't let the two of them do this because I know the moment that Mila agrees, Bryan is going to run to Kieron and they're going to overrule me.

I know the minute I've lost.

Bryan looks to Mila, who nods at him, and they both turn to me with understanding and apologetic looks.

Bryan's lips are pursed and his eyes full of understanding and pain. He knows that by agreeing to this, by even discussing this, it means sending Mila into the arms of the one who wants her dead. I can see the set of his jaw that he wishes he could stop this somehow. His hand is balled into a fist and rests against the back of the couch showing me that the silent one of the group has some big feelings about what has to happen next. Bryan looks away suddenly, anger and pain lacing his features.

Knowing I've lost, I turn to Mila, hoping maybe I can change her mind. But before I can even look at her, I feel her gaze on me. Of course, she put the pieces together before I did.

There is sadness in her eyes, as if she can see right through the frustration and small glimmer of hope that she wouldn't do this that I had, right down to the hurt and fear that sit heavy on my chest.

Mila's thin fingers thread with mine and she pulls me so I'm looking right at her.

"Trust me, Killer," she whispers. "I know you're scared. I

know you're concerned and that you'd gladly be the one racing in and putting yourself in danger instead of me. But this is my domain. I know how they think, how they act, I know how best to defend myself. You like to forget that I was the most feared, most elite assassin for a long time." She says this jokingly, chuckling and squeezing my hand. "This is my mess to help clean up. This is my, *our,* future they're threatening and I won't let that be taken from us." Her determination is unmistakable, etched into every line of her face.

I realize I have to let her do this. It's not about me. It's about letting her gain her power back, by herself. I sigh; anxiety clawing at my throat, but I have trust in her. I trust that she'll do what's best for her and keep herself as safe as possible.

She's looking at me patiently, waiting for me to work through this overwhelming amount of emotion I'm feeling. It goes against everything I want to do, everything I've been trained for, everything I promised I'd protect her from. Mila holds my hands between us and smiles softly.

Fuck it. This isn't about me. Whatever I'm feeling is nothing compared to what she is.

"I do trust you. That's not, and never has been, in question. It's…" I take a deep breath and close my eyes. "This will be very hard for me to do, but only because I never wanted you to have to deal with those shitheads ever again. I promised you and myself the moment we got married that I would put myself between you and any danger that came our way. But instead, only a few months into our marriage, everyone is asking me to let you run head-on into danger." Mila opens her mouth to try to reassure me, but I just put a hang up to stop her. "I know you're the famed, dangerous *Prizrak,* but you're *my wife.* My wife. Mine to love, mine to hold, mine to protect. You're also mine to trust." I cup her chin with my hand, forcing her to look at me. "I'll do whatever I can to support you and keep you safe. I promise."

Mila's eyes start to water and I almost worry that I'd made her upset, but then she shifts from my Mila into her Ghost-mode. The look that crosses her face is multifaceted, but what I see most is thirst. She's out for blood and it's very much a turn-on.

In this moment, I know that she is willing to do whatever it takes to ensure our plan's success, even if it means putting herself in harm's way. And as we lock eyes, a silent under-standing passes between us, a shared acknowledgment of the dangers ahead and the sacrifices we were both willing to make for the greater good.

"Then let's go get this son of a bitch and take down the Bratva," Mila says with a sinister smile.

The Plan

Cillian

"You know what this means, right?" Kieron's baritone voice comes through the speakers of my computer as the three of us crowd around to be a part of the video call. He's speaking directly to me, knowing that I would be the one to cause the most issues with the plan simply because it involved using Mila. Something I never, ever wanted to do.

We'd called Kieron through the secured server Bryan had encrypted on my hard drive and immediately gotten to work. Kieron went into the plan in a little more detail, but overall, it depended quite a bit on getting Aleksander to show himself.

"Yes, Kieron. I know what this means." I do my best to refrain from answering like an annoyed teenager, but even I can hear that my tone is clipped.

"Look, I know that this is going to be hard. I had to send Talia in undercover, right into the lion's den, and it was the most torturous hour of my life. Do you really think you can handle this? Tell us now, because if you fuck this up by

249

running in there, you're done. Benched, until we can get the problem with the Smirnovas sorted." Kieron looks tired and I feel somewhat bad for adding onto his exhaustion, but he has to understand.

This is my girl. My *wife.*

"I understand. I won't do anything to jeopardize Mila," I promise.

"Good." He runs his fingers through his hair anxiously. "We have a lot to do in a very short period of time. I want this done and settled before Sergei is able to get his foot soldiers organized. That means we are a go in twenty-four hours." I look down at my watch. It's 5:30 pm. By tomorrow evening, this will all be over. For the better, hopefully.

No, screw that. Not hopefully. It *will* be better. We will have won, Mila and I will be free to do what we choose to, and the Bratva will know not to fuck with the Clan.

"Wow, that's—" Mila sucks in a breath. "—so soon."

"It needs to be," I say, looking at her meaningfully. "It's already been going on too long." Cupping her cheek, I trace her cheekbone with the pad of my thumb softly and I smile when she leans into my hand. "You deserve to be free," I whisper, low enough that she's the only one that hears.

She'd taken the colored contacts out so instead of the muddied brown, I can see her bright, brilliant blues. In those azure eyes I can see her gratitude, her love, her fear, but mostly her determination.

"So, y'all,"—Trent's jovial tone and big, goofy smile pops on screen—"how are we going to do this?"

"I have an idea," Bryan pipes in.

"We're all ears." Kieron sits back in the leather chair of his office.

"The Haunted, or Aleksander as we now know, is collecting information on Mila, on her whereabouts, but she doesn't have any sort of online presence. I've looked into it and scourged the internet trying to find a shred of information about Mila Smirnova and have only been able to obtain the basics that everyone else knows. Whomever you have working for you to keep you off the grid, I'd like their information. I have a lot to learn." Bryan says the last part directly to Mila, completely seriously.

She chuckles and nods.

"Add that to the fact that we haven't texted, emailed, or posted any information about the woman we found that night, and have not insinuated Mila in any way, really helps in keeping her whereabouts unknown. Based on the information from the meeting with Sergei, they aren't having any success with the different avenues to find her, so they're starting to get desperate. If we give them some information, targeted, specific information from an unknown source, then it might be enticing enough for him to come get her himself."

"Why would he come himself for some random tip? They must get those all the time," Trent asks, scratching his head.

"Because." Bryan sighs "I'm going to send it as me."

My eyes widen, nostrils flare, as I try to process what he just said. Why would he…. How would that make it any better?

Kieron leans forward, one eyebrow raising accusingly, and his mouth starts to open to yell or ask a question, but I don't know which.

Bryan's calm demeanor is replaced by a restless energy. We all wait for him to explain, and watch him closely. His brow is furrowed with worry, and I can see the tension etched into the lines of his face. It's very unlike him to be so visibly unsettled, and that shows me just how much he knows we aren't going to like what he's done.

"What did you do?" I ask, attempting to sound as non-confrontational as I can, even though I want to snap, yell, scream. This isn't the time for secrets, especially not from my friends.

"Look…" Bryan starts to fidget; sitting up straighter, then leaning over again, reaching to scratch the back of his head, then dragging a hand down his face. "I've been talking with The Haunted for a while now. As Bryan O'Conner."

It seems like time stands still for a moment before all hell breaks loose. Trent starts screaming obscenities through the line. Mila gasps, but quickly recovers as she tenses up beside me, speaking quickly and menacingly in Russian. It's kind of impressive how fast and how darkly she's speaking. If it was pointed at me, I would've definitely been a bit afraid of the assassin.

I don't say anything. I don't react. I clench my fist, every muscle in my body tense with a mixture of rage and betrayal. The weight of betrayal bears down on me like a suffocating blanket, fueling the fire within.

Without any warning, my fist flies out and connects with Bryan's jaw, and a surge of primal satisfaction courses through me, momentarily drowning out the chaos of emotions swirling inside me. The impact reverberates through my arm, sending a shockwave of raw power rippling through me.

Bryan staggers back, his shoulders hitting the other arm of the couch as he immediately tries to determine if he needs to defend himself for another blow. I've never seen the look on his face before, a mixture of understanding, shock and frustration.

I don't know why he's fucking frustrated. It's not like he's been betrayed here. It's not like someone he loved and cared about went behind his fucking back and fed information to the enemy, resulting in who knows what.

The more I think about it, the angrier I get. The more I feel like beating him bloody is the only acceptable answer. Leaning forward, I twist the collar of his shirt to drag him back to sitting and yank him closer.

"Give me one good reason why I shouldn't kill you right now," I say through clenched teeth. "I'm begging for a reason."

"Cillian!" Kieron's voice screams through the speakers. "Let him go!"

His order doesn't deter me. Trent and Kieron are hours away. By the time they got here, Bryan's body would already be cool.

"Come on, man. What reason could you possibly have to do this to me? To *her*? We know how you feel, so how could you? *How could you?*"

Bryan doesn't make any move to defend himself as I punch him a second time, letting go of his shirt so he falls back against the couch again.

"Why?!" I scream, the anger heating my skin, making me feel as if it's stretched too thin over my body.

"Cillian, I mean it. Let him go. *Now!*" Kieron's voice booms so loudly the speakers crack and clip.

I shoot a look at Kieron. His frustration is clear through the monitor.

"Stop, just stop." He sighs. "Bryan, we discussed not telling him yet."

The fuck did he just say?

"You two have one minute to tell me what is going on, or

I swear, I'm walking and I'm taking her with me." I release Bryan's shirt from my grip and push him back down again.

"Fuck, fuck. *Fuck*," Bryan hisses, touching his nose gently. "I think you broke my nose."

"The least of what you deserve."

"Why is it you two that's always fighting?" Trent teases on the other side of the call.

"Shut up, Trent," Bryan and I say at the same time.

In the aftermath, a heavy silence descends, broken only by the echoes of my ragged breaths.

"Someone fucking talk!" I bellow.

Mila wraps her fingers around my bicep, pulling me back toward her.

"Okay, okay." Bryan grunts, sitting up softly. "I was working the tech angle and Aleksander caught on to me."

"When we discovered that The Haunted had essentially caught Bryan, we used it as a turning point. Bryan came to me with a backup plan, and I okayed it. So if you're going to be mad at anyone, Cillian, be mad at me. It was my call to keep it a secret." Kieron shakes his head. "When Bryan was discovered and The Haunted ID'd him, he thought that if he gained The Haunted's trust, over time, that when he asked for information on Mila, the real, whole story would be given and we could use the trust in Bryan's word for one very well-timed need. Like telling him exactly where Mila is going to be, even if she's not actually there."

"He's not stupid. He'd know you were double-crossing him, he's methodical," Mila jumps in, peeking her head around my arm, but not getting closer to Bryan. She's come such a long way in recovering from her trauma, and the betrayal from Bryan, even if it was to help her, is hitting her hard.

"That's why the information I had to leak to him was real," Bryan whispers.

"Oh damn." Trent drops his head.

"Excuse me? The fuck did you just say?" I snap. I can't believe this. I can't believe that Kieron would sanction this. "You gave our enemy, the one who is after *my* wife, *real* sensitive information about her, us, and the Clan. You okayed this?" I point an accusing finger at Bryan, but stare down Kieron.

"I did. We took the proper precautions and made sure that Mila was safe, but it was worth it. The Haunted confided in Bryan and now we have a sure way of getting him to fall for our trap. Mila will be off-site the whole ti—" Kieron's cut off mid-word when Mila whispers.

"It was because of you two."

"What?" Trent says. "What did she say?"

'I said," Mila enunciates overtly, angrily, "it was because of you two. The Haunted knew which apartment in HQ was Cillian's and tried to attack me there. He killed the lights and tried intimidating me. He knew where I was, who I was with, because of you." She speaks aggressively, leaning further around me, but her hand tightens on me as if she wants to take charge, but is too anxious to.

"I'm so sorry, Mila," Bryan says quietly.

"So Aleksander has known where I was the whole time? You told him exactly where I was. You lied to me." She's close to tears.

"This was the only way I could protect you," he says simply.

I do my best not to react in any way. I knew how he felt, I knew that he was either in love with her or the feelings were headed there. To do this, though, this means more.

The room is silent for a few miserably awkward beats. I want to scream at him that I'm hers. She chose me. That I can protect her just as well as he can, better even. But when I look at him to tell him off, I see a broken man.

He's hurt. Bryan has put everything out on the line for a woman who doesn't even love him back, and never will now, but more, he's lonely and wanting what the rest of us have found. Love and partnership.

Kieron sighs deeply, and leans forward on his desk with both elbows. "What I said before still stands. Bryan only acted under my orders."

"So you told him to tell the man that's trying to kill me exactly where I was?" Mila snaps off at Kieron.

I can't say I blame her.

"No, that's not what happened," Bryan cut in.

"There's no excuse anymore, Bryan. You helped him. You betrayed me," she says harshly. It's as if the room stops breathing. Everyone can hear the sadness in her voice, and the raw emotion is breaking my heart.

Before anyone can say anything else, I step in, letting Mila step back and sort through what she's feeling. "Why did Sergei act like he didn't know where Mila was if Aleksander knew where she was and that we were helping her?"

"I convinced Aleksander that it would be better and more satisfying if he were to get to Mila first. Life-long revenge and all that," Bryan explains.

"Oh good, so on top of betraying me, you also helped plan my kidnapping and murder. Fucking fantastic," Mila snaps.

"Let's get back on track," Kieron mumbles.

The awkward tension is rising, and I can't blame Mila at all. If I was in her shoes, I'd have strangled the fucker already.

But she's sorting through everything, and I don't know how she'll feel on the other side of it.

I take over, saying, "Mila isn't going to be anywhere near the pick-up site. We can plant hints for him to buy that she'd frequent whatever place you're wanting to pick him up, but she will not be there when Aleksander is."

"Absolutely not!" She stands up, pacing the room and commanding everyone's attention. But instead of elaborating, she just continues to pace. Eyes wild, fingers twisting together over and over, her chest rising and falling quickly.

"Doll?" I try to bring her back, but she snaps her fingers and points at me.

"Don't."

All four of us are watching her closely, eyes glued to the magnetic and strong presence.

She stops suddenly and turns to face us. "What I'm about to say next is going to piss you off, Cillian, but you're going to listen and there's not going to be anything you can do to change my mind."

"Goddamn it." I shake my head and push off the couch to stand by her. "Please."

"No, no. I'm going to be there. That son-of-a-bitch is trying to kill me, he's threatening to hurt you all and he's turned my uncle against me which means that my own father is in on it. And approves of it!" She laughs humorlessly. "I'm going to be at the sting. Make sure you get Aleks and then I'll scurry off and hide."

"That sounds fair," Trent pipes in.

I aggressively stick a finger up to shush him while throwing him a 'stay out of this' look. "Well, it is."

"There's no way—" I start to tell her off, explaining why I

absolutely don't want her there, the different plans I think would work instead of her putting herself in danger. But she's made up her mind. I can see that. I know how important this is to her, and I don't want to be the reason she doesn't have some kind of closure. "You decide to do whatever is best for you. I'll be there to watch your back either way," I say softly. The words taste terrible as they leave my mouth. Every bit of my being is telling me this is wrong, that I need to keep her and hide her away to keep her safe. But I trust that she knows what she's doing. I trust my boys.

"Good." With raised eyebrows, she nods in relief. "We'll talk about this later. But for right now," she says, squeezing my hand and turning to face the guys, "we have a lot of work to do."

* * *

"Everyone clear on the plan, then?" Kieron asks one more time. No one is writing anything down, taking notes, there is no paper trail, no digital footprint. We've repeated the plan, over and over until we could recite it in our sleep. There will be no refreshers.

"In twenty-four hours, Bryan will alert The Haunted that Mila was spotted at the coffee shop on the first floor of HQ for the first time without Cillian. He'll make sure to really sell it that Cillian "had to be pulled away on business" but that she's going to be untraceable and untrackable for a few moments after leaving the cameras in the coffee shop and entering into our building. Remember to add that once she steps inside the building, Cillian, or any of the rest of us will be able to get to her within moments," Kieron reminds Bryan.

"Got it," Bryan says, his eye puffy and starting to turn dark from my punches earlier. He crosses his arms over his chest and stares out in front of him, deep in thought.

"Mila will put on a wig that replicates the length that her hair was before. We have to make it easy for him, don't we?" Trent picks up explaining.

"I will be sure to mention how Kellan brought them back from the safehouse because of the deal with Sergei," Bryan pipes in, rubbing his jaw slightly after speaking. "Mila will head to the cafe at exactly 10:45 am tomorrow morning. Order, sit at the booth by the back door, be seen, then after fifteen minutes, instead of going to Cillian's apartment, you'll be going to Kieron's office in the penthouse. Cillian will be watching from there, ready to go if anything happens."

"Bryan, Trent and myself will be waiting at three locations; loitering by the front door, inside the lobby of our building and in the lobby. Eyes will be on Mila and the surrounding area. Cillian will have all access to the security cameras and will be able to see every inch of the building and surrounding areas," Kieron says.

"You guys have an older photo of Aleksander you will send through the secure server to Cillian and myself, and I will be sure to let you know the moment I notice him if he falls for the bait," Mila says firmly. Authoritatively. Her tone is so dominant that all that's missing is her hands on her hips and her bedroom eyes. I feel my cock harden and twitch in my jeans and I shift to adjust myself.

She misses nothing though and smirks at me as she pointedly looks at my dick that's pressing painfully into my thigh, trapped under the denim, ready to bury itself in her heat again as soon as possible.

I cough awkwardly as everyone looks at me, waiting for me to continue the plan or maybe throw a fit about keeping Mila from the mission.

Only she smirks, her eyes bright with arousal and humor. She knows what she's doing to me.

"After Aleksander is apprehended, we will immediately convene in the basement for… creative questioning," I say, looking at the group. "Bryan will make sure to download Aleksander's contacts and hack into The Haunted's server. Sergei kept him alive for a reason; we need to know why."

"After we get answers from Aleksander, we will take it to Kellan. Once it's in his hands, The Bratva will be dealt with accordingly," Kieron says.

"And what will become of Aleksander?" Mila asks, leaning forward so her elbows rest against her thighs.

"He will be dealt with. Just know that he will never see the light of day again." Kieron shrugs. His eyes narrow and a sick smile curves on his face.

"Promise?"

Trent and Kieron look at her in surprise, their shock written clearly all over their faces.

"I can promise you that, no problem," Kieron reiterates, his dark eyes piercing the screen. "And I can promise that it'll hurt."

I don't know what I was expecting from Mila, but the determined, bloodthirsty look on her face wasn't it.

"Good."

The Night Before

Mila

"The message will go out to The Haunted in twelve hours. Cillian and Mila, you're expected to be back in Boston by tomorrow morning at 7 am at the latest. But you need to make sure no one knows you're back, so plan accordingly. I suggest early morning before any of the commuters start to make their way in," Kieron orders.

I nod. That means we need to leave here by midnight if we want to arrive with the cover of darkness and the odd early-morning hour.

"Not a problem," Cillian says. He looks so handsome, so strong, and determined. I love who he is in totality, but there's something so special about the softness and vulnerability he shares with just me. When it's the two of us, he melts. He's sweeter, kinder, like all his rough edges are smoothed over.

It's those moments I want to keep working for. Those bits of time that are just Cillian and I, sharing a peaceful state with each other and getting to be who we truly are. Together.

"I bet they won't sleep a wink." Trent laughs, his jovial smile spreading across his face.

"And on that note, I'm leaving." Bryan pushes himself up off the couch, and crosses our small living room quickly. He picks up his leather jacket and reaches for the front door.

I don't know if he will look at me after this. I don't know if I want to be around him ever again after this.

He holds the front doorknob, but doesn't turn it. His shoulders are dipped, heavy with burden and regret, as he turns back toward us. Toward me.

"I really am sorry that I had to betray you in order to save you. If I could've done it any other way, I would have," he says, those dark eyes locked on mine. The words are nice, but I've been around darkness for too long in my life to believe it wholeheartedly. I just can't let it go, can't let the betrayal leave my mind. I never thought one of Cillian's best friends, one of the men that I thought I could count on and let in, besides Cillian, would do this to me.

He nods sadly, understanding that I'm not going to say anything, that I'm not going to forgive him soon, and leaves quickly. It's awkward, no one speaking as the words Bryan said and the apology I didn't accept hang in the air.

"Until tomorrow then." Kieron nods and the computer screen goes blank.

There's a strange mixture of apprehension and relief swirling within me, like two opposing currents vying for dominance.

For so long, I've been caught in this whirlwind of constant motion, always chasing after something. Whether it was something ordered of me, away from danger, or for my life, I've been running—running from my past, running from my fears, running toward an uncertain future. A future I now have within my grasp. A future I've always wanted desperately.

As I look at Cillian, a surge of emotions floods my heart, so overwhelming, yet familiar. There he is, the man I've chosen, standing before me with his gentle eyes and soft smile.

With him, I find solace, security, and excitement for tomorrow. Things I've never had. Despite the uncertainties that loom on the horizon, I find comfort in knowing that he's by my side, ready to face whatever challenges may come our way.

But intertwined with the warmth of love is the chill of fear, a nagging apprehension that tugs at the corners of my mind. Tomorrow everything will change.

What will happen? Will he be able to let me walk into the line of fire? Will I be able to hold myself steady when faced with the cousin who has done all this to try and kill me?

Will we be able to prevail, or will we be torn apart?

In the face of what's to come, a notion takes hold of me—a desire to make our last night count, to cherish every moment we have together. I want to etch this memory into my heart, to hold onto it like a beacon of light in the darkness. Cillian, my light in the dark.

Tonight, I want to love him with every fiber of my being, to show him just how much he means to me.

* * *

"That was one of the hardest things I've ever done. And I know it will be nothing compared to tomorrow." Cillian shakes his head, mumbling.

"What do you mean?" I pull back the covers of the bed we share, slipping in between the cool, soft sheets.

"I know how much this means to you, to be a part of taking The Bratva down. But you have nothing to prove. You know that right?" He's getting ready for bed, brushing his teeth, naked except for his boxers. The domesticity of it makes me smile.

"I know that, Cillian."

"I just… If you wanted to let a decoy go tomorrow, instead of you, I wouldn't be opposed."

"Cillian…" I groan, shaking my head. I don't want to have this conversation. I just need him to let this happen and stop trying to stand in between me and danger. I love that he cares and takes care of me, I love it so much. But he also needs to let me protect myself. I've done it my entire life and I'm not about to stop now.

"I know, I know." He leaves the room and I hear the water run before shutting off, and see the lights switching off in the living room. Cillian walks in and sits at the end of the bed. His shoulders slump forward and he sounds defeated as he says, "I had to try."

This sweet, kind man.

I slip out of bed and stand in front of him, kneeling at his feet. Holding his knees in my hands, I look up at him. He looks different than he did all those months ago when he saved me from that terrible fate.

His clean-shaven face is now covered with a medium-length, dark-chocolate-brown beard that I've grown to love feeling against my skin as he kisses me passionately. His buzz-cut short hair has grown out and is curling over his forehead. I think it's adorable because he's starting to push it up and back with his fingers and it's just the most sexy, innocent gesture ever.

"I'm going to be okay." I cup his face softly with both hands. "I can handle this. Can *you?*"

My poor husband looks so torn, and I can understand why.

It's ingrained in your psyche when your whole world is life or death at every corner to protect the ones you love dearly. He's promised me over and over that he would keep me safe by any means, and now I've asked him to do the exact opposite.

"I don't have a choice, do I?" he says softly, though he knows exactly what my answer would be.

I shake my head, and stand, wrapping my arms around his head. I pull him closer, letting his head rest against my chest.

"I have to do this," I whisper. "For us, for our future."

"I know."

"If we want a future; kids, careers, the whole thing, I need to make sure that this ends with Aleksander and my Uncle. I won't be able to really live with one eye always looking over my shoulder." I pull back and stare at him. "I want to live, really, fully live, with you. I want everything life has to offer *with you.*"

"I want that too."

"Good." I smile, then feel my smile turn more sultry. "Then tonight, for the next few hours that we have left, we will make them the best we have."

"What did you have in mind?" Cillian's eyes sparkle with arousal and curiosity.

"Go lay back on the bed."

* * *

Cillian

All my attention is on Mila as I climb backward on the mattress.

"So sexy." She smirks seductively. The pink of her lips darken as she licks them. I get to see her pure blues staring at me hungrily.

She exudes a natural confidence that's so fucking sexy. Mila stands up straight, pushing her short hair over her shoulders. It falls forward as she looks at me lovingly, cupping my beard-covered cheek.

"You take such good care of me, don't you?" she coos.

I nod, emphatically. I will take care of her for the rest of time. Until my last fucking breath, I'll take care of her.

"Lay back, Killer. Cock up," she orders.

If I wasn't hard before, I am now.

I lay down, my arms stretched out and my dick straining so hard against my briefs that they're tented. My head hits the small headboard but I don't let it fall, instead I stay watching her. Mila slips the shirt from her head, and my mouth waters at the dusty-pink nipples hanging so sweetly in front of me.

Mila bends over and crawls up the bed, her hooded eyes locked on mine. Without warning, she takes my whole cock in her mouth all the way to the base, and hollows out her cheeks, sucking hard like she wants to suck out my very soul through my dick.

"Mi… Mi…" I struggle to get her name out as she bobs her head, twisting her tongue all the way to the top.

She pops off and stares at me as I sigh with relief as I get a moment to collect myself. "Yes?"

"Don't stop," I say breathlessly as she resumes working my dick with her mouth like a pro. My hands go immediately to her hair, holding it away from her face as she goes back to work. Mila bobs and sucks, soft and sweet for a beat and then furiously fast. I thrust up and she gags.

And how that sound is music to my ears.

I groan, already feeling my orgasm building quickly.

When her eyes roll back in her head, I'm done for. The understanding that I was bringing her just as much pleasure as she was bringing me is too much.

"If you don't want me coming in your mouth you need to stop now," I warn through my clenched teeth.

Instead of moving, she holds my thighs tighter, sucks harder, licks longer, and I explode in her mouth. And like a good girl, she swallows me down.

Every last drop.

With my orgasm comes the need to make her do the same. She sucks slower, pulling her naughty lips off my softening cock, and I sit up swiftly, grabbing her neck and kissing her deeply.

She tastes like me and I love it.

"It's my turn to drive now," I whisper against her lips. In one movement, I reach around her waist, pulling her to me, flipping us both so that I am now on top of her..

I kiss her hard, pushing her against the bed. My semi-soft cock brushes against her wetness and I moan. If I can get her to squirt again, I'll be ecstatic. It was one of the sexiest things

I've ever done or seen.

I continue to kiss her down her neck, while my hands go wandering. Her skin is so smooth, so warm. My hand slips up her body, over her ribs, and I squeeze her tit before swirling my fingers around the pink peaked nipple and pulling lightly.

Mila arches her back under my hands and moans.

My other hand goes the opposite way. I run my fingers over her hip, down between her thighs. As she squirms, I bite down on the spot she likes; the base of her neck where her shoulder starts. She responds by wrapping her arms around my head, keeping me against her tightly. My hand continues to wander, swirling my fingers in her wetness until I find her pulsing clit.

I start rubbing small, hard circles and I fucking love feeling her thrust up to chase the sensation. I move my hand so my thumb continues to run her clit, but my two fingers slip deep inside her cunt.

"Ahhh! Cillian!" She cries in my ear, and her fingers dig into my shoulders, leaving little fingernail marks all over.

Her walls start to clench around my fingers and I pull them out suddenly. I sit up, wrap my hands around her thighs, pull her legs to me and fuck into her in one motion. I shimmy us successfully so the crook of her legs are being held up by my arms. This way I can watch every time I hit a spot that makes her toes curl.

I slide all the way out, then yank her to me and watch with total attention as her eyes roll back and she bites her lower lip. Her head rolls to the side so I can't see her face completely.

"Oh no, that won't do." I move her so both legs are held in one arm—*fuck me she's even tighter this way*—and I use the other hand to hold her chin so she has to look at me.

Moaning at how tight she is, I growl, "I want to see every bit of your beautiful face. I want to see how every move I make makes you feel. Don't you dare look away."

I release her chin, happy with knowing she won't turn away from me again. I slide out of her heat, only to slam back into her, smirking when I hear her yelp, then moan. Keeping her legs together, draped over one arm, I lean forward, propping myself up over her with my other arm. This position gets us closer and I'm able to kiss those sweet lips of hers.

As we kiss, our movements get sloppier and as we push against each other it becomes more intense.

The small room smells of sex and sweat, the only sounds are our damp skin slapping against each other and the groans against each other's lips.

"I can't hold back," she whispers against my lips, her hot breath fanning my face.

"I don't want you to. Come for me, I want to feel you clench around my cock. Milk me hard," I whisper harshly in her ear.

At my words, her back arches, her fingers grip my shoulders tightly, and I can feel her thighs start to shake under my hold. I feel the familiar and welcome tingle building in my balls. I drop her legs to either side of me roughly. The moment I do, Mila lifts her hips and rocks aggressively in time with my thrusts.

"That's it! That's it, right there! Cillian, Cillian!" Mila screams, her entire body going tight with the force of her orgasm. From her fingernails cutting into my skin, to her walls fluttering tightly around me, to her toes curling as her heels dig into the mattress to hold her up higher. Wetness spurts out of her around my cock with each thrust, dripping down onto the bed and landing in big patches on the sheets.

Fuuuuccccckkkk, I groan mentally. My eyes close without my permission and I roll my neck trying to keep thrusting through her orgasm.

It's like we've turned on a faucet between us and it sounds obscene. So fucking hot. Her cries, the wetness of her cum squishing with each thrust, her hold on me, it's all too much.

"Mila, baby!" I shout, painting her walls with my cum.

Goddamn, just the sheer force of coming is making me shake and moan. I bite down on Mila's shoulder to keep from shouting again.

"Ah!" she cries, but holds the back of my head tighter against her.

My hips stutter as I feel my orgasm come to its end. I feel her walls clench, holding me tightly inside her for as long as possible, before I feel all my muscles relax and I let the full weight of my body rest on her. On this wonderful woman that I call mine.

"Oh my god," I say, completely and totally out of breath. "Mila, that was…"

"Fucking unreal." She sighs, sounding like she's in a daze. Satisfied in totality. Spent.

"We've made a mess of the sheets," I say, not fazed at all. She looks at me and chuckles, her cheeks turning red from a blush.

"I'm sorry, but I'm not really that sorry," she whispers.

"I don't want you to be. I love it." I slip out of her and sit back, watching the creamy white of my cum slide from her open legs as her ass sits in a puddle of her own wetness. Holding her legs open with my hands on her knees, I can't help but stare.

"The two of us together… we make art, baby. What we just

did, every single moment, was perfection." I bite my lip and lean down to kiss her again, breathing her in deeply. "I love you."

"I love you," she whispers back, with a bright smile shining at me.

The Heist

Cillian

We spent our last few hours at this safehouse in each other's arms. Slow, lazy kisses and sweet words whispered into the shared space between us. But two in the morning comes much too quickly. We both shower in silence, getting ready for the day, and getting dressed so we can leave in the darkness.

Mila and I look very similar to when we arrived here; she's wearing my shirt and leggings with sneakers on her feet, and I'm back in my usual jeans and t-shirt with my leather jacket over top, with biker boots. My uniform. Like the past eight months never happened. But they did, and they were some of the best months of my life.

Leaving this place feels like tearing away a part of myself that I'm not quite ready to let go of. It's like trying to walk away from a chapter of my life that isn't quite finished, leaving behind a myriad of emotions and memories that still cling to me like invisible chains. Every corner, every familiar nook of this shitty little safehouse that I hated so much when we first arrived, they all whisper to me, begging me to stay a little longer, to hold onto the comfort of what's known between Mila and I.

Slipping my duffel bag and hers over one of my shoulders, I look around the small house one last time. This place wasn't fancy, but it was just what we needed.

"Ready?" I ask with a deep sigh.

"Do we have to leave?" I can hear the reluctance in her voice that matches my own.

"I don't want to. But you know we have to."

I watch her eyes trace the rooms of our temporary home, and I can't help but notice the sadness etched into every line of her face. Her eyes linger on the little places, the details that have become a part of our daily existence. It's as if she's trying to memorize every inch of this place, knowing deep down that soon it will all become nothing more than a memory. The weight of her reluctance to leave hangs heavy in the air, so heavy in the air that I can almost reach out and touch it.

"I know." She sighs sadly.

"Let's get going." I reach out to take her hand in mine and lead her out the front door of our surprising little oasis.

* * *

She looks so serene sitting in the passenger seat, fast asleep. Her face is only illuminated by the dashboard lights and the occasional highway light as I turn into the city. In the silence, I let my mind wander and try to prepare myself for what we are walking into.

273

What I'm letting her walk into.

When we get Aleksander, I'm going to kill him. He's done nothing but bring darkness to our lives, and we know now that he's able to do pretty much anything he wants through his computer. Tracking her, terrorizing her, perpetuating the horrors she's lived through. She'll never feel safe again, I'll never feel like I can protect her completely if he's alive and free.

That thought brings me to Bryan.

I can't believe he'd do that. Work with the enemy, feed him information on someone he'd sworn to protect, hide it all from us. Even if it was sanctioned by Kieron. I turn my attention to my task, getting us to headquarters safely without anyone tailing us.

The city is so peaceful at this time of night. No one's awake, it's too early for the work rush but too late for the party people. The skyscrapers loom over the car like silent sentinels, their towering forms reaching up toward the star-studded sky. The windows are dark, the residents inside them lost to their sleep. Occasional bursts of color flicker from the neon signs that are on various storefronts, casting strange patterns of light and shadow across the deserted streets. Each one lighting up Mila's face for a few moments, bathing her in colored glow.

As I navigate through the familiar maze of streets, I can't help but feel a sense of awe at the beauty of the city in the stillness of the night. It's a different kind of beauty, one that's tinged with a hint of mystery and silence, but no less intriguing for it.

I turn us smoothly onto the correct street and see Headquarters, turning quickly into the parking garage entrance. I enter my code, our first step at showing Aleksander we're back in Boston.

Parking the car in my spot, I turn the engine off and turn to Mila. Her eyes flutter open almost immediately after the engine turns off.

"We're here, doll," I whisper, and push a stray lock of her raven hair around her ears.

"I'm sleeping," she grumbles.

I chuckle. "Very deeply it seems."

"Let's go up to your apartment and get a few more hours of sleep." She rubs her eyes.

"That sounds perfect." In silence, we make our way to the elevator and up onto my floor. There's a mix of disappointment, nervousness, and finality in the air.

I take a deep breath as the elevator opens onto my floor and Mila pushes forward.

"I don't want to live in Boston anymore," I say suddenly, surprising myself even.

Mila stops walking and turns to face me, shock and surprise clear on her face. "What? Why? Your family is here, your apartment is here, your job is here."

"I know. And you know as well as I do that I don't want to leave the Clan. But I don't want it to be my entire life anymore. I liked our little life undercover in Maine. And I know you did too. It fucking sucks that we have to come back." One of us had to say it. We were both stepping around it, even if it was clear to see that both of us were disappointed, neither of us had come out and fully said it. That we didn't want to leave.

"It does suck." Mila smiles softly with a sadness in her eyes and her shoulders drop. She turns to walk toward the front door, holding her hand out for the keys, and I toss them to her.

We unlock the front door, and step over the threshold, and it's like being sucked through a time portal. Everything has been left untouched in all the time we've been gone. There's a thin layer of dust covering everything, but it's nothing a good cleaning can't fix. Setting our bags down, I make sure to lock the door. I know Aleksander's method of warfare has been psychological, never actually getting his hands dirty, but that doesn't mean I'm okay with being lax on security. I pull my gun from my waistband, and check all the rooms, behind the curtains, in closets, under the bed. Everywhere where someone could be laying in wait.

"It's clear," I say as I walk back into the living room and motion for Mila to come with me into the bedroom. We wordlessly change the sheets and top blanket before falling into bed, still in our clothes.

Don't get me wrong, it's nice to lay in my bed, surrounded by my things, in my hometown. But the commonality in those things is that they are mine when I want it all to be *ours*.

* * *

Mila

"I'm not going to insult you by asking if you've got this, because you are quite literally trained to be a shadow, but I wanted to know if you need anything before this whole thing kicks off?" Trent asks me as the four of us ride in the elevator down to where the trap will start.

Kieron, Bryan and Trent came to Cillians at 7:00 am on the dot, waking the both of us from a dead sleep. They all look completely different; wigs, contacts, and maybe even prosthetics galore. None of them looked like themselves, so much so that I almost threw a punch when I opened the door.

Kieron's dark long hair is nowhere to be seen, hidden under a short black wig. He still has his beard but it's significantly shorter, cut much closer to his face. With aviators covering his eyes, he looks unrecognizable at a passing glance. Add that to the cargo shorts and plain t-shirt, he looks like someone on vacation, just here to see the sights.

Trent's red hair is gone, replaced with a shaggy blonde wig with a cut reminiscent of Justin Bieber in his younger years. He's clean shaven like normal, but he's wearing a turtleneck and slacks like he's a hot college professor. He has fake—or I assume they're fake—dark-rimmed glasses on his face to complete the transformation. I can't say it's a bad look on him. At all.

Bryan looks the most different. His face, normally covered with dark chestnut facial hair, is bare. He's shaved, showing off his sharp cheekbones and even sharper jaw. It's amazing how square his jaw is. Without his beard, his brown eyes sparkle. He's wearing a suit and tie, cut sharp to his figure, and carrying a briefcase to finish off his look. Wow.

Kieron handed me a long black wig and without asking, walked into the bedroom to get his cousin. Thankfully, Cillian was fully dressed.

"We need to go over what happens when we get Aleksander. In private," we all heard Kieron say to Cillian before he shut the door. The other two told me I needed to get ready. Their only saving grace was that they brought us donuts and coffee.

Two-and-a-half hours later, and here we are. I reposition the earpiece in my ear that connects me to all four of them. It's a nice surprise having someone in my ear, supporting me. A team that's got my back. It's also great because I'm connected to Cillian, I'll be able to hear him and know exactly what's going on.

"I'm okay, thank you though." I half-smile at Trent.

"Trent will be in the coffee shop with you, a professor taking advantage of the free wi-fi. Do not sit by him, do not make eye contact. I'll be a tourist on the street, taking photos and on my way to stop for a morning coffee. Ignore me completely," Kieron instructs. "Bryan is a businessman and will be the one in the lobby. He will take the elevator up to the penthouse with you while Cillian meets Trent and I with Aleksander. If it gets that far."

I nod, breathing slowly through my nose.

"From there, we'll get the information we need and he'll be out of your hair forever." Kieron pulls his shoulders back, standing straighter, and looks forward.

"Forever?"

"*Unless you want to be there for the questioning?*" Cillian's deep voice sounds loud and clear in my ear, so strong and sure, like he is only bending for me.

"No," I say quietly, though I know everyone can hear me, "there isn't anything I need to know directly. Get the answers I know we need and be done with it."

"*I'll make sure it's done, doll,*" Cillian promises.

I know he'll be thorough and bury this issue for good.

"All right, are you all ready?" Kieron asks.

We all nod.

"Cillian, you can see everything from above?"

"I can see everything, thank you, Bryan, for tapping into the coffee shop's surveillance."

"Good," Kieron answers.

I take a peek at Bryan and see him look downward, probably picking up on Cillian's snappy tone. The elevator starts to slow down as we approach the ground floor.

"From now on, this line stays clear unless absolutely necessary," Kieron says sternly.

I take a deep breath, narrowing my focus like I used to on missions as the elevator dings and the doors open slowly.

And it's go time.

Bryan lifts his phone to his ear and nods along with his pretend conversation, head down, speed-walking out of the elevator like a man on a mission.

Kieron pulls a map from his back pocket and starts to unfold it as he steps off the elevator.

Trent follows quickly, his backpack holding his laptop as he goes straight for the coffee shop.

"Let's do this." I nod.

Damn it. Kieron said to be quiet.

"You've got this, Mila. I love you." Fuck, just Cillian's voice makes me smile.

"I love you, too," I whisper, grinning from ear to ear.

"Come on guys, as cute as this is, focus up." Kieron sounds exasperated and I can't say I blame him. He did tell us.

I roll my shoulders back, flip the fake hair over my shoulder, and walk out of the elevator ready to end this.

* * *

I stride with purpose through the lobby and out the front door. The whole point is to show my face, make Aleks think he can slip in and abduct me in broad daylight.

Making sure to turn with my face toward the camera to look over my shoulder, I push the door of the lobby open and step into the hub-bub of mid-morning, downtown Boston. The sidewalks are full of both tourists and natives, pushing past each other to get to their destinations. I lift my face to the sun. If I close my eyes and try to ignore the sounds, I can almost imagine I'm still at the beach on one of my walks.

It smells of car exhaust and coffee mixed with fresh air, definitely different from the salty sea air on the beach.

God, I want to go back.

Focus, Mila.

I turn, surveying the area and the people around me and I see Trent already seated in the coffee shop, right by the window. Kieron is walking back and forth in front of a cathedral that has lots of attention from a tourist group. He's taking pictures, but the way he's standing, I can tell he can see the street and the coffee shop entrance.

I play up the nervous look on my face, shifting the wig so my hair covers a bit more of my face as I open the door.

Ding! The bell rings out overhead and the strong smell of coffee beans overpowers my senses as I walk through the door.

Don't look at Trent. Don't look at Trent. Don't look at Trent. I chant in my head as I walk toward the counter.

"One medium vanilla latte," I say softly, handing the barista a ten-dollar bill. With a smile, she takes it and gets to work on my coffee. While her back is turned, I look around discreetly. There's three teenage girls who are obviously ditching school crowded together in the corner by the window; all wearing too much makeup and talking way too loudly. A blonde girl sitting at a table in the middle of the room with big headphones and typing furiously on her laptop. A man in a three-piece suit behind me who has checked his watch twice since I placed my order. Trent is sitting at a barstool at the table lining the window, hunched over a laptop and writing something on a notepad right beside it.

"Here you go!" The barista places my drink in one hand and my change in the other. "Have a good day," she says with a smile, which I half-heartedly return.

I turn to go sit at a table in the back, like instructed, and turn directly to see Aleksander standing in my way. My breath hitches and my reflexes are the only thing that keeps me from dropping the cup in my hand.

"It's been a long time, cousin," he says, letting out a deep sigh. "I didn't think you'd be so ignorant and foolish as to show your face so freely."

Aleksander gestures to the side, indicating to me that he's going to follow wherever I go. Taking a deep breath, I walk toward the back table and slide into the booth facing the door. Aleksander's got a sick smile on his face, like a fox that has a rabbit in its sights. Only he doesn't know that this rabbit has a pack of wolves behind her.

I take a split second to look at my cousin, to feel the weight of the guilt that's been on my soul for years. Ever since I had to skin that man alive, a man who I thought was the one standing before me. I don't know who it was I killed, and the fact that I won't ever know makes me uneasy.

Aleksander is definitely older. The time since I last saw him hasn't been kind. Wrinkles line his eyes and face, his black hair is starting to gray at the temples. He's not the polished and collected man I knew, instead more calculative, more desperate. But his blue eyes, crystal-blue just like mine, can't be mistaken. He's dressed in an inconspicuous way; just jeans and a gray hoodie, and he looks more arrogant now that he seems to think he's caught me.

"Aleksander. What an… unpleasant surprise," I say, sipping my coffee nonchalantly. There's no need for preamble, for acting or hiding. We both know what the other is.

Aleksander stretches an arm out over the top of the booth looking pleased with himself.

"That's him," Bryan says in my ear.

"I have eyes on them both," Trent answers, low and hushed.

I see him shift in his seat, moving his laptop to where I can see the high-definition camera that's watching us.

"I'm on my way to you," Kieron says loudly, the sounds of everything going on outside audible in the background.

"Mila, absolutely nothing is going to happen to you. Keep him talking, and we won't let you out of our sight." Cillian speaks clearly in my ear, and his voice soothes me.

My eyes go to the camera on the ceiling in the corner of the room and I swear I can see it zoom in.

Ding! The bell on the door goes off again and I don't need to move to see Kieron stroll in, his eyes surveying everything casually before they lock on me.

"How'd you find me?" My words come out all scratchy and I take a sip of my coffee.

"It wasn't that difficult." Alexsander shrugs. "Everyone has a web trace. Everyone."

"Cut the bullshit. How are you alive?"

"Careful baby, we don't want him to do something rash," Cillian says nervously.

"That's the million-dollar question, isn't it? How am I alive after you so brutally murdered me, *us*, in cold blood." He sneers, sitting forward, with all traces of arrogance gone. All that remains is fury and vengeance. He threads his fingers together and leans on the table. "After Sergei ordered our execution; the execution of his own sister and her children, *his blood*,"—Each word is spoken with more anger than the one before—"everyone left the room and I bartered. I took the one useful tool he taught me and I negotiated. I lived, but I was in exile. Never to be seen again in Boston. But I had a skill that was useful for him. So he kept tabs on me, forcing me to become what I am now."

Aleksander's jaw ticks as he clenches down. "In exchange for my life, Sergei said I had to work for him from afar. To everyone else, I was dead, but to him, I was his. I did what he wanted, I hacked who he wanted, when and where. I built viruses and bugs to destroy the rival gangs in moments. I kept track of his… wayward assets. The man you so brutally and so heartlessly *murdered*, was a prisoner that had been in the basement for years, rotting away." His blue eyes flicker over me like with obvious disgust. "I wanted nothing more than to kill you both. To see your heads on spikes for what you'd done to my family. It's what's kept me going all these years since I watched you murder my mother and brother. Like it was nothing, like they weren't your family. You could've refused, asked for a different test, but no, you took the one way that you knew would grant you favor." Each of his words are like daggers to my heart, my guilt is threatening to overtake me at each punctuation. It also shows me that Aleksander knew nothing of the threat to my sister. He thinks that I was doing everything just to be favored by our uncle.

"You had no choice, Mila," Cillian whispers, giving me a small piece of light to hang onto.

"You don't know what really happened. I didn't want to, he had my sister. Please, you don't know everything," I say softly, but his hand slams down on the table loudly. I stay seated, rooted to the booth like nothing happened, but I can see Trent white-knuckling the countertop and Kieron's eyes throwing daggers at Aleksander.

The whole shop turns to look at us, but it's like he has nothing to lose, because he keeps talking.

"I know everything I need to. You're a murderer," he sneers, then spits in my direction. "And now, you're going to pay."

"You know that isn't going to happen."

"Why, because you think your Irish husband is going to save you?" Aleksander laughs and it's an unhinged sound. "Come here," he says, motioning with a crooked finger for me to lean closer like he was going to tell me a secret.

I stay where I am.

"No one's coming for you. I have someone working inside the Irish Clan. Someone who works very closely with your husband and who promised me that he, and his little ragtag group, would be busy and unable to come to your aide. That's if he actually wants to help you." He smirks, sitting back in his seat like he's dropped the mic. The implication that Cillian might not love me hits me, irrationally, as my brain tries to tell me that Aleksander is just trying to get under my skin.

"He's just trying to throw you off, babydoll. Don't listen to him.

Don't react. I'm here," Cillian says passionately in my ear, his words soothing the hurt that Aleksander's caused.

"You don't know Cillian," I snap.

Alexsander laughs wickedly again. "Do you? Married in under a year. You're not the smart, infallible *Prizrak* that Sergei always boasted about. You threw yourself at a man hoping he'd take you from your guilt, from your duty to the Bratva, and he will resent you for it. Everyone will come for you, everyone that knows that the *Prizrak,* the Ghost, is real, will come for you with everything they have. What will be of your husband then? Do you think he cares enough for you to fight against the Bratva? No, not at all. You're just a pretty face. And once your looks turn from age and the darkness of your soul, you'll have nothing. No one." Each word calculated and evil, designed to prey on my insecurity and desire to belong. I try to fortify my mental walls and I hope it works so that my face shows him nothing.

"Don't listen to him. You're everything. Everything to me."

"Nothing," Aleksander snarls.

"My world."

"Useless."

"Amazing."

"Evil."

"My savior when I didn't even know I needed one," Cillian says wholeheartedly.

"And I'm going to correct a mistake that was made a long time ago."

"Not here," I blurt out.

"Of course not here." Aleksander rolls his eyes. "Why Uncle chose you to be *Prizrak,* I'll never know. I have no clue on how you've survived this long."

"Why would I go with you anywhere? I'm not as stupid as you think." I take another sip of my latte.

"Because I have my inside man waiting at the ready. He'll kill your husband if you don't. He might not love you, but it's plain as day that you love him."

"You actually got him to believe you'd kill Cillian? Way to go, Bryan," Trent whispers.

I let the fear, the shock, the desperation I feel to have this work show freely on my face.

"No, please. He doesn't know who I am. I'll… I'll go with you. Just leave Cillian alone," I say softly, with faux sobs catching every few words. "Let them all be, they've done nothing wrong."

"Except harbor you. It should've been Los Muertos who tried making a deal with Sergei, but they were too short-sighted, too dim-witted, to see what they had." Aleksander rolls his eyes.

"You told them I was her sister. Why?" I gasp.

"You needed to be brought down a peg." He shrugs. "I wanted you wrecked, mentally and physically, before I end your life. You deserve it. Whatever they did to you and more," he says, hatred behind his eyes.

My jaw drops and I'm finding it very hard to breathe.

He did this.

He manufactured all of this.

All the nights of sleeping on the cold cement floor, shivering in terror that someone was going to come for another round. All the days screaming inside for the pain to stop. All the hours drugged off my ass, trying desperately to say anything but not able to even open my mouth.

It was all because of him.

"I'm going to kill him. Slowly. Painfully. In every single way, big and small, to cause him pain," Cillian snarls in my ear. I almost don't hear him because I'm starting to hyperventilate. *"Baby, breathe. You can't let him get to you."*

Easier said than done.

"Hell, I even gave them some torture ideas. I'm sure I know every little thing they did to you. You're completely ruined." Aleksander leans over the table, speaking the words quietly but with such passion that they seem like they're screamed at me. "You're disgusting."

"Stop," I whisper, closing my eyes and shaking my head.

"Why should I?" He laughs. "The fun is just beginning. Because once you're dead, the entire Bratva will fall to their knees for me. Both you and Uncle will pay for what you've done."

"Trent, Kieron, get her out of there before I come down there and rip his motherfucking head off myself. I swear to god, I'll skin this fucker alive, for real this time, for doing this!" Cillian roars in our ears.

"Just end it," I whisper, closing my eyes and letting my head drop. "I'm done being a part of this. I just want to be done, I'm so tired."

And the sad part is, I *am* tired.

I'm tired of this life. I'm tired of always running. I'm tired of the violence and the treachery. I'm tired of looking over my shoulder and constantly feeling like someone is going to betray me. I'm tired of feeling like the other shoe is going to drop.

I'm tired of being *The Prizrak*. The Ghost.

I'm tired of being Sergei's niece. The oldest female heir.

I'm tired of being targeted.

I'm tired of being Mila Smirnova.

My eyes meet Aleksander's and I see the victory he feels. He thinks he's been successful in breaking me. And truthfully, maybe he has been.

But what he doesn't realize is I'm no longer the woman, the weapon, the assassin with nothing to live for except orders.

I'm Mila Tavish. Russian Bratva by birth, and Irish Clan by choice.

I have a lot to live for now.

"Please." I throw in a whimper, desperate to get out of his presence once and for all.

"Just get him out of there and you'll never have to see him again. Never have to hear his name. I promise," Cillian says.

"Fuck," Kieron swears.

"He promised. You know what that means," Trent says.

I can hear the smile in his voice.

"The demon in Killer is about to come out to play."

"It's going to be a masterpiece," Bryan says, and from his tone I can hear just how angry he is.

I fight back a smile because I realize now that I have a family. Because Cillian chose me and I chose Cillian, they've adopted me too. By doing this, by being okay with going to war for me, by helping protect me, they're choosing me.

Aleksander rolls his eyes and scoffs. "Stop sniffling and get up. Don't even think about running." He pulls out an iPhone with a message already made out to an unsaved, unknown number. "All I have to do is send one text to this number and your precious Cillian is gone. Don't fuck with me."

"I'll come quietly. I know better than to mess with the Bratva. I'm not going to jeopardize Cillian's life," I say, rising to my feet.

"Go back toward the front door, go back to the Irish lobby and we'll go from there," he snaps, heading toward the door. It's not until he reaches the front of the coffee shop that he turns around, shakes the iPhone at me with a sick smile, and walks in the direction he told me to go.

"Well, at least this will be an easy clean-up," Kieron says. *"Cillian?"*

"Already on my way."

I move quickly through the shop, walking back out into the city air, and nearly run to headquarters. The sooner Aleksander grabs me, the sooner this will all be over. I hear footsteps behind me, and I know without turning that the guys are trying to stay close enough, without their covers.

I rip open the door and the air conditioning blasts me in the face. It's dark in the lobby, and Aleksander is nowhere to be found.

Feeling his presence before I see him, I grab the arm going for my neck and twist it around his body, behind his back and angle it up, hard. So hard, I hear a pop.

"You said you'd come quietly," Aleksander sneers.

A shadow moves behind him; a suit and familiar, yet unfamiliar beardless face. A silencer is pointed at the base of Aleksander's skull.

"And you must be stupid to believe that she wouldn't have backup," Bryan snaps.

Aleksander's nostrils flare with anger and his fists clench at his sides as his eyes dart around. He's trying to figure out a way out of here.

"You were wrong, Aleksander," I say just as Cillian comes running from the elevator. "You're wrong about a lot of things. But I will say you showed me something about myself I didn't know."

Trent and Kieron walk in, drawing their guns. Trent's backing us up in case Aleksander decided he needed backup other than his 'insider' who wasn't really on his side, and Kieron keeps his sights on Aleksander.

"You showed me that I'm done with this life. That I don't ever want to be, or have ties to, Mila Smirnova again. That with your death, I don't ever have to be that person again. I can be Mila Tavish. My own person," I say, letting a deep breath leave my lungs. With that exhale, it's as if every bad thing falls away. Cillian's staring at me over Aleksander's shoulder and in the midst of all the chaos and danger, he smiles.

He knows.

Of course he does.

Because he gets me.

"You think you can just decide to be done and walk away? That isn't how it happens. You'll never be free. Ever. The Bratva will never let you go," Aleksander snaps, each word fighting for the same hatred and confidence, but instead coming across desperate. Like he wishes he could get away too.

"If she wants out, she'll get out," Cillian vows. "That woman is my wife, *my wife*, and whatever she wants, she gets. If she's saying she wants to never be a part of the Bratva again, then I'll make that happen."

"Regardless, Aleksander," Kieron says, stepping closer to him, gun still raised. "You won't be alive to see it."

And with that, Bryan lifts his hand and pistol-whips Aleksander on the back of his head, sending him promptly to the ground.

The Basement

Cillian

After getting Mila secured in my apartment with a cup of tea, a pizza and the remote, I triple-check the lock on the front door and leave to meet the boys in The Basement.

I want to stay with her and make sure she's okay emotionally, but I have promises to keep. Pain to inflict.

When I brought up leaving Aleksander to Kieron, Bryan and Trent, Mila immediately told me that she would feel better knowing that I was there, to know without a doubt that he's gone.

After all she's gone through, I can understand that. And if it brings her a little peace, I'll do it.

I get on the elevator and hit the button for bottom floor, sub-level 6. That's the technical last floor of the building... legally. On the blueprints there are only six sub-levels, but in reality there are closer to ten. Kellan made sure when he built it that The Basement was off the records in each and every way.

The Basement is where nightmares are realized. It's the dark and scary underground that's filled with monsters, demons, creatures that lurk, and the thing that's hiding under your bed. There are at least twenty rooms, all designed specifically for maximum discomfort and torture. Then there's the dungeon. The first step for all our "guests".

I step off the elevator at sub-level 6, and it's just another parking garage, filled with cars for the other members that work and live in the building. Moving through the cement-and-steel space, I quickly move to the back wall that's lined with storage shelves. Opening up the third cabinet, in the second drawer, I pull up on the first screwdriver and the hinges for the fake door release with an audible hiss. I return the shelves and drawer to the way they were, and open the door that is camouflaged with industrial shelves, closing it behind me.

Submerged in darkness, I hear the click of the generator for the motion sensors and light by light flickers on illuminating the descent to hell.

As I descend the narrow staircase, each step echoes in the dimly lit corridor, the sound reverberating off the cold, concrete walls. At the bottom, a steel door looms. The only other thing is the keypad embedded into the wall next to it. The faint glow of the display casts an eerie light against the metallic surface. Reaching out, I enter my code quickly, eager to get inside and get justice for Mila.

With a heavy metallic groan, the steel door before me begins to slide open, revealing a dimly lit, empty room. Kieron, Trent and Bryan, are all changed out of their disguises and back into their regular clothes, standing in a loose circle talking. Whatever they're talking about, Kieron does not look pleased. His arms are crossed tightly over his chest with his skin stretched taut over his knuckles as he clenches his fists. With his beard cut so short for the trap, I can see how he's grinding his teeth and how his nostrils flare with anger. Trent is talking in hushed tones, his hands moving quickly in front of him and it looks like he's trying to calm Kieron down. As usual, Bryan is quiet, standing off to the side with his chin in between his forefinger and thumb as he thinks.

"What's wrong?" My voice echoes through the room. All three sets of eyes turn to face me, with varying degrees of concern.

"Technically, nothing is wrong." Trent shrugs.

"But…"

"But, Aleksander had a cyanide pill somewhere on his person and he took it before we could get him talking," Kieron snaps.

My eyes widen with understanding. "No."

"I'm sorry, Killer," Kieron says, walking over to me. "He dropped dead as soon as we closed the door behind him."

Looking at each of them, I can see that it's true, but I need to see for myself. I turn to the one steel door that holds inside of it another room we call 'the dungeon'. It serves as a place to hold our captives and begin the psychological torture. A place to break them down before the real fun begins. It's exactly what it sounds like: a wall of metal bars, the room encased in cement blocks, a leaky wooden bucket for piss and shit, and a cot in the corner. But instead of being greeted with Aleksander's smug face lined with worry and fear at what is coming, I see him lying facedown on the cement floor. Not breathing. Dead.

Fuck. *Fuck.* "Goddamnit!" I roar, hitting the bars. I look closer at the body, making sure it's not a goddamn ploy, and I can see the foam around his mouth and how he'd pissed his pants.

Fucker took the coward's way out.

"I'm sorry," Kieron says. "At the very least though, he's gone. He can't hurt her again."

"But do we know that he didn't have anything planned? Do we know that he didn't dump all the information on the dark web? Do we know what he'd planned on telling Sergei? No! We don't. Now, we just have to wait and hope that nothing else is going to happen." I run my fingers through my hair and storm out of the dungeon.

"You need to look on the dark web and make sure he didn't do anything before he killed himself. Hurry," I tell Bryan, ordering him around like I'm the Second-In-Command, but Kieron doesn't say anything.

Bryan takes his phone out of his jacket pocket and starts tapping away.

"You guys, we need to prepare for when the Bratva comes to our doorstep. All we know is that Aleksander was forced to work for Sergei, for cyber warfare, and he had a vendetta for Mila, and he knew who she was, what she did. That means—"

"Wait," Bryan says, holding his hand up. His eyes are still glued to the screen. "He... he didn't do anything."

"What?" I ask, a flicker of hope that Mila's identity and the Clan are safe.

"By the time you're reading this, I'll already be dead," Bryan reads from his phone. "He sent me a note to the dark web account. It's time-stamped right before we brought him down. I thought we took his phone." Bryan looks at Trent, who nods.

"I did," Trent says, holding up a burner phone. "I even frisked him to make sure he wasn't packing anything else. Wait..." Trent starts patting himself down frantically. "He took my phone."

"What does it say?" Kieron cuts in.

"By the time you're reading this, I'll be dead. I know now that the person I had thought turned from the Clan, you, was simply using me like I'd hoped to do to you. Normally, I'd be furious and retaliate, but something my cousin said struck a chord with me.

She said she was tired.

That she didn't want to be a Smirnova any more.

And was willing to die to be free of all the pain.

I knew you would never let me see the light of day again. I knew exactly what was going to happen to me. I know this foils your plans, but I want to go out my way. I've spent too much of my life being controlled.

I'm tired.

I don't want to be a Smirnov in any way anymore either.

I want to be done.

Mila killed my family, but I see now that I've been manipulated by my Uncle just as she was. I've set the files to delete and I've forwarded you all the accounts on the Bratva I've compiled. Let Mila be free and make sure our Uncle suffers for us both. Now I can finally rest."

Bryan finishes reading and looks at me in shock.

"This can't be real, can it?" Trent asks.

I'm feeling the same way. It's too good to be true, too much to hope for.

"Look, all the files are downloading to my external server right now," Bryan says, holding his phone up to show the code lining the screen over and over.

My jaw has dropped and I'm almost too scared to hope. I look at Kieron, hoping that he can help me make sense of it all. He looks just as stunned as I do.

Clapping me on the shoulder, he turns me so I'm looking at him. "Pain makes people do unexplainable things."

"Holy fuck, he's got so much dirt on Sergei that we can bury him for the rest of his life. He won't make another dime if we don't say it. He won't live to see tomorrow if we don't want him to. Oh my god," Bryan gushes, sifting through the code on his phone. Each file he opens makes his eyes widen even more. "We can fucking shut the Bratva down for good if we want to."

Kieron looks at me, one eyebrow cocked and a question clear in his eyes.

"I need to talk to Mila."

* * *

The guys had asked to be there when I told Mila what happened. They are genuinely concerned about how she'll take it, and it warms my heart that they care about my girl so much. That they care for Mila as a sister-in-law, enough to be there when she hears hard news. That they care about me enough to embrace her with open arms.

Bryan holds back the whole way to my apartment, not saying much, but still showing his support the best way he can. I appreciate whatever he can stand, I'm not going to push him.

The herd of us walk in, footsteps echoing against the tile and Bryan slams the door shut behind him. Mila jumps from the couch, ready to throw hands. She had clearly been napping. Her eyes are hooded with sleep and her shirt is askew.

"It's just us, doll," I say with a smile. "You can lay back down."

Mila sighs in relief, her hands slowly dropping from in front of her. Standing up straight, she sees the guys behind me and her eyes widen. "What happened? Where is he?"

"That's actually what we wanted to talk about, Mila. Would you like to sit down?" Kieron steps forward, trying to be diplomatic. His tone is reminiscent of when he speaks to other figureheads.

Her gaze jumps to where he's gesturing for her to sit, back in her rumpled-up nest I made for her on the couch, and then snap back to me. "Cillian?"

"Something happened," I tell her honestly. "Aleksander killed himself. It looks like he popped a cyanide pill before we got him to talk more. Or at all." I don't mince words or beat around the bush. She wants to know, and I'm not going sugar coat it because I want to soften the blow.

"What?" The word leaves her like a breath.

"I wasn't actually there when he died, but I saw the body. Foam at the mouth, urination all over, he wasn't breathing, no heartbeat. We all checked."

After Kieron and I left the dungeon, I'd asked the other two to make sure that there was no way he was somehow faking it. But he really had died.

"What did he do?" she asks, terror evident in her eyes. "Everyone knows I'm the Ghost, don't they? Oh god, I need to get out of the city." She starts speaking fast. Almost too fast for any of us to hear, but she goes on and on like she's in a trace; planning and spiraling, worrying and plotting.

I watch her for a second before I grab her biceps roughly in my hands and shake her out of it. "Mila, Mila, come on."

"I have to leave, Cillian. So many people are coming after

me. Dangerous, dangerous people. Worse than my Uncle. Worse than Aleksander." Her eyes lock with mine.

"He didn't expose your identity," I say softly.

"What?" she asks again, incredulously. "Of course he did, why wouldn't he? It's the perfect revenge."

"It seems he had a change of heart at the last moment." Kissing her forehead, I can't resist pulling her in for a quick hug. I need it maybe more than she does. Feeling her warmth and heartbeat proves to me that she's alive and well. "He sent Bryan a letter."

"He figured out you betrayed him?" Worried, she looks around my side to where Bryan is standing awkwardly by the door, leaning on the wall.

"He did." Bryan shrugs. "But he also deleted your file. Mila Smirnova doesn't exist according to the internet and there is absolutely no mention anywhere of the Ghost." He puts his hands in his pockets, one of them pulling out the cell phone. "He sent us every single file he compiled on the Bratva and a letter, too."

"A letter?"

Bryan holds the phone out for her to take. Mila slowly reaches out, looking at the device as if it's going to grow hands and attack her like Aleksander tried to. Her hands shake ever so slightly as she holds it.

"You should read it," Bryan says gruffly.

Mila nods absently, her eyes never leaving the phone. "I'm, uh, I'm going to go to the bedroom," she tells us, walking away slowly. Once the door closes, I turn to the guys.

"Well, that could've gone worse." Shaking my head, I head to the kitchen. "I need caffeine and liquor. Anyone want anything?"

* * *

Mila

"I'm tired," he'd written. *"I'm done."*

How many times had I thought about suicide just to end the torment? Hundreds? Thousands of times? I'd contemplated suicide every day while I was being tortured by Los Muertos, but never let that part of myself win. I'd never come close. I fought. Over and over again, I fought for myself.

But Aleksander realized he was wrong and instead of reuniting, he used my words and decided to fucking die?

I… I feel sick to my stomach. The guilt I felt before is *nothing* compared to how I feel now.

For someone who's killed her fair share of people, I should be used to the feeling of death. Of bringing death to people who may or may not have deserved it. But Aleksander using my words as the ones that resonated with him, the ones that convinced him he was done living… it strikes me down.

I fall to the floor, my heart beating too fast and my stomach twisting in knots. I don't know how I can live like this. With this knowledge. That I was responsible for this, when maybe after talking with him I could've helped him. It's the knowledge that things could've worked out positively, that I could have had a family member by my side, but this happened instead.

"Oh, Aleks…" I whisper. Tears prick my eyes and begin to fall. I don't stop them as they drip steadily down my face.

A soft knock sounds on my door. "Mila?"

Surprisingly, it's Trent that's at the door. I hastily wipe my eyes and call for him to come in.

"How are you doing?" he asks kindly, sitting on the edge of the bed that's still rumpled and unmade from the nap Cillian and I had in the early hours of the morning. Had that really just been earlier today?

A sob starts to build in my throat, but I try to swallow it down. "I'm okay."

"Really?" He looks at me so sincerely, like he actually cares, like he actually understands.

The sob rips from my throat uncontrollably.

I watch as he shifts uncomfortably in his seat, his eyes darting quickly around the room as if he's searching for an escape route. I can see the concern etched across his face. His brows furrow with worry.

"Do you want to talk about it?" he asks, scooting closer.

It's clear to see that his movements are hesitant, as if he's afraid of intruding on my space. I try to catch my breath as his words hang in the air between us like a lifeline.

"I just… it's been a rough day," I say, my voice wobbly.

He nods slowly.

Another lump forms in my throat as the events of today, of the last eight months, the last… lifetime, all catch up with me. I shake my head, unable to find the words to articulate the storm of different emotions raging inside me. But his presence alone is comforting, a silent reassurance that I'm not alone in my pain.

He reaches out, his hand hovering in the air before gently resting on my shoulder. The warmth of his touch is a soothing balm to my wounded soul, and I can't help but lean into it, seeking a moment of peace.

"I'm here for you, we all are," he whispers, his voice barely above a breath.

And in that moment, I know that even in the midst of my tears, I am surrounded by the unwavering support of a true friend.

"Thank you," I say brokenly.

"This isn't your fault. I know it feels like it at this moment, but it isn't," he says. "I was in a situation similar to this back when I was undercover in the Italian Mob."

"Really?"

Trent nods, and explains, "I had to prove myself to them… in the worst way I could think of. It really fucked me up. I couldn't get myself out from under the weight of my guilt. I pretty much drank until I was blackout drunk, day in and day out, to keep myself numb."

"How'd you get through it?" Wiping my eyes, I look at Trent. At this man who has been through so much, and is still willing to sit with me and share his story, even if it's painful.

Trent scratches his head absentmindedly and sighs. "In the beginning it was drinking. Partying would keep my body and mind busy so I couldn't think about it. But that didn't work for long. The nightmares became too much, and the guilt was about to suffocate me. I eventually stopped checking in with Kieron and that's when he'd had enough of my wallowing. Funny enough, that's when he sent me on a mission to guard his sister-in-law."

"How did that help?"

"Because looking after her forced me to be vigilant. I had to be on the lookout and on point to keep her safe. In the beginning it was just a job, then it turned deeper and I had to keep her safe because she was my girl. I wanted to be better for her, and after I told her everything, I felt like there was someone in my corner. Someone who supported me when I needed it most. She supports me and helps me through my guilt every single day. It's never going to go away, this feeling, but it will lessen over time. Let people help you, and don't try to numb the pain."

"But it's all my fault." The weight of my words sit like a weight on my chest making it hard to breathe.

"It's not. It's not your fault." Trent takes my hand and holds it in his. He takes an uneasy deep breath. "Just like it wasn't mine."

I watch as his eyes turn haunted and get misty. Squeezing his hand, I give him a tight-lipped smile. A hard one, but genuine nonetheless.

"Thank you," I whisper, my voice hoarse. It's very obvious I'm holding back tears.

"No problem." Trent nudges my shoulder with his and slaps his hands on his thighs before pushing up off the bed. He coughs, wiping his eyes with his thumb and forefinger roughly before putting his hands on his hips. "Take your time, but I think Kieron wants to talk to you before we leave. I'm also very sure that Cillian wanted to kick us out the moment you walked in here."

I'm sure he did. My man is nothing if not protective.

I let out a loud laugh and stand up. "I'm sure he did. He's a good man, and a great partner."

Trent smiles fondly. "That's really good to hear. Shall we?" He holds out his elbow for me to take.

After a beat, I slide my hand through. "After you."

* * *

When Trent and I walk back into the living room, it's painfully obvious that they all heard me cry. Kieron purses his lips and nods, looking away from me and to Bryan. A clear sign he's moving on and not going to draw attention to me, which I'm very thankful for. Bryan doesn't look at Kieron though, he's staring right at me.

It's clear as day to see the turmoil swirling within his eyes. There is a depth of sorrow there, an undeniable weight pressing down on his shoulders. He's carrying the burden of regret, and it's etched into the lines of his weary face. I can sense his guilt, it's almost palpable in the air around us. It hangs between us across the room like a heavy fog, thick and suffocating. And yet, despite it all, there is something else there too—a longing, a desire that he's tried so hard to conceal.

A longing for something that I can't give him. At least not yet. Forgiveness.

Cillian comes up to me, pulling me out of the awkward tension with Bryan, and wraps me in his arms tightly. In that one move, I feel at home. Like I can breathe again.

I hug him back, holding him as tightly as I can. I may not have much anymore; no family, no connections, hell, no real name, but I have him. I have Cillian. And that's more than enough. Whatever happens, we'll face it together like we have everything else. He'll be the one to catch me when I fall.

"I don't think I should be saying that I'm sorry he's gone seeing as I was literally going to kill him myself, but I'm sorry you're sad," he whispers, kissing my forehead.

"It's a lot." I shrug.

"I know."

"So what do we do from here?" Trent asks, putting his hands in his pockets.

We all look to Kieron, who sighs and rubs his forehead.

"I have to give this over to Kellan. There's so much blackmail here, we can basically have the Bratva do whatever we want. I really don't know what he's going to want to do."

"I know what we have to do," I say. There's only one option here. Only one way to go.

I owe it to myself, to Aleksander, to everyone that's been squashed under Sergei's hand.

"We're going to take down the Bratva."

The Takedown

Mila

"I don't care how it happens. I don't care what assets Kellan or you guys want. I just want Sergei dead, and the Bratva taken down. For good." My mind's made up and the need for justice is surging through my body so strongly it's overwhelming. "And I want him to be the one to kill him."

And maybe I'm feeling a little bloodthirsty.

Cillian smirks, pulling me in tighter to his side and holding me to him with a big, possessive grip on my hip. Claiming me for everyone to see as if I wasn't fully, legally married to him and he thought I might run away.

The guys all look at each other, but my gaze is on Kieron. He's the one that would be able to grant me this. He's watching me right back, but his expression is utterly unreadable as he considers my request. Time stands still as I wait with bated breath, and my heart hammering in my ears.

I need this. I need to see the demise of an evil, corrupted man, a man no different than the ones he made me kill for him. Maybe that makes me just as evil, but I'm willing to spend the rest of my life trying to be better. How can I do that if I don't rid the world of him first?

At long last, Kieron crosses his arms over his chest, takes a deep breath, and nods. A measured, deliberate, shake of his head tells me that he agrees to my terms. He holds a hand out for me and as we shake, I know we have a mutual respect and understanding. I'm giving him and his this complete control and power, and he's giving me the ability to return my life back to myself.

"I'll have to tell Kellan," he says.

I nod. "I know. You tell him he can have whatever he wants, do whatever he wants to the organization. Keep my sister alive, send her off somewhere safe, but I don't care about the rest."

"Really? That's millions, potentially *billions,* that you're giving to him. To us, to the Clan. Not to mention power. You could be the next Tsarina of the Bratva." Kieron furrows his eyebrows, looking at me somewhat skeptically.

"I don't care about money. I never have. And I definitely don't want that power. Fuck no." I step back next to Cillian, wrapping my arm around his waist and looking up at him. I have everything I want, or I will, soon. "I just want to be free to be myself."

"Okay then." Kieron claps his hands together loudly as a big toothy smile forms on his face. "This is going to be great."

* * *

Two weeks later...

As per my request, Kieron, Cillian, Trent and Bryan didn't tell me anything about the business side of the takedown, but there were whisperings. I would walk around the building and hear of how the Clan acquired five new businesses from the Bratva. The next day it would be that the Irish moved their boundary lines further into Russian territory. The next it was how the Clan took over the vendors and dealers from the Bratva, costing them hundreds of thousands in product. They were slowly but surely taking over. It was smart how they decided to go about it. It happened slow enough that no one was the wiser.

I'm sure Sergei's life is on fire, stressful and awful, as everything he's worked so hard for is being ripped from him piece by piece. And worse, given to his enemy.

The thought almost makes me smile.

I'd decided to take my time killing Sergei. I wanted him to see his life go up in flames before ending it. And tonight is the night.

For the last time, I don my *Prizrak* gear: a black bodysuit that covers me from head to toe, with a thin layer of carbon-fiber plates sewn into pockets across the suit to give me protection while still allowing for movement. It has a mask that covers my face, head, and neck, and special eyewear that lets me see in the dark and in infrared. It was designed so that not a single inch of my skin is showing. No showing skin means no DNA or prints.

The suit itself holds twelve knives; four across my shoulders, two on my hips, a knife strapped to each thigh and each ankle with two on my forearms. It was created to be as stealthy as possible, but also provide the maximum amount of fatalness possible. In the darkness, you'd never know I was coming for you. No sound, no movement, no scent. Just steel.

I fucking hate it. It's suffocating. The weight of the pressure and guilt when I wear it is too much for me now.

One last time though.

"Mila, are you—" Cillian swings the bedroom door and stops in his tracks when he sees me. "Tonight's the night?"

I nod, slowly.

"No wonder they call you The Ghost. You look like something straight out of a nightmare."

"Thanks, baby," I say, rolling my eyes. My voice is muffled and quieted by the mask, but he hears me.

"That's what the *Prizrak* is meant to be though, a nightmare."

"Not anymore. After tonight, it really will just be a ghost story."

Cillian steps forward and puts his hands on my shoulders. "Go take care of business and come home to me. I'll be waiting in bed for you," he says, whispering the last part in my ear before kissing my temple and stepping back.

A shiver runs down my spine in anticipation as I open the window and slip out into the night. Like a ghost ready to haunt Sergei to his unmarked grave.

* * *

Slipping through the compound Sergei had built for himself isn't hard to do. I grew up there, so I know the ins and outs. Not to mention that I'd spent the last two weeks going over every detail in my head, to make sure I didn't inadvertently alert anyone in any way that I was back.

I stand at the edge of the treeline, bathed in shadows as I look at the place of horror. The moon is full tonight so I have plenty of light to see without needing to turn on my mask. I hide in the shadows, peering through the dense foliage at the imposing mansion. A shiver of anticipation runs down my spine. Every window is dark, meaning that hopefully, everyone inside is asleep. The dead of night keeps my cover as I sleuth through the small clearing toward the mansion. I know this place is heavily guarded, its security measures designed to keep its occupants safe from people like me. But I've spent my whole life doing this. Living, moving, and breathing in darkness.

I run to the brick perimeter of the estate and press my back to it, hiding from the cameras in a shadow. Sergei has them everywhere, but I pay very close attention to the blind spots and watch as they rotate, trying to catch every angle. When the camera across from me rotates to show where I'm standing, I slip underneath it and stay completely hidden. The only sound is the wind blowing softly, whistling in the trees.

I know that Sergei sleeps in the northwest room, the master suite. Thankfully, the shadows from the moonlight cover the entirety of that side of the mansion. Perfect.

His room has massive windows that are great for this purpose. The one window I'm able to lockpick is right next to the drainpipe I can climb up. My gloves help my traction as I start to climb, and the only sound is a small groan from the metal as I ascend. His room is on the second floor, so when I get to the right height, I toe the small ledge and hold myself to the wall with my fingertips and toes. No matter how strenuous it is, how much it hurts, how much my muscles burn, I can't make a noise. Not a groan, not a sigh, not even too loud of a breath.

The sweat starts to build under my mask, but I keep holding. Transferring all my weight to one hand, I take out the knife hidden in my forearm sheath and slip it under the frame, slicing through roughly.

Clink!

I don't move, I keep still even under the strain, and hold my breath.

Nothing happens for a few moments, except the mechanical sound of the automatic rotation of the cameras right below me. Mentally breathing easy, I return my knife back to its sheath, then slowly, silently, slide the window up just enough for me to slip inside.

I close it behind me, leaving it open mere centimeters so that the cameras don't pick up on the open window and the wind doesn't alert anyone inside.

With a deep breath, I step forward. Each of my movements are cautious and deliberate. Sneaking swiftly into the room, shadows and darkness surround me.

He sure does like to pretend he's royalty. His decor is just as bad. It is all dark red, dark mahogany wood, and golden fixtures. It looks like he held up a picture of the inside of Buckingham Palace and said, 'I want my room to look like this'.

What a fucking joke.

In the middle of the grand room, there's an extra-large bed with dark wooden bed posts and golden knobs. In the middle, there is one lone figure breathing deeply. I step onto a shag carpet that covers most of the hardwood flooring. I can be a bit quicker with my movements as the carpet absorbs most of my sound. The figure on the bed is moving up and down slightly with every breath, in deep sleep, based on the length of inhale.

Perfect.

Softly, I slide onto the bed, being careful not to disrupt the covers or pull on the sheets until I'm at the same level as my uncle. He's sleeping deeply, albeit snoring, and he looks anything but peaceful. His eyebrows are furrowed, the lines of his face seem even deeper than they were last I saw him. Everything that has happened since Aleksander died looks to have aged him decades in the span of weeks. Even in sleep, he looks evil. The man of my nightmares who started me on this awful path. The man who only cares for people if they can be of use to him. The man who cares for no one's happiness but his own. The man who morphed me into this monster.

I pull the knife from my right thigh holster out. It's the sharpest one I own, and I look on in satisfaction as the moonlight shines off the steel. With one motion, I slide the tip of my knife into the side of his neck, making sure to hit the carotid artery. He'll bleed out in minutes.

The moment the knife is embedded in his neck, Sergei's eyes snap open in fear and pain. They're wild and frightened, frantically searching for what's caused him to wake up. Slinking back, I leave the knife in place. Watching the blood seep from the wound gives me an odd feeling, one I can't place just yet.

Sergei's hand slips up to his neck, and I can tell he almost thinks that it's a nightmare. That it's just a phantom pain. Until his fingers touch the hilt.

Just like I knew he would, he pulls the dagger from his neck and looks at it in confusion. When his brain connects what happened to what is going to happen, he tries to scream for help.

But he can't. I made sure to slice his vocal chords as well. It's amazing how precise you can get when your victim isn't moving.

He's got maybe ten seconds left before his entire life force flows out of him, slipping from the wound on his neck and spraying across the bed. I step into his line of sight slowly, moving with precision and fluidity. Like a Ghost from his nightmares.

Recognition lights his eyes, an understanding that it is *me* that's brought him his death. His personal little assassin that he sent out to kill those who he deemed worthy, come back to kill him.

"Nug, nnnuuuggg." He tries to speak, but it's too guttural, too soft, for anyone to hear anything. His last words are full of fear and despair, all because of me.

I watch with a morbid smile as the fear never leaves his eyes, even as the light behind them fades. It brings me a sense of justice for Aleksander that Sergei died feeling scared. Feeling played and betrayed.

I wait an extra minute before I check his pulse. The blood has stopped flowing from the hole in his neck, and when I check his wrist, there's nothing there. Prying back his fingers from his death-grip on my dagger, I run to the other side of the bed where the back of his head is visible. It's easy and quick work slicing an inch by inch square from the middle of his skull, ensuring hair follicles are still attached. It's almost like riding a bike.

Normally, I would have to carry this little disgusting piece of scalp with me and bring it to Sergei, proving that I'd done my job and that I deserved to live another day. But instead, I put the piece in his own hand. Let whoever finds him figure that out.

I wipe my dagger on a section of the duvet that is clean, making sure to get the last piece of that disgusting animal off me, and slide the knife back into its sheath.

Leaving the way I came, I relock the window and shimmy down the drain pipe once again. The cameras automatically rotate and it gives me a window to run to the treeline, immersing myself in the protective shadows.

I did it. I fucking did it.

It's over now.

It's well and truly over.

* * *

Slipping back into the open window of Cillian's apartment, I see that he's been true to his word and is waiting in bed for me.

Asleep.

I turn around silently, close the window and take my first free deep breath, letting it out in a sigh of relief.

He's safe. I'm safe. We're safe. I immediately feel all my muscles unclench for the first time in years. All the monsters are gone.

I need a shower, maybe two, to get all of the guilt and blood off of me. Moving quietly into the bathroom I start to undress.

The mask drops to the floor, followed by my arm pieces, then my boots. And finally my bodysuit falls to the floor with an audible thud. I'm going to burn it all. Melt down my knives. I never want to see any of it ever again.

Reaching into the shower, I turn it to scalding. I want my body to be sanitized and stripped of every bad thing I've ever done or had done to me. I want to be clean and new moving forward. The room starts to fog and the shower calls my name. Stepping under the hot water is heavenly. Amazing. The most relaxed I've ever been.

"How long have you been home?" Cillian's gruff, sleep-filled voice sounds on the other side of the shower curtain.

"Not long." I grab the bottle of shampoo and start to lather my hair, the green-apple scent filling the warm air.

"Are you okay?"

"Never better," I say with a smile that he can't see.

"Did it… did it go the way you wanted?"

The shower curtain opens suddenly and with it the cold air barrels in.

My nipples harden at the cold and it doesn't escape Cillian's attention. His gaze settles on my breasts.

"It did."

"Do you want to talk about it?" He leans against the wall, arms crossed over his shirtless chest, so I can see him, but still shower.

"There's nothing to talk about really. He got the death he deserved. The one that he never wanted." I lean back, and let the hot water wash the shampoo away. When I open my eyes, Cillian is looking at me expectantly. "What?"

"How'd you do it?"

"Dagger to the jugular, slicing through the carotid artery

and vocal chords in one motion. Bled out in minutes," I say, shrugging my shoulders. Continuing to rinse off my past, I let the hot water roll off my shoulders, drip down my chest, and cleanse my body of the darkness that's taken over my life.

"Nice. Simple. I like it." Cillian smirks, kicking off the wall to stand.

"Easy. Messy," I say. "Then I left the *Prizrak* calling card in his hand."

He nods in appreciation and I find it so odd that we both are talking about death and gruesome horrors, things that will damn our soul, as if it's nothing. An accomplishment to be congratulated on.

We're definitely going to hell.

But at least we're going together, him and I.

"I waited for you in bed, like I promised, but I got a little tired," he says plainly. "I'm going to let you get all clean, so we can get dirty." Cillian winks at me and walks out, leaving me turned on.

Rolling my eyes with a smile on my face, I make quick work of the rest of my shower.

I have a sudden, very strong need to get to bed.

* * *

I open the bathroom door and the steam rolls out around me. I'm shaking the water out of my hair with a towel and another wrapped around my body.

I feel refreshed and clean, in more ways than one.

I'm Mila Tavish, through and through now. And I couldn't

be fucking happier. Despite everything, a smile hasn't left my face since I returned.

"God, your smile is beautiful." Cillian sighs. He's sitting on the end of the bed, hands on his knees as he looks me over. "You're beautiful."

"Thank you." His words touch my heart, making my confidence soar. "You're beautiful, too. And I don't just mean your looks." I step closer to him and his hands immediately reach out to hold my waist, as he rests his chin on my chest.

"I didn't mean just yours either." His eyes lock onto mine and I see how much he loves me, how much he believes the words he says.

Cupping his cheeks, I whisper, "Kiss me."

"Always," he says with enough passion to knock me over before surging up from the bed and taking my lips with his. This kiss is full of love, full of acceptance, full of excitement. This is it: The rest of our lives, and I'm so grateful.

Cillian picks me up and throws me on the bed, ripping my towel off in the process. I bounce on the soft mattress.

"I want to take your mind off of everything but pleasure. You just lay back and *feel.*" He prowls forward, slipping his underwear off before getting on the bed himself. His face slowly lowers to my flat belly, and he presses a kiss on my belly button. "Please."

It's the 'please' that really gets me. That takes my breath away.

I nod, my eyes never leaving his. "Thank you," I say softly. His returning smile takes my breath away as his hot breath warms the skin of my lower belly as he moves lower. And lower.

My breath hitches as he flattens his tongue and expertly

slips it between my folds, instantly finding my clit.

"Oh fuck," I hiss, arching my back to push my pussy into his face.

He slips his tongue down lower and plunges it in, twisting and curling to make sure he gets a good taste of me. His fingers graze my inner thigh until they reach my lips and two slip inside me.

"Cillian!" I cry as he angles them up slightly, making sure to hit all the delicious dark places inside me with each pass. "More, please, more," I gasp.

"As you wish, babydoll," he says against my cunt with a wet, sloppy smirk. I can see my wetness covering his chin and beard. He's going to smell my cum with every breath he takes until he washes off.

That thought drives me wild. He's mine, and he'll know it until the end of his days.

Cillian crooks his fingers and starts to slide them in and out shallowly, teasingly. Just enough to drive me freaking wild.

"Deeper," I moan, turning my face into the pillow.

"I like it right here," he says, not letting me change his tempo or mind.

"Cillian," I groan, pushing my hips up to try to force his fingers deeper.

He pushes my hips down with his other hand.

"Tsk, tsk, tsk." He shakes his head and moves positions so he's able to see both my face and my pussy at the same time. It must be a better angle because he gets more sure with each thrust. Each thrust of his fingers gets slightly deeper, slightly more forceful, until he's fingering me fast and hard, and I feel like I'm going to explode. I lift my hips up and he counteracts that with his hand over my lower belly.

"Holy fuck." I start to sweat. It's all too much. "Shit, shit, shit." My voice is getting louder and louder, but I could care less.

"Come on, baby. Give it to me. Let me taste your squirt, come on." He's talking as roughly as he is fingering me and it's devastatingly attractive. The fact that he wants me to spray him again…

"Let go, Mila," he whispers in a groan.

I can feel myself come with his words and scream out my release. My eyes close, my fingers grip the comforter and my heels push down even harder as my spine goes rigid.

I can feel the cum cover my thighs and Cillian moves on the bed to be directly in between them, putting his face right at the apex of my legs.

"Yes, that's it," he moans.

I open my eyes as I'm coming down, to see what I've done to him.

And that image is going right into my mental spank-bank. I'm going to want to repeat this to get him looking like that again and again, over and over.

Cillian's face is dripping wet from his forehead to his chin, drops of *me* slipping down the hair of his beard that he hasn't shaved off yet. His eyes are bright and feral, like he wants to take a bite of me. His breathing is rough and quick, like mine is, like he's just finished running a race. And as he sees me staring at him, he slowly and deliberately licks his lips.

If I hadn't just come, that would've made me. For sure.

"Come here," I groan, pulling him to me.Threading his fingers through his longer hair, I crush my mouth to his.

He pulls back and looks at me with dark eyes. "You like the taste of yourself, don't you? It's so fucking sweet, I love it."

He drives me crazy.

I must drive him crazy too because his cock is so hard I can feel it throbbing against my core, begging for entrance.

"Fuck me bare. Please," I whisper in his ear.

My words have an immediate effect on him because my man wastes no time thrusting his magnificent cock inside me. I'm so wet and so made for him that it just takes one thrust for him to be inside me completely.

We both moan, holding onto each other tighter as a shiver rolls through us.

"I've been wanting to do this from day one. Every time." He groans in my ear, pulling out and pushing in slowly, shallowly. Never pulling out fully.

"Yes," I moan softly. My voice is breathy and broken with each thrust. I'm still sensitive as fuck from my first orgasm and I can feel a second quickly approaching.

He snaps his hips hard enough that the breath is knocked out of me. "Tell me you want this."

"I want this."

"Tell me you're going to come for me again."

I moan as his fingers slip between us and he starts to rub at my clit.

"I'm definitely going to come for you again."

"Tell me you're mine," he grunts, his hips snapping into mine faster. The sheer power behind each thrust is making the bed squeak.

Grabbing his toned, sexy-as-fuck ass, I bite down on his neck and lick over the spot softly to soothe the pain.

He groans and his head drops to my chest for a split second before he lifts it and looks into my eyes. "Say it, Mila. Say you're mine and that I'm yours. That you want this, you want me." His dark-chocolate eyes are pleading with me, but there's an undercurrent running in the golden flecks.

"I'm yours," I say, dragging his head down to mine and kissing him sloppily. "And you're mine. Forever."

He kisses me deeper, our mouths moving together to create something dynamic instead of fighting for dominance. We know where we stand now, what we are, what we like.

And it's only going to get better with time.

"Oh god, oh fuck." He grunts and he thrusts faster, like a man possessed. I clench my walls around his cock and his fingers go back to my clit. "You're coming with me," he demands.

"Yes, fuck yes," I moan, my head falling back. Goosebumps cover my skin as my pussy tightens again.

Fuck, this man and his magic cock.

I thrust up as much as I can to meet him and it's like fireworks. An explosion goes off inside me and I scream as my body jerks. Cillian grunts my name, moaning in my ear as his hips stutter and stall. His warmth floods me, threatening to overflow.

As we're both coming down from our sex high, I cuddle into him. Feeling him against me like this reminds me why I worked so hard to be free. So nothing would ever happen to the man in my arms. He's safe and we can be together.

Giddiness overwhelms me and I start to giggle.

"Okay weirdo, laughing after sex isn't good for my ego," Cillian mumbles into my neck.

"I'm not laughing at you." I smack his back. "I'm just so happy," I say, my voice full of tears. Tears of happiness. "I'm so fucking happy."

* * *

The sex between us is electric. Fantastic. Addictive. But the after... it's the after I love.

Cillian's sitting up against the headboard, his arm around me as I lay my head on his chest. I rub slow circles across his skin over his chest, where his heart beats for me. We lay together, holding each other and basking in our shared glow. Soft touches, sweet kisses, and whispered declarations of love and commitment.

It's just the best.

"Can I ask you something?" Cillian breaks the silence, and kisses my temple to apologize.

"Of course." Shifting up, so I can look him in the eye, I rest against the headboard.

"Why did you say you killed him "the way he deserved"? Wouldn't it have been what he deserved if it was slow and painful? I would've wanted to see him cry and beg and plead for his life."

I sigh. "Uncle always wanted the most. The most power, the most money, the most attention. He got what he wanted every single time from the moment he became head of the Bratva. He's always liked, wanted, and needed attention. Before my first mission as *The Ghost*, Sergei inspected my gear and told me that my job was to bring the most influential men, women and children the ending they deserved. To take them out without anyone knowing they were already gone. A death without the chance to be saved."

Memories threaten to take me back, but I fight to stay in the present. I thread my fingers through Cillian's and he brings my knuckles to his lips, kissing them softly.

His touch grounds me, and I continue.

"He always talked about how he wanted to go out the way that warriors do. In battle. But really, what he wanted was for his death to spark more fire in his underlings. If he had to die, he wanted it to be spectacular and moving, a cause for war. Instead, he got what he never wanted: to be taken out without anyone knowing or caring. And because you guys have been working on dismantling the Bratva through other avenues, it means his death was meaningless. In the end, *he* was meaningless."

Cillian looks away, nodding absentmindedly before meeting my eyes again. He sits up straighter against the headboard, putting his other hand on our joined ones. Whatever he's going to say, he's really gearing up for it.

It makes me nervous. Is he having second thoughts about me? He hears me talking like this and suddenly I look differently to him. Worse. A monster, like they all told me I was. Anxiety claws at my throat and makes my heart beat unevenly.

"I have a question I need to ask for my own sake," he says, biting his cheek.

I sit up, mirroring him.

Whatever he says, whatever he needs, I'll give it to him. I'll be, or do, whatever.

Even if what he needs is for me to go because he can't be with someone with such darkness in their soul.

"Now that you're able to live how you want to, be who you want to be, do you still want to be with me?" he asks, his voice gruff and low, like he's forced himself to speak.

My eyebrows shoot to my hairline and I jolt back as if I've

been pushed. "What?"

"I told you in the beginning that I'd never keep you prisoner or hold you back from your dreams. I stand by that now. I want you to want to be here. I want you to want to be with me. I want you to choose this." Pulling my hands together and lifting them to his chest, he lays my hands flat over his heart. "I'm yours. My heart is yours. You're all I want," he says.

His emotion is making my heart clench. I can't help but feel tears prick at my eyes. My breath hitches when he speaks again.

"But what I want more, what I *need*, is for you to be happy. However that is."

This man.

This wonderful, sensitive, thoughtful man.

I cup his cheek, making sure he's looking right at me. They say your eyes are windows to your soul and my soul, as damaged as it is, is his.

"I love you more than I thought possible. I never want to be without you. I'm here, and I'm yours, for as long as you'll have me." I put as much love and hope as I can into my words, letting the love I have for him shine through and lay my hand over his heart again. "I don't ever want you to think that again. I don't *need* to be here anymore, I never needed to be. But I *wanted* to be, and I still do. Desperately." I smile softly. "You're my family, Cillian. My best friend. My lover. My husband."

The sound he makes is akin to a sob mixed with a chuckle and a wide smile crosses his face as he looks at me with the same level of love that I have for him.

"Forever, baby," he says softly before closing the gap between us and sealing the deal with a life-changing kiss.

The Ending

Cillian

Six months later...

If someone would've told me two years ago that I would become happily married to the Bratva heiress, I would've sworn they were smoking something deadly.

Sure, I had hopes I'd find someone who I felt comfortable with, someone I could tell my secrets to, someone I could be vulnerable with. But never in a million fucking years did I think my perfect woman would be Mila Smirnova, the niece of the Tsar of the Russian Bratva.

The morning Sergei was discovered dead, the news of his death spread like wildfire through the world of organized crime in Boston. As Kieron and Kellan anticipated, there were Sergei's heirs who tried to take over, tried to come to the Clan to barter for their property and dealings that had been taken with the information from Aleksander's files, but my Uncle held strong. Going so far as to ensure that no one would trade, deal, or barter with any Smirnova who come their way. When they couldn't get momentum going, soldiers started deserting the Bratva left and right. The Smirnov reign was no more.

Mila stayed true to not wanting to know about any of it. I would try to check in with her every so often, sharing information that Kieron passed onto me, but she would plug her ears and walk away, telling me she didn't want to know any of it. She really and truly wanted none of the power of position that came with her name.

Kellan, in the name of the Clan, made millions from the takeover. We're talking triple- digit millions. And my girl wanted none of it.

She told us over and over that she simply wanted to be left alone to live her life as Mila Tavish.

"Let Mila Smirnova die with the Bratva," she's told me more than once. But since then, she's gone through a few rough spots, just within herself, trying to figure out who she actually is without any of the pressure, any of the death, she was forced to be around.

The first few days after Sergei's death, Mila slept around the clock, only getting up to go to the bathroom and eat before crawling back under the covers and sleeping more. I was worried she was sick or maybe depressed and thought about bringing in the Clan doctor, but she told me she was just finally able to sleep well.

All those years in fight-or-flight mode caught up to her, and when her body finally felt safe, it took what it needed.

Once she got her fill of sleep, she started joining me in the gym. It's really great getting my ass handed to me by a woman that weighs maybe half of what I do. Trent still pesters me to find out the days she's sparring with me or Kieron, and comes to our workouts just to laugh like a fucking hyena when we're knocked out.

I secretly love it though, because when she manages to pin me down, she has a glint of mischief in her eye that promises more sparring, completely naked, later on when it's just the two of us.

The sex, *holy fucking god,* the sex is phenomenal. She's a goddess walking among us. I thought that when we were at the safehouse that we were at our peak together. I thought that was the best it would get because we were so attuned with each other and somehow seamlessly passed the metaphorical baton back and forth when we knew the other needed it.

But fuck me, have we just gotten better. Our honeymoon period hasn't ended yet. Every touch is lingering, a silent question asking if the other wants to go further. More often than not, the answer is yes. Every look lasts just a little longer, so we can memorize the other one's features. Every smile is genuine and loving.

It's simply the best. Being married is everything I never knew I wanted and everything I need and more. The only thing that would make it better, Mila and I have both agreed, is getting a place of our own. I don't want to live at Headquarters forever, and I'd eventually like us to buy a house. A fixer-upper that we can make our own. I want to give her her dream home and I know that right now, where we are, isn't her dream.

I'm working on it.

Today, Mila and I have an appointment with Kieron. He's asked us to meet him in his office that he's using more and more now that he's getting more responsibility from Kellan with the acquisition of the Bratva contacts. I don't know what he wants to talk about, but I know that it's important because he actually sent me a calendar invite.

The man barely uses his phone usually.

"I'm ready, let's go," my bride says, smoothing back her hair. She tucks the front of her—my—white shirt into her denim cut-offs in that sexy way girls do, showing off her small waist and muscular long legs.

She walks past me, reaching her fingertips out and dragging them across my chest playfully. Darting a hand out, I grab her by the waist and pull her to me.

"We don't have to go, let's stay here. I know of a few things we can do," I whisper in her ear before taking the lobe between my teeth and grazing it.

She moans and I see the goosebumps that form down her neck and arms. I bet if I was to pull her bra down her nipples would be hard. Fuck.

"Come on," I whisper deeply, in the way I know she loves.

"Don't tempt me," she whines, wrapping both arms around my shoulders. "We have to go. You know it's something important."

Damn, she's right.

"Fine," I grumble. My hands slide from her waist to her hips, before sliding down to her ass and grabbing two handfuls. "Then promise me we'll get to play later." I lean down, touching my forehead to hers. "Can I please you tonight?"

A shiver runs down her and I love that I still have the power to make her feel like that.

"I mean…" She shrugs teasingly. "I guess that would be alright."

I raise an eyebrow and lean back. "You guess?"

"I could be persuaded." She smirks, looking up to the ceiling like she's thinking about it.

"Oh, I'll persuade you all right. When I have time to get on my knees and make you beg for me."

"I do like that."

"I know you do." I kiss her neck quickly and breathe in through my teeth. "Let's get this fucking over with so I can get you naked."

Mila laughs wholeheartedly, throwing her head back. I watch her, feeling my heart swell with love. She's beautiful. She always has been since the moment I saw her all that time ago, but now, now she's radiant. Like a flower that's been placed in the sun for the first time.

She's just… bloomed.

"Come on, big boy." She drags me by the hand out of our apartment and I follow her like a puppy.

I'll follow this woman anywhere.

* * *

"I like what you've done with the place," I say to Kieron, looking around his office. The space used to be constantly covered in a fine layer of dust because he never really used it. We would all meet up at his apartment or mine and go through whatever shit needed to be handled. We never needed—or should've had—a paperwork trail.

Now, he's a big boss in the penthouse, working alongside his dad properly. Talia, his wife, has been a good influence on him.

"Thanks," Kieron says from the heavy leather chair behind

the solid wood desk as he closes the laptop in front of him. A few papers are scattered about, showing me that Kieron actually is working and not just calling us up here for shits and giggles. "Talia doesn't want me bringing any of this stuff home and Rosie is starting to grab at everything and make it impossible to actually work, so the office it is."

"It's very… cozy," Mila says, nodding in agreement.

My gaze is drawn to the rich mahogany bookshelf that dominates one wall. Its polished wooden surface gleams in the soft light filtering through the window. The shelves are neatly lined with rows of leather-bound books, their spines embossed with gold lettering, exuding an air of timeless elegance.Of course there wouldn't be a plastic binder in sight.

In the corner of the room sits a plush leather chair that matches Kieron's but is noticeably smaller. Like in Kellan's office, Kieron is keeping a fully stocked drink cart with multiple decanters filled with amber, clear and dark brown liquors next to scotch glasses and a silver ice bucket.

The room is filled with a sense of quiet sophistication, from the scent of aged wood mingling with the faint aroma of leather to the gentle ticking of the clock on the wall. It's a nice space, but I can see why he tried to work from home for as long as he did.

It's stuffy. It's dark. It's very clear that it's all about work here.

And from the pinched look on Kieron's face as he looks around the space with us, I know he agrees.

"Well, let's get down to business, shall we?" Kieron stands up and points to the two leather chairs right in front of his desk. I put my arm around Mila and motion for her to sit first and once she does, I do.

"You've got me nervous, Kieron. What's going on?" Mila asks, crossing her legs and putting her hands on top of her knees.

"It's nothing bad, I promise. But what I say cannot leave this room, understood?" He raises both eyebrows, looking at us pointedly until we agree.

"Everything that I'm going to say, I kept off books. Bryan, as agreed, scrubbed the dark web and as many documents as he could of Mila Smirnova. Mila Smirnova is gone."

Mila's eyes widen. "You did it?"

"You knew about this?" I look at Mila, shocked. I knew she was done with the Smirnovs, but I didn't think she wanted everything gone.

"I asked him to." She has an electric, bright smile on her face and it's clear to see just how happy she is.

"We changed the name on the marriage license from Smirnova to Smith like you asked, too. So, to the world, Mila Smirnova doesn't exist. She never has." Kieron crosses his hands as he rests on them on his desk.

"Thank you so much. You don't know how amazing this is. How much I've wanted and dreamed of this. Thank you, really." I can hear the tears in her voice and reach out to hold her hand.

"You're very welcome." Kieron stifles a full smile, and nods. He's being modest, because I can't imagine that doing something of that magnitude was easy. Bryan's good, but he isn't that good at rewriting documents. It would've made our lives easier many times if he was.

"I'll have to tell Bryan thank you," she says softly, looking to me as if I am to remind her.

The tension that fills the room is thick. It's awkward and I know exactly why. Kieron's eyes widen and he looks to me, then to Mila and back to me quickly. Like he's trying to say, 'you better fucking tell her because I'm not going to'. Asshole.

"Um, baby," I say softly, biting my lip. I don't know how she's going to take this. We both know how Bryan feels about Mila, how awkward it was for us when we got together and he found out. I know that while she didn't feel exactly the same as he did, she is fond of him. "Bryan left."

"What?" She breathes out the word like she's been sucker-punched.

"He took a vacation," Kieron jumps in. "He's expected back in a few months. He just needed some time to clear his head."

Mila, understandably, looks shocked. Her eyes, usually bright and full of life, now hold a shock and disbelief. Her lips tremble ever so slightly, betraying the turmoil she's trying to hide. My mind races, searching for words, any words, of comfort. Yet at this moment, all I can do is wait for her to pull herself out of her guilt.

All I want to do is hold her in my arms, promise her over and over that this isn't her fault. That she hasn't ruined anything, to help her heal from the betrayal and forgive. But for now, I can only watch as she argues with her demons.

As quickly as the shock dawned on her face, she forces all emotion clear away. Squeezing her hand for support, she bites her lips and nods. Because accepting Bryan's choice to leave when he knows how much he hurt her, is her only choice. "Well, tell him how thankful I am."

"Of course. Next time he checks in." Kieron nods. "Now, the second thing I wanted to tell you affects you both." Kieron turns in his chair to face the wall of documents. He pulls a thin leather binder out and turns it so Mila and I can look through it.

"What is this?" I ask him, opening it to read the papers inside. They're full of legal jargon.

"When the Clan took over all of the Bratva's assets, we turned around and sold them off. Well, the ones we didn't think would be of use to us, anyway. Your uncle owned an obscene amount of vacation homes and apartment buildings. After talking it over, Kellan and I decided that we didn't want any of those so we sold them. For a shit-ton over market value." He flips us through the pages. "A lot of the profit had to go into the Clan's account. However, I decided we needed to pay off one of our outstanding accounts." He points to the last page that shows seven million dollars in an account for a management company. "This account is only accessible without a trace one time. So when you get to the bank, I need you to transfer the whole sum through this wire. It will send the cash through a number of offshore accounts thus making it incredibly difficult to trace the origin of the funds. Once it's been through the accounts, you guys are good to use it when needed." Kieron explains all this like we are following what he's saying.

"You're giving us this money?" I ask.

"No, I'm giving you *your* money." He looks at Mila. "I know it's not enough, but it's what I could hide. Anything more and my father would've been curious."

"I didn't want any of it." Her eyebrows are furrowed as she cocks her head and looks at Kieron accusingly.

"I know."

"I didn't do all this for the money."

"Trust me, we know. It would've been amazingly easier for you to just take over than for you to go through all this for fortune." Kieron chuckles. "But you deserve it. You're starting over, Mila. You have no credit to your name, no savings account, no banking information. Any job you apply for will need to be in your new name and information. This is to get you started. Cillian makes good money, and I know because I make sure of it. But you seem like the kind of woman who doesn't want to rely on anyone. This means you don't have to."

Well fuck me. Kieron's really put some thought into this. I always planned on taking care of her. My money is her money and I have no issue providing for us both. In fact, if she wanted to stay at home for the rest of our lives, I'd encourage it. But I know Mila. And Kieron's right, she's far too independent to be restricted that way.

"Thank you." Mila accepts simply.

"That's it?" He narrows his eyes at her, obviously prepared for a fight.

"That's it. You're right. Thank you for looking out for me, for us," she says, putting her hand on mine.

"You're family. We look out for our family." Kieron smiles at me.

I nod at him, hoping he knows I'm appreciative. Being in the world of organized crime is gruesome and deadly, it's full of moles and people who are just waiting to stab you in the back for what you have, or even what they think you might have. People you love will kill you in an instant over insignificant things. It's very rare to find those who are genuine and will have your back no matter what.

That's why I cherish my family: Kieron, Trent and Bryan, so much.

Clearing my throat, I ask, "Is there anything else you wanted to talk to us about?"

"No," he answers with a pursed, restrained smile. "That's it, brother."

The both of us stand at the same time, and shake hands. I know what he's done for us and I'm incredibly appreciative.

"Thank you," I say softly.

"Anytime." He claps me on the shoulder with his other hand, squeezing for a moment before letting go and picking up the binder. "This has all the account numbers in it. After you write them down somewhere, burn it."

"Got it." I take the leather-bound book from him.

Mila offers her hand to Kieron, but instead of taking it, he leans in and gives her a surprise hug. "Take care of my little cousin, okay? He may play at being a big tough guy, but we all know he's a softie at heart." He smirks playfully at me over her shoulder and Mila laughs loudly.

"I'll be in touch for the next job, but take a few days, Cillian. It's been a lot," he says before sitting down and returning to his work. Like the boss he is.

Being obviously dismissed, Mila and I leave his office heading back to the elevator to go to our apartment in silence.

* * *

Mila's been silent for a long time.

Too long.

"Are you okay?" I ask after we get to the apartment. "Are you mad?"

"No, no I'm not mad," she replies softly. "I'm just... I'm very happy. I feel guilty because I'm happy. Bryan had to leave because he was so hurt by me, but instead of feeling badly, I'm happy with how my life has turned out."

I put the book down on the counter and turn to Mila. "You don't need to feel guilty. You're allowed to be happy and Bryan knows that, he wants that. It's not your fault. He'll come around and it will all be good. You'll see." I pull her to me, my hands hold her hips to mine.

"I know. It's just still raw."

"I get it. I do." I nod. "Time heals."

"Thank you, for understanding."

"Of course, babydoll." I kiss her chastely, not expecting it to go anywhere beyond that, but Mila pushes us further.

She reaches up and grips my shirt tightly with her fingers. I feel her tongue pry my lips open before I open them willingly. She tastes like mint and coffee, an intoxicating combination. The ferocity in which she's kissing me leaves no room to play it cool. Her grip on my shirt is strong and confident, a sure sign that she's going to take what she wants from me. There will be no discussion about it.

And I can't fucking wait.

Just her kissing me like this has my cock hard. It's pressing painfully against the denim of my jeans, begging to be released and buried in her.

Abruptly, she pulls back and we're both breathless.

"Go get in bed. I need to freshen up but expect you naked when I get there," she orders, but her eyes never meet mine. Instead she stares at my lips like she's barely able to contain herself.

"Yes, Ma'am." I wink.

Mila steps back stiffly, like she's forced herself to let go of me, and I watch her every move, her every shiver, like a hawk. My chest heaves with each quickened breath and we stare at each other with a deeply heated gaze before I step backward once, then twice. I keep walking until my back hits the bedroom door.

Mila watches me like she's a predator, ready to eat me.

And I'm here for it. I feel trapped in the best, most exciting way. I slip inside the bedroom, keeping the door cracked and immediately take my shirt off, throwing it into the hamper in the corner, pulling my socks off and unbuckling my belt before snapping it out of the loops on my pants. She watches me with hooded eyes as I wrap the leather around my hand.

I place the wrapped up belt on our dresser, and unbutton my jeans with the other hand. Feeling desperate, I fight the urge to wrap my hand around my cock and stroke it. I don't want to start without her, so I lay back on the bed and try to even out my breathing.

Biting my lip, I try to ignore the throbbing hard-on in my pants.

"You're so sexy," Mila coos. I hear her feet walking on the soft carpet and I shiver.

Slipping my pants down, I look at her. She's changed from her shorts and my shirt to an all-black leather outfit. She's in a bralette with lace triangles covering her tits. It's perfect because I can see her rosy nipples peaked against the lace. I barely keep the drool inside my mouth when I see the matching black g-string and garter belt holding up thigh-high fishnet stockings.

"You look…" I stutter horribly. "You look, holy fuck, babydoll. I can't… oh god."

"You like?" She twirls for me slowly, shaking her ass, and I bite my fist when it jiggles.

"So much," I say breathlessly.

"I want to try something." She bends over and whispers in my ear, her breath making me shiver. She's hovering over me and my cock is pressed against her tight stomach. I wait for her to tell me what she wants, knowing that I'll give it to her.

"I want to finger you. Just like we've talked about. Do you want to?" she says softly, almost shyly even though we've talked about it before.

"Okay." My voice cracks with nerves. I've always been interested in being pegged, but I've never been comfortable with even discussing it, not until her.

"Okay then. Pants off, big guy."

When I tell you I've not scrambled to the bed faster, I mean it. Excitement and anticipation have taken over my body. I'm nervous, but I trust Mila with my whole being. I'd never even think about doing this if I didn't.

"Turn around," She commands with a seductive smirk.

I swear I've never been harder.

I do what she says and rest my upper body on the bed, leaving my ass exposed. It's uncomfortable being this vulnerable, but then Mila runs her hands over my asscheeks while she praises me and I relax.

"I'm going to go with just my finger, okay baby? But first..." Her voice drops lower and softer in my ear. "I'm going to get you all wet."

A dribble of cold liquid lands unexpectedly on my crack and I jump.

"Sorry, Killer. I should've warmed it up for you." She tugs on the head of my cock with her other hand in apology.

"Oh fuck!" I call out.

The gel warms as it slides down my crack and pools under my balls. Her small, wet fingers slide up and down, slipping easier with the lube, until she distributes it all thoroughly. Each pass of her fingers puts me closer and closer to coming all over the bed. Searching for any kind of relief I start to grind against the sheets.

"Wait, baby, wait," she says softly, her fingers circling my asshole. One of her fingers is putting pressure on my ass, but not pressing for more. She's waiting for me to tell her I'm okay with this.

I'm so fucking okay with this.

"Fuck me," I choke out as she presses on.

And it's fucking... I can't even...

"Breathe," she whispers in my ear, kissing my lobe.

It's too much pressure though, it burns and right before I tell her I'm done, she starts to jerk me off slowly, taking the attention off of the discomfort, to emphasize the pleasure it's bringing.

"Oh god," I groan, dropping my head to the comforter.

"It's good, right?" she murmurs in my ear. "It brings all the sensations to a higher level. It's just taboo enough that it makes everything you're feeling heightened." Her words are dark and sultry, whispered hotly in my ear as her finger goes deeper before pulling out.

She's almost got me, I'm right fucking there, but I still need...

"Make yourself come. Do it," she orders. She always knows what I need before I can voice it.

Moaning, I grab my leaking cock and start to twist and tug, jerking it rapidly.

"When you come, you come knowing that my finger's in

your ass and that I love you. When you come, you scream out *my* name, understand?"

Fuck me, that's the hottest thing I've ever heard.

I stroke myself faster, my hand flying over my cock, gripping tighter. She's starting to match my rhythm with each pass of her finger, and the rest of her fingers caressing my balls. I'm rocking back and forth, humping the bed as she presses into me from behind.

"Mila! Fuck, Mila. Mila, Mila, Mi—" I cry out, and come like a fountain all over my hand.

"You're so fucking sexy. That was… That was amazing. You did so good for me." She moans in my ear seductively.

I groan long and low as I come down. Letting go of my cock, I drop down on the bed, no longer having the strength to hold myself up in any way.

"Relax, okay? It'll hurt less," she says softly, and I could not be more relaxed if I tried. But she starts to pull her finger out of me and I see what she means. It's quick and then I go right back to letting myself be numb with pleasure.

Mila lays beside me, giving me space to recover, but lightly rubbing my shoulders. I breathe heavily into the comforter, coming down slowly.

"You did so well, I'm so proud of you."

After a few minutes, I flip over and pull her into my arms. I'm covered in cum, but she doesn't seem to mind. I lean over and kiss her deeply.

"I love you. With all of my heart and darkened soul." She smiles.

"I love you too, with all of my heart and darkened soul."

II

Other works by Alina Martyn

The Heliander Chronicles
Secretly Born
Living In Secret
Secrets End

The Men Of The Clan
From My Past
Towards My Now
Embracing My Future
Through Time - coming 2025

Author's Note

A huge, huge thank you to the readers, to the people who asked for Cillian's story and pushed me to continue. I started *The Men Of The Clan* series with *From My Past*, thinking it would just be a standalone and was met with many questions about the rest of the guys. So then came Trent's story, and now Cillian's. :) Thank you all so much for showing your love for my guys and for asking for more. I hope I've done you proud.

Thank you to my wonderful husband. He's the best. Always.

Thank you to my cover designer, Maja. (@_m_design3) Check out her work! She never misses, I mean, how hot is this cover?

Thank you to my editor, Rayanna! I honestly learned so much from you and am so happy to have worked with you!

One more to go guys. Bryan's ready to tell his side of things...

Follow Me On Social Media!

www.alinamartyn.com

Tik Tok
@alinamartynwrites
@authorlina.martyn1

Instagram
@authoralina.martyn1

Threads
@authoralina.martyn1

Join My Facebook Group!
Alina's Spicy Angels